Also by Pam Webber

The Wiregrass

Moon Water

Life Dust

Life
Dust

a novel

Pam Webber

SHE WRITES PRESS

Published 2022
Printed in the United States of America
Print ISBN: 978-1-64742-091-8
E-ISBN: 978-1-64742-092-5
Library of Congress Control Number: 2022908445

For information, address:
She Writes Press
1569 Solano Ave #546
Berkeley, CA 94707

Interior design by Tabitha Lahr

She Writes Press is a division of SparkPoint Studio, LLC.

For Jeff

Spring 1971

Chapter 1

NETTIE

Nettie took the back stairs from the emergency room to the second floor two at a time. Glancing left and right, she darted across the hall into the pitch-black recovery room. She needed an oxygen regulator fast, and this unit always had plenty. They just didn't like to share after-hours. Clicking her penlight on, she hurried past rows of stretchers toward the supply closet but froze as startled shadows thrashed in the corner ahead.

"Bloody hell," hissed a low, male voice.

Eyes wide and heart racing, Nettie released the button on the penlight and backed up. Panicked whispers and whiffs of perfume followed her out the door, the scent a favorite of the hospital's most contentious evening supervisor, Genevieve Woods.

Slipping out the door, Nettie ran down the hall to the intensive care unit in search of anonymity and the needed equipment. Just inside, she bumped into Dougie, the short, quiet fellow who delivered linens throughout the hospital from seven at night until seven in the morning. Nettie leaned against the wall, breathless from angst more than effort. "Hi, Dougie."

"Hey, Miss Nettie, are you okay?"

Straightening up, she peeked through the door's small window at an empty hall and closed recovery room door. "Yeah, Dougie, I'm fine. How about you?"

"I'm good. Working hard. Lots of sick people, so lots of laundry. Are you and TK still going to the cafeteria for dinner?"

Nettie's preceptor, TK, had befriended Dougie years ago by sharing a cafeteria table with the shy young man. They'd been friends ever since. When Nettie started the hospital's nursing internship program earlier in the year, Dougie decided any friend of TK's was a friend of his.

"Yep, we'll be there."

"Okay, see you in a little while."

Nettie moved aside and opened the door, peeping around the tall cart as Dougie pulled it into the hall. The door to the recovery room now stood ajar, a dark figure hovering just inside. "Gotta go, Dougie." Darting past moaning patients, beeping monitors, and pulsing ventilators, Nettie found the charge nurse and requested the needed regulator. After signing an equipment form and promising to return it within twenty-four hours, she headed back to the ER.

"What took so long?" TK asked, whipping the regulator out of its sterile bag and replacing the faulty one. Tall and slim with short, curly brown hair and wire-rimmed glasses, TK seldom wasted time.

"I couldn't get it from the recovery room. I had to go to the ICU," Nettie replied, opting to stay quiet about what she'd witnessed. Speculating about the identity of the two people in the recovery room wouldn't accomplish anything. Even if she had proof, she wasn't sure what to do with it. Hopefully, they hadn't recognized her, either.

"We need to get this patient undressed," TK said. "The

cardiac catheterization lab will be ready for him any minute. You get his shoes. I'll get his pants."

The unconscious man looked like a gentleman. Slender, hair carefully trimmed and styled, close-shaven, with soft hands and manicured nails, he had walked into the ER a short time ago and collapsed. TK and the code blue team had managed to get his heart started again, but the monitor still showed a heart attack in progress.

As TK unbuckled the man's monogrammed, leather belt, he woke and sat up in a panic.

"What do you think you're doing?" He slapped TK's hands away and kicked at Nettie. "Get away from me." Dazed, his head and shoulders wobbled.

TK raised the head of the stretcher so he could lean back. "Sir, you're in the emergency room of the Northern Virginia Hospital."

"I know where I am, dammit. I drove myself here. What I don't know is who the hell you two are." He slapped at TK and kicked at Nettie again.

They both stepped back.

Always calm, TK introduced herself and Nettie. "Sir, you passed out as you walked in the door. It looks like you're having a heart attack. We're giving you medicine in your vein to help, but there's a clot in one of the arteries supplying your heart that we need to—"

"Another heart attack? Then, the last thing I need is you two bedpan Betties. Get a doctor in here."

"A cardiologist has already been here, Mr. Pepper," TK replied, patiently. "She's gone to the cath lab to get things ready. We're going to take you there as soon as her team calls."

"Don't talk to me like I'm an idiot. I've had heart attacks before. I know the drill." He stared at TK. "You went through my things. That's how you know my name." He looked at his right hand. "Where's the ring?"

"Your ring and watch are in the safe along with your wallet. We had to know who you are, where you're from, and how to reach your family," TK replied.

"My name is William Edward Pepper. There is no family. You don't need to know my address in Hawaii. And I want the ring back, right now!" Mr. Pepper banged the rail. "And get that damn doctor back in here!"

TK winked at Nettie. "Stay here. I'll be right back."

As she left the room, Nettie moved to the side of the stretcher, worried Mr. Pepper's agitation might land him on the floor.

"What are you looking at?" he snapped.

She looked him in the eye. "A jackass."

Mr. Pepper sucked air as his mouth fell open.

Nettie put her hands on the rail and leaned in. "TK is trying her best to save your life. Why don't you settle down and let her?"

"Who the hell do you think you are?"

"Just someone who knows you're scared to death and in a dozen different types of pain."

Mr. Pepper's eyes narrowed. "You know nothing of the sort."

Nettie waited.

He lolled his head back. "Did my heart actually stop?"

"Yes."

"I'm sweating like crazy." He wiped his brow. "You all must have given me morphine. I always sweat when I get morphine."

"Yes, sir. It eases the pain and lowers the heart's workload at the same time."

He looked at her name badge. "Nettie, I need to get that ring back."

The pleading in his voice spoke to more than a ring. "If TK doesn't bring it when she comes, I'll get it for you. I promise."

"I want it—"

The alarm above the stretcher sounded as Mr. Pepper's eyes rolled back and he slumped to the side, deadly ventricular fibrillation wiggling its way across the monitor. Nettie hit the code blue button on the wall, lowered the head of the bed, gave him two quick breaths, and began pumping his chest. "Please God, lift him up, ease his pain, and heal his heart," she whispered as others rushed to help. "Don't go, Mr. Pepper, not now, not like this."

THE VENTILATOR CYCLED STEADILY NEXT to Mr. Pepper's stretcher. Still unconscious, he had just returned from the cath lab where the clot blocking his left coronary artery had been dissolved, but not before it caused permanent damage.

Nettie pulled his signet ring from the valuables bag she'd retrieved from the ER's safe. The ring's weight, muted gold glow, and hundreds of minuscule scratches spoke to its quality and long years of wear. She couldn't separate the swirly initials on the top, but they didn't appear to be Mr. Pepper's. Returning the ring to its home on his right hand, she wrapped it in surgical tape to ensure it stayed on his finger, then wrote "Do not remove" and her initials on the tape.

TK appeared in the doorway. "CCU is ready for him. I'll get his chart while you pack his things."

Mr. Pepper's dress shirt had been cut away during the first resuscitation and the rest of his things thrown across a chair during the second. Nettie put his tailored suit and cashmere overcoat on hangers, then covered them with a long clear plastic trash bag. While not the best protection for elegant things, it was better than nothing. Laying the bag across the bottom of the stretcher, she placed his intricately tooled leather shoes, matching belt, and monogrammed socks and underwear in a plastic bag and stowed it in a basket under the mattress.

Rolling Mr. Pepper into his assigned CCU room, TK left to talk with the charge nurse while Nettie positioned the stretcher and put his things away. She stepped back as two CCU nurses quickly changed monitors, placed an automatic blood pressure cuff on Mr. Pepper's arm, arranged the pumps and poles holding multiple IV lines, and covered him with a hypothermia blanket. In a few minutes, his body temperature would drop to ninety degrees where it would stay for twenty-four hours or more. The cold would decrease his body's demand for oxygen and lessen the workload of his hurting heart. Nettie put his socks back on his feet, then covered the top of his head with a folded towel. These small pieces of cloth would help minimize shivering and further reduce his demand for oxygen. Underneath the hum and systematic beeps of the life-saving equipment lay a hurting and unhappy man. The least she could do was try to make him a little more comfortable.

Outside the door, TK and the charge nurse studied Mr. Pepper's latest electrocardiogram. "Left anterior descending infarct," the nurse whispered. "Widowmaker."

Nettie wrapped her hand around Mr. Pepper's and whispered in his ear. "Your ring is on your finger and God is in your corner. Feel better soon."

His eyelids fluttered, and for a split-second Nettie thought he might wake up. But his lids went smooth again as he drifted back to wherever the mind goes when traumatized and drugged.

Leaving work later that night, Nettie couldn't stop thinking about Mr. Pepper. "There's no family," he'd said. The only thing in his wallet besides cash and credit cards had been the name and phone number of a lawyer in Hawaii. Tomorrow, one of the hospital's social workers would call to see if they could get more information. Until then, the only people who cared about this man were strangers.

At home, Nettie brushed her teeth, slipped into her pajamas, and had just turned down her bed covers when the phone rang. She rushed to stop the clanging before it woke Win, her best friend and roommate. *No one calls this late at night. Something's wrong.*

Wisps of steam radiated from the asphalt as Nettie brought the car to a stop in the shade of the rain-heavy loblolly pines outside the entrance to Fort Benning. Instead of delivering a cool start to an unusually hot, spring day, the fast-moving storm had created a stifling morning sauna. Already disheveled from the all-night drive, the humidity made her hair droop, skin sticky, and clothes wilt. Plus, her breath had to smell like coffee. She didn't want to say goodbye to Andy like this. Without warning, his orders had been changed and moved up. Instead of participating in the next level of tactical training in Georgia for three months, he would be leaving for South Vietnam in a matter of hours.

"Everyone's restricted to base until flight time," he'd said last night. "I can't even meet you halfway."

"If I leave now, I can get there before you go."

"No, honey. It's too late to be on the road. I—"

"I'm on my way." Nettie hung up before he could object again. She called TK, then left a message with the ER charge nurse explaining that she wouldn't be in tomorrow and why. Andy, the love of her life, would be gone for a year, maybe longer. She quickly changed clothes, filled a thermos with instant black coffee, and left a note for Win. Grabbing her wallet and the keys to her old Oldsmobile Cutlass, Nettie headed for I-95, the new interstate highway that made it possible for her to travel from Northern Virginia to Columbus, Georgia, before Andy had to leave.

She'd tried to pull herself together during the long drive, but the closer she got to the military base, the more rogue tears escaped. *Get a grip, girl. The last thing Andy needs is to see you puffy, red-eyed, and bawling.* She blew her nose, blotted her eyes, brushed her hair, and stepped out of the car to tuck in her blouse. Straightening her shorts, she took several deep breaths. The sharp citrusy smell of the pines helped clear her head. Climbing back behind the wheel, she pinched her cheeks, bit her lips until they blushed, popped a Certs mint in her mouth, and headed for the guard gate.

Checking Nettie's driver's license against the expected guest list, the military policeman waved her in. From memory, she turned right, drove through a tunnel of overhanging hickory trees, and entered a village of austere, white clapboard buildings. The sign on the first one said Visitor's Center.

Andy jumped from the steps and trotted toward the car as Nettie pulled up, relief flooding his handsome face. Tall and tanned, his uniform accented his broad shoulders, slim waist, and muscular build.

Thank God he's strong. He'll need to be.

Andy leaned in the window, cupped Nettie's face, and gave her a quick kiss.

She slid to the middle of the seat as he climbed in and put his arms around her. He smelled good and felt better. His second kiss was long and sweet.

"I'm sorry you had such a long drive, but I'm so glad you came," he said, kissing her hair.

"Me, too." She took his hand. "Why the sudden change in orders?"

"I'm not sure. Rumor has it a North Vietnamese offensive may be in the works, so they want us in-country and up to speed as soon as possible."

Nettie shivered.

Andy pulled her close. "Just a lot more of what we've already been doing, honey."

She knew better. It was more, dangerously more. As hot, humid, and miserable as summers in Georgia were, there was no comparison to the hellish heat and wetness of the jungles of Southeast Asia. And there would be no pretending, he'd be dodging real people and things intent on killing him. Nightly television news reported the horrors of fighting a jungle war and never failed to update the American public on the numbers of soldiers killed and wounded on a weekly basis. "Is everyone going early?" she asked.

"No, only those who've completed Long-Range Reconnaissance Patrol training. The rest will follow later."

"Your mom must be beside herself."

"I called her last night. She wasn't surprised. The army used to do the same thing to my dad. Would you call her when you get home? See if she's okay?"

"Of course. It's an awfully long flight. Will you have any layovers?"

"Not really. We fly to Alaska today, refuel, then head to Okinawa, Japan. From there we fly to Da Nang Air Base in South Vietnam. After that, I have no idea where I'll be sent."

"You're a lieutenant. That's a good thing, right?"

Doubt flashed in Andy's eyes. "I don't know if it's good or not. I have to lead men I've never met, in a country I've never seen, in a war no one seems sure about."

Nettie squeezed his hand. As the son of a military family, the words were not easy for Andy to say, but she understood why he said them. To date, the United States had lost over fifty thousand men and their allies, South Vietnam's Army of the Republic of Vietnam, the ARVNs, had lost over two hundred thousand in their attempt to stop a hostile takeover by the communist controlled North Vietnamese Army, the NVA. With the brutal war playing out on television, many citizens were questioning America's continued involvement. Even the politicians in Washington, DC, couldn't seem to decide if they wanted to stay the course or just get the hell out.

Andy drove to the western edge of the base. Parking in front of a forested area, he pulled a colorful, patchwork quilt from the trunk. Hand-sewn from squares of cloth cut from the clothes Nettie and Andy grew up in, the quilt had been an engagement present from their mothers.

Following a curvy path through the woods, they came to the bank of the picturesque Chattahoochee, the river of painted rocks. Spreading the quilt near the water's edge, they sat shoulder to shoulder watching the morning fog lift in lazy drifts. They'd discovered the serene glade during Nettie's first visit to the base and made a point of visiting it every time she came. The secluded spot reminded them both of River's Rest, their favorite hideaway at home in Amherst.

In the middle of the river's sauntering current sat a small, W-shaped structure made of colorful granite boulders. Placed by Native Americans a century ago, the structure provided an easy way to secure food. The boulders' quartz and feldspar sparkles attracted fish that became trapped in the W-shaped design, making them easy targets for spears.

"I've been thinking," Andy said, watching the osprey and cormorants dive for their breakfast. "I'm going to be gone a long time, and I don't want you worrying. I know you'll be busy with school and work, but I also want you to go out with friends, have fun. Like you always say, I want you to choose to be happy."

Nettie's mantra flew back at her hard. "Andy, don't—"

"No, listen, this is important." He took her hand. "I can do whatever I have to do over there, but it will be a hell of a lot easier if I know you're okay. For decades I watched my mother worry herself sick whenever my father deployed in harm's way. I don't want you going through that."

"Worry seldom accomplishes what fear does," Nettie replied, remembering the words of Win's grandmother, Nibi, a full-blooded Monacan Indian.

"What?"

"It's something Nibi told me once. She said worry spins us in circles while fear motivates us to act. I'll stay busy with school and work, and if that's not enough to keep the worry at bay, I'll find something else to do, something constructive. I promise."

"Who would have thought fear could be a friend." Andy pulled a stem of white clover and twirled it back and forth. "It's the unknown that has my attention, what I fear. The army's prepared me for a lot. And I'm sure I'll learn more from the guys who've been in-country for a while. But still—"

"Don't underestimate yourself, Andy. You're smart, you see things others aren't even looking for, and you're the bravest human being I know." Andy had risked his life to save hers during the flooding after Hurricane Camille in 1969. He'd demonstrated a level of courage that defined heroism.

He kissed her, then pulled a small version of the New Testament from his breast pocket. Inside was a picture of Nettie and him.

"You had it laminated?"

"The monsoons over there keep everything wet. I didn't want it to get ruined." He slid the picture between pages marked with a small, red ribbon. Several lines on the page were underlined.

"First Corinthians 13:13?"

Andy nodded. "And now these three remain: faith, hope, and love. But the greatest of these is love." He wove his fingers through hers. "I love you, Nettie. I have since the day I met you in the sandbox, and I will love you until the day I die and beyond."

Tears Nettie had been trying to corral for hours broke free. Andy pulled her close. "It will be okay, baby."

"No. Nothing will be okay until you're back home."

"Look at me." Andy lifted her chin. "Nobody wants this, but if we have to do it, let's do it our way. Let's stay focused on the jobs we have to do, and take it one step at a time, one day at a time." He kissed their engagement ring. "A year from now, this will all be over, and we'll be having a picnic at River's Rest and putting the finishing touches on our wedding plans. Deal?"

Nettie managed a weak nod. "Deal," she whispered.

He slid the New Testament back into his pocket and wiped away her tears. "I have to go."

Nettie started to get up.

"No, stay here. I don't want you standing behind some rusty, chain-link fence on a sweltering tarmac. I'll walk back." He kissed her, holding her tight for a long moment, as if trying to imprint the feeling deep in his memory.

She held onto his hand as he stood. "Come back to me."

"Count on it." He put two fingers to his lips and blew her a kiss as he walked away.

She held the air kiss until she couldn't see him anymore, her heart breaking. Numb, she laid down on the soft quilt. Since childhood, Andy had been there, her rock, her port in every storm, and she'd been there for him. Now, she couldn't help him, and he couldn't help her. Loss, loneliness, and the insanity of war pulled her into an exhausted sleep.

Hours later, a gusty breeze signaled the approach of another storm. Groggy, Nettie got to her feet and wrapped the quilt around her, Andy's scent still present. The path seemed longer and rougher as she stumbled her way back to the car. Opening the trunk, she brushed the grass and twigs from the quilt, folded it, and placed it inside, resolving not to unfold it until she and Andy were together again.

Rain drops and tears wet her face as she got into the car. *Get a grip, Nettie. You can't do it this way. You promised Andy. If he can do what he has to do, you can, too. You have school and work to concentrate on, and before you know it, he'll be home. So, suck it up buttercup, and get on with it.* Taking a deep breath, she turned the windshield wipers on, put the car in gear and headed for home.

THE NEXT AFTERNOON, AT THE 3:00 P.M. change of shifts, a dozen ER nurses gathered in pairs across the glass-enclosed nurses' station preparing to give and receive report on each patient. Having the additional eyes and ears around did little to deflect Genevieve Woods's dressing-down of Nettie, the graying supervisor intent on humiliation.

Twice, Nettie tried to explain that she'd missed work the previous day because her fiancé's deployment had been moved up unexpectedly and that he would be in Vietnam for a year. And twice it didn't matter. In fact, Nettie's reason for being gone seemed to infuriate the woman even more.

"You had an obligation to be here, regardless of what's going on in your personal life," Mrs. Woods insisted, her once pretty face distorted with feigned indignation. "Illness and death in the immediate family are the only acceptable excuses. You demonstrated a flagrant disregard of hospital policy, which constitutes grounds for dismissal from the internship program."

Some of the ER nurses turned disbelieving eyes toward the angry woman, others kept their heads down to stay out of the line of fire.

"Ma'am, I didn't disregard the policy. I followed it exactly. I notified—"

"You were expected to be here. Others in this department were counting on you."

TK entered the nurses' station, after standing in the door long enough to hear what was going on. "Mrs. Woods, Nettie had my permission to be away."

Mrs. Woods spun around. "TK, you're not authorized to give anyone a day off, much less an intern."

"Ma'am, we're interrupting report, why don't we talk in here." TK opened the door to a side office and motioned Nettie in. Mrs. Woods followed in a snit, her perfume trailing in her wake.

Not bothering to sit, TK pulled a notebook from the bookcase. "Mrs. Woods, the new *Nursing Internship Manual* says the designated preceptor, which in this case is me, can adjust the intern's schedule as needed. Nettie had my permission to be off yesterday."

Mrs. Woods snatched the manual, her eyes narrowing as she read the policy. "At any point did you consider notifying me or another supervisor of the change in staffing?"

"No," TK replied matter-of-factly. "The manual also says interns are not to be counted in the daily staffing schedule, so her absence didn't inconvenience or cause a hardship on anyone. Why would a supervisor need to be informed of a problem that didn't exist?"

Touché TK. Nettie braced for an acidic comeback but watched Mrs. Woods surrender to logic instead.

"Regardless, supervisors need to know what's going on in their units."

TK had mastered the skill of allowing people to save face, even when they didn't deserve it. She opened the office door, scattering those who'd huddled nearby. "I see your point, Mrs. Woods. We'll try and remember that next time."

"Good." Mrs. Woods nodded stiffly at TK, shot Nettie a dark look, then left.

"Come on," TK said to Nettie as the supervisor disappeared. "We've wasted enough time on this nonsense." Grabbing stethoscopes, she and Nettie headed down the hall.

"Thanks for the help back there, TK," Nettie said when they were past curious ears.

"No need to thank me. Woods was out of line." TK stopped. "I got the feeling she was angry about something else altogether. Any idea what it could be?"

Nettie shrugged, unwilling to drag TK into speculating about who was in the recovery room that night.

"Well, don't let her get to you. She's an unhappy person."

"Any idea why?"

"Lord only knows. Seems like it's a choice she made a long time ago."

"What a miserable way to live."

"Exactly."

"Her perfume doesn't fit her personality," Nettie said. "In fact, I'm surprised she wears perfume at all."

"No hospital staff is supposed to, but Genevieve Woods has gotten away with it for decades. Unfortunately, it hasn't helped her disposition." TK frowned. "I don't know why she is so wound up about you, but stay out of her way. People who can't control their own happiness will try to control yours."

Chapter 2

ANDY

The heavy, vibrating drone of the C-130's four turbo-prop engines made sleep impossible, even if Andy and the other soldiers had wanted to close their eyes. Back-and-forth chatter had ended hours ago. Now most of them just stared at something no one else could see. Once they landed in South Vietnam, his platoon would be separated, shipped off to reinforce other recon platoons who'd lost men to the enemy or home. He looked around. *How many of these men will make the return flight in a body bag? Will I?* Andy moved his hand over his left breast pocket, the outline of its contents filling his palm.

"So, what's in that pocket, Lieutenant?" asked Luca Moretti, the platoon's New York City street-smart, badass, funny man. "You've touched it a half-dozen times since we've been in the air. She must be something," he added with an irritating grin.

Dammit, Andy. Keep your hand down. He knew better than to give any of these men, especially Moretti, a reason to needle him.

"I don't have a girl," Moretti continued. "Maybe when we get home, I'll find one and we can go on a double date."

"Moretti, you find a girl crazy enough to go out with you, and we'll do it."

Small, wiry, and barely meeting the army's height and weight requirements, Moretti had been in a half-dozen scuffles or outright fights since joining Andy's unit. Even now, his face showed evidence of a recent encounter with someone's fist.

Andy pointed to the black-and-blue eye. "How'd you get the shiner this time?"

"Tripped, sir," he replied, winking with his good eye.

Moretti had a quick temper, but it seemed most of the fights occurred because he refused to back down when provoked. Despite being battered and bruised, Moretti never squealed on the other guy, even if it meant taking the blame and punishment himself. The higher-ups at Fort Benning had wanted to send Moretti packing long ago, but Andy fought to keep him. "If nothing more, he's a good man to have in a fight."

THE BLAST OF SCORCHING HOT, humid air stole Andy's breath as he exited the plane at Da Nang Air Base. Georgia summers were paradise compared to this furnace. Squinting against the glare and waves of heat rolling off the white tarmac, he reached for the Ray-Ban aviator sunglasses Nettie had given him for his birthday. They fogged up before he could get them adjusted.

"Try shaving cream," Moretti said, matching Andy's stride.

"Pardon?"

"Shaving cream. It will keep your sunglasses from fogging up. Spread a little dab on each lens, let it dry, polish them, and you're good to go."

Andy cocked his head. "Where the hell did you come up with that?"

"Hints from Heloise. My mom reads her column every day."

Following the crowd into a massive and only slightly cooler hangar, Andy stopped at the first table to pick up his assignment. Following instructions to wait under the Camp Eagle sign, he refused to let his disappointment show. Located in Military Region One, Camp Eagle sat just south of the DMZ, the demilitarized zone separating North and South Vietnam. Also known as I Corps, the region recorded more American and ARVNs killed or wounded than the other three military regions combined. Andy studied the assignment in his hand. He would be leading a long-range reconnaissance platoon out of Camp Eagle.

Moretti joined Andy. "Looks like you drew the short straw, Lieutenant. I'm in your platoon."

"Lucky me," Andy joked.

When a dozen men had gathered under the Camp Eagle sign, a corporal wearing a blaze orange vest approached Andy, the only officer in the group. "Sir, if you and the others will follow me to the supply tent, we'll get you equipped. After that, we'll grab some chow and I'll get you back here to catch a chopper up to Eagle."

Two hours later, Andy and Moretti were back at the airfield dressed in lightweight jungle fatigues and waiting for the next step in their journey. Each carried a steel helmet, an M16 rifle, a bandolier with six magazines of ammo, and a utility belt with two canteens and a knife. Their rucksacks held a soft, wide-brimmed boonie hat, a poncho, long range patrol rations that were nicknamed LURPS, chlorine tablets, compact day and night binoculars, a first aid kit, extra socks, a small brick of C4 plastic explosive, and any personal items whose weight they were willing to carry.

The corporal pointed to the first of several Chinooks lined up on the tarmac. "Lieutenant, that's your ride. It's warming up so you all keep your head down and watch out for the rotors, it's windy."

Andy gave him a thumbs up, then he, Moretti, and others destined for Camp Eagle crossed the tarmac and climbed aboard the powerful chopper. As it lifted off, the view below changed quickly from hangars and concrete runways to palm trees, acres of jade-colored rice paddies lined with irrigation ditches, scattered huts, villages, and massive stretches of dense jungle canopy.

A splayed, peach-colored sunset nestled above the low-lying mountains in the distance as the Chinook approached the front-line base. From above, Camp Eagle had the appearance of a midsize city. Hundreds of buildings and tents of various shapes and sizes filled the clear-cut acres. Roads full of jeeps, trucks, and scurrying people crisscrossed the camp. On the south side, dozens of helicopters were taking off and landing, their multicolored lights blinking codes like fireflies.

Once on the ground, Andy and the others gathered in yet another large hangar and were separated by assignments. Those going to the recon platoon were directed to a corner where a sergeant with hazel skin and graying temples waited.

Saluting Andy, the sergeant stuck out his hand. "Lieutenant Stockton, I'm Gus Griffin, platoon sergeant for special recon. Welcome to Eagle."

"Thank you, Sergeant." Gus's handshake felt firm and friendly.

Once all the names on Gus's clipboard had been checked off, he waved his assistant over, then addressed the group. "Gentlemen, grab your gear. The private will show you to your barracks and where the closest mess hall is located. Tomorrow at 0800, we'll meet in the briefing building across from the barracks to start your orientation and begin updating your advanced jungle training."

"When can we call home?" a voice asked from the back.

"You can't," Gus said. "Outgoing calls from here are few and far between. We're too close to the front and stand to lose too much if somebody says the wrong thing. But you can write. Mail is delivered a couple of times a week when you're in camp. Long-range recon patrols get their mail when they surface to be resupplied, or they can pick it up at the post office when they get back to camp."

Andy hung back as the rest of the men followed the private. "Sergeant, I heard a rumor about an enemy offensive in the works. Any truth to it?"

Gus nodded. "It's possible, sir. We've had reports that the Viet Cong, the guerrilla faction of the NVA, have increased their activity along the southern border of the DMZ. That could mean NVA regulars are preparing to follow. Colonel Clark, Camp Eagle's commander, wants to increase the number of small reconnaissance squads close to the border to monitor what's going on. That's what our platoon will be doing."

The angst in the pit of Andy's stomach worsened. "How long have you been in-country, Sergeant?"

"Just started my third tour, sir."

"Lifer, huh?"

"Yes, sir. Looking to retire after this one."

"Have you always done recon?"

"Yes, sir."

"Then I imagine you can teach us new guys a lot."

"I'll try, sir. Come on, I'll give you a ride to your barracks."

Driving toward the center of camp, they passed supply tents, multiple mess halls that smelled like dinner, laundry tents, horseshoe pits, clubs for officers and those who weren't, and a large mobile army surgical hospital, or MASH unit, where patients lounged on benches or strode around dressed in layered hospital gowns and bandages. Nettie's friend and long-time nursing mentor, Linda Howard, was stationed with this MASH unit. He'd be sure to look her up.

After stowing their gear, Andy and Moretti toured the camp, filled up on a fried chicken, mashed potatoes, green beans, and apple pie dinner, then separated to pen letters home. There wasn't much to write about, but at least Nettie and his mom would know he had arrived safely. Once the patrols started, there would be few chances to let them know anything.

The next morning, Gus greeted Andy with a salute and warm smile as he and the rest of the platoon entered the briefing building. Leading Andy to the front of the room, Gus's tone went flat as he introduced a tall, thin, balding officer. "Lieutenant Stockton, this is our company commander, Major Smith."

"Sir," Andy said, offering his hand. He fought the urge to wipe his palm on his pants after the major's sweaty, indifferent shake.

Gus turned toward two men standing off to the side, warmth returning to his voice. "Lieutenant, this is Due Le and Quy Tran, our ARVN interpreters."

The handshakes of the two men were welcoming. "Pleasure to meet you both," Andy said.

Gus motioned for the four of them to sit in the front row as Major Smith called the group to order. Welcoming everyone to the briefing in a bored voice, he introduced Andy as the platoon leader and Gus as his second.

Andy wished it were the other way around.

Moving to a large map of Vietnam, the major used a black-tipped wooden pointer to trace the southern edge of the DMZ. "We have reports that the Viet Cong—VC for short—have infiltrated the DMZ and are attempting to establish control of strategic villages on this side of the border. If true, NVA regulars may follow and try to use those villages to stage an offensive in the months to come." Moving the pointer west, he added, "Lieutenant, your platoon will be split into two squads and conduct deep cover reconnaissance patrols here, in the Vinh Lee District."

Andy studied the topography markings and noted mostly mountainous jungle, with widely scattered villages in the valleys and plains.

"The VC commonly set up cadres of sympathizers in villages they want to control. These spies suppress any resistance, often violently, and divert the village's resources north. They also try to recruit young men and boys from the villages to join their ranks or those of the NVA. If the boys refuse, they are conscripted or taken by force." Laying the pointer down, Major Smith turned to Andy and Gus. "We want your squads to find out which villages have cadres, which ones are actually occupied by VC, and determine if the NVA is showing any signs of following. Other recon platoons will be doing the same eastward along the DMZ. Questions?"

Seeing no hands, the Major continued. "The two most dangerous times for an American soldier in Vietnam are his first and last patrols. We've learned to dramatically decrease casualties by providing in-country training above and beyond what you learned at Fort Benning. To that end, your activities for the rest of this week will include advanced jungle survival and reconnaissance techniques. Next week, you will practice these skills in overnight patrols in the jungle surrounding the base. During these practice patrols, Lieutenant Stockton and Sergeant Griffin will be assessing your abilities. Afterward, they will divide the platoon into two squads. Each squad will then conduct a two-week patrol along the closest boundary of your primary reconnaissance area. You will then come back to Eagle to debrief, make any needed personnel adjustments, and prepare to conduct longer patrols further north in your assigned area. Long-range patrols can last between thirty to ninety days, sometimes longer."

The inexperienced soldiers in the room became restless at hearing how long they could be in the jungle. Andy stilled them with a glance.

Major Smith motioned for Gus to come forward. "I'm

going to turn the briefing over to Sergeant Griffin. He will fill you in on the logistics of your training."

As Major Smith left the building, Gus strolled over to a box sitting on a long folding table in the front of the room. One by one he pulled out packs of cigarettes and chewing gum, bars of soap and candy, tubes of toothpaste, containers of deodorant and commercial bug repellant, and toilet paper. "As a recon platoon, our job is to reach our target, collect data, and leave without anyone ever knowing we were there, especially the VC, NVA, and their sympathizers. Living a covert life in an unforgiving jungle is not easy. In fact, it's damn hard and unbelievably dangerous. To survive, there are rules you must follow. The first is that you will not pack items like these." Gus motioned toward the table.

The moans and groans started immediately. Andy raised his hand, again commanding silence as Gus continued.

"We can't afford to let commercial smells or trash of any kind give away our position. Either could get us killed."

"Sir?" a voice asked from the back. "If we have to use leaves for TP, how do we know which ones are safe?"

"Good question. Each of you will receive a laminated handout of plants to avoid. I suggest you pay attention to it."

Some of the inexperienced men sent raised eyebrow looks to one another. The experienced ones just nodded.

"The second rule is don't fight the jungle. Use it to your advantage. It provides food, water, and cover against the enemy and the elements. Its noise, as well as its silence, warns you if someone or something is approaching. It even has medicines for some of our most common ailments. However, if you ignore or disrespect it, the jungle will kill you. Pack out everything you pack in. Leave the environment exactly as you found it and keep your eyes open and moving.

"Rule three. Protect yourself. Keep your steel helmets on even when your perimeter is set. Keep your sleeves down and buttoned and your pants tucked into your socks. If you don't, the bugs will eat you alive and the bot flies will use your skin as an incubator for their larva. Use lemongrass, basil, and plain old mud as bug repellants. Put it on all exposed skin, including your head. Assume unknown plants, vines, and snakes are poisonous, bathe when it rains, keep your feet dry, and don't drink any untreated jungle water unless it is in the form of rain.

"Rule four. Take care of your rifle. Here, the enemy has one goal and that is to kill you."

The room went still.

"While our mission is reconnaissance, don't take your rifle for granted. Keep it clean, keep it within arm's length, keep a bullet in the chamber, and remember, if the enemy is in range, so are you. If you need to hit the ground, keep the barrel of your gun up. If it's raining hard, keep the barrel down. And always carry at least six magazines. That being said, we will not—and I repeat—will not engage the enemy in any offensive action. We fire defensively and only if needed to save a life. Remember, our goal is to avoid detection."

Reminded of their covert status, Andy relaxed a little. He never relished the idea of taking a human life, but he also wasn't about to let someone take his without a fight.

"Rule five. Never forget where you are. Walk heel first, look left, look right, and look down every third step. It's the best way to keep yourself from being blown up, impaled on a punji board, dropped into a spear pit, or bitten by a poisonous snake. The VC have few weapons, and the ones they do have are usually scavenged from us. However, they're great at conniving other ways to kill us, even more so than the NVA. Expect the unexpected," Gus emphasized. "They'll distract you in one direction, while someone tries to kill you from another. They like to use foot traps attached to spear boards and are great at setting tripwires attached to grenades.

If you hear the soft ping of a pin being pulled, you have two seconds to hit the deck. Understood?"

Gus and Andy looked around at the nodding heads.

"The VC are also very good at hiding," Gus continued. "Tunnels, caves, treetop canopies, dead tree trunks, ledges, and dense brush. They'll hit you when you're vulnerable, run like hell, then hide and hit you again. They'll also hide in plain sight. VC and their cadres roam the villages, supposedly to help people, but more often terrorizing and brutalizing to ensure submission. They've murdered hundreds of thousands of South Vietnamese civilians this way. So, when villagers are around, pay attention to where they are looking. Those living in fear will look down and avoid eye contact. Actual VC and cadre members will have their eyes up and watching everyone."

"Time to remember that class on body language," Moretti joked, lightening the mood in the room.

"Exactly," Gus said. "Sometimes body language can say more than words." He picked up a long, narrow piece of brown cloth from the table. "The VC do not wear uniforms, but they do favor black tunics as do their cadres." Tying the brown belt around his waist, he picked up a knife and a pistol and hid them among the folds of the belt. "Always assume the enemy is armed, especially if they are wearing belts similar to this one."

Gus removed the weapons and belt and moved to the center of the room. "The last and most important rule is one word. Team. When you arrive in-country, it's all about you. What you need to learn, what you need to see, what you need to hear, and what you need to do to stay alive. Out there, it's not about you, it's about your team, your squad, and what it needs. Your squad lives or dies based on the skills of its weakest link. You don't want to be the self-centered ass that gets someone killed."

"And if the enemy spots us anyway?" someone asked.

Gus looked at Andy and winked. "Try to look unimportant. They may be low on ammo and only shoot at the officers."

Laughter rippled across the room.

"Seriously, follow the rules and they will get you back here in one piece. Now, does anyone have questions?"

"How often do we get supply drops when we're out on patrol?" someone asked.

"If we're out for a month or longer, we'll get drops every couple of weeks, but only when it's safe. If we're close enough to the enemy to do our job, the choppers can't come in without giving away our position, so be prepared to live off the jungle more times than not."

The double doors in the back of the room opened, and an aproned private pushed in a cart holding a tall coffee pot and stacks of Styrofoam cups.

"Let's take a ten-minute break," Gus said.

Most of the men who were in-country for the first time stayed seated, not even bothering with social chatter, their expressions reflecting a sobering reality. Andy got a cup of coffee and walked outside. He felt good about being paired with Gus. He outranked the sergeant but understood the value of experience and common sense in keeping soldiers from becoming mortality statistics. They just had to be willing to listen.

TEN DAYS LATER, ANDY JOINED Gus in the mess tent. Except for Moretti, he barely knew the men in his platoon, yet he already had to make critical decisions that could influence the rest of their lives. The platoon had finished orientation and completed the overnight practice patrols using experienced soldiers to guide the new ones and testing different combinations of men to discern who worked together best. Earlier in the day, he and Gus had divided the platoon into two squads of ten, including the two ARVN interpreters. Now they had to assign men to key positions within each squad before heading north into the jungle tomorrow morning.

"Ready to review position assignments, Sergeant?" Andy asked, taking a seat across the table.

"I think so," Gus replied, sliding his list toward Andy. "I put those with in-country experience in the key positions to start and will rotate the new guys in as I get to know them better."

Andy studied the list while Gus got them both a beer. During his time at Fort Benning, Andy had trained for all routine patrol positions, including the most dangerous ones— point, slack, sharpshooter, and rear security. As point man, he walked ten yards ahead of the rest of the squad, scanning for anything out of place, learning to expect the unexpected and anticipating what's coming next and from which direction. In the slack position, he stayed five yards behind the point man and at least five yards ahead of the squad, scanning in the opposite direction of the point. As third man in, the sharp-shooter position, his rifle stayed up and ready to take out targets spotted by the point and slack. And, when covering rear security, he'd learned how to do 360s while still moving forward. The rest of the squad stayed in the cradle or middle.

Once promoted to lieutenant, Andy had evaluated soldiers and assigned them to each of the positions, but at Fort Benning, the enemy and bullets weren't real and a good meal, shower, and comfortable bunk waited for each man at the end of the day. None of that applied here.

"Your assignments look good," Andy said. "See what you think of mine." He slid both lists across the table. "On point, I have Ronnie Mays, the one nicknamed Strawberry." Andy wasn't crazy about nicknames based on an individual's most vulnerable characteristics, but in this case, the man with red hair and freckles preferred his nickname. "Strawberry's been in-country the longest and has the most experience on point. His peripheral vision is incredible. He picked up small trail signs others missed on some of the practice patrols. And he always looks twice if he doesn't trust his first glance."

"You notice a lot for a new lieutenant."

"Beginner's luck," Andy replied, half-kiddingly. "I've got Skip Rawlin as slack. He's quiet, but he and Strawberry have a smooth rhythm. If Strawberry's looking up, Rawlin is looking down. If Strawberry's looking left, Rawlin is looking right."

Gus nodded. "You're right, they are a good team. Rawlin also has a reputation as a fixer. If something isn't working, he usually knows how to fix it, including rifles and radios."

"That's good to know," Andy replied, marking Rawlin as backup radio man. "I put Dan Chase as third man in, the sharpshooter position. He's cool under pressure, and he's got icy precision with a rifle. He put six shots in the bullseye in less than thirty seconds at the range yesterday."

"I saw that. Impressive."

"Next is John Wayne Taylor, the one the guys nicknamed Cowboy. He's been cocky and a little sloppy on the practice patrols. For now, he stays in the middle where I can watch him."

"Good move. It will be interesting to see how he'll react under pressure."

"Damn, Gus. I'm not sure how I'm going to react under pressure, much less Cowboy and the rest of these guys."

"I'm not worried about you, sir."

Andy wished he shared Gus's optimism. "I put Paul Trent, a.k.a. Doc, in the cradle. He watches out for everyone. He spots men with blisters before they start limping and those with bites before they start scratching. And he's obsessive about the men keeping their feet dry and skin covered."

Gus laughed. "He'll be a good one to have on long patrols. Who's your rear sharpshooter?"

"Matt Hollis."

"The one they call the philosopher," Gus tapped his temple. "He's an exceptional shot and is always analyzing and questioning what he's seeing. This is his second tour."

"A sharpshooting philosopher. Interesting combination," Andy said.

"He'll be a steadying influence on your new guys. How about rear security?"

"Scott Sirocco," Andy replied. "He has a good eye, steady aim, and a can-do attitude."

"He also has an infectious laugh. He'll help keep things light," Gus added, looking at the list again. "So, that leaves Moretti as your radioman."

Andy nodded. "He's small but strong as an ox, hears like a bat, and has a clear, low voice. He covered the radio for me at Benning."

"He's scrappy. I had to break up a scuffle between him and one of my guys."

"Let me guess," Andy chuckled. "The other guy started it and Moretti ended it."

"That's about the size of it. My guy made the mistake of calling him shorty. The next thing I knew, Moretti was pounding the heck out of him."

"Did Moretti shake the man's hand after?"

"Yeah, he did."

"He's a good man to have in a fight."

"Your lineup looks good, Lieutenant. If you're agreeable, Quy Tran can go with you to translate and I'll take Due Le with me."

"What can you tell me about Quy?" Andy asked.

"He's young, smart, and hardworking. He blends in well and knows how to get close enough to hear things without getting caught. I've worked with him before. He's a good man."

"How did he learn English well enough to become an interpreter?"

"Quy is what Asians call 'life dust' or one who is left behind. He's the son of a French soldier and a South Vietnamese woman. Neither wanted him, so he ended up in a missionary orphanage, which is where he learned to speak and read English. When fighting broke out, he joined the ARVNs. They eventually transferred him to Camp Eagle because of his language skills. He's one of the best we have."

"Never underestimate the power of what you leave behind, huh?" Andy said.

"That's right. And just so you know, Quy is a master of the martial arts and carries at least two concealed knives. He can also handle an M16 as well as anyone in your squad."

"Good to know." Andy folded his assignment sheet and stuck it in his pocket. "Any other last-minute details we need to cover?"

"No, sir, that about does it."

"Okay. See you at 0500?"

"Yes, sir. Sleep well."

"You, too, Sergeant."

Andy headed back to the barracks. He wanted to write Nettie before his squad headed out. He found a quiet place where there was enough light to write, but he could still see the stars. He filled page after page with things about the camp, his men, what he was learning, and what he wished he could tell her in person. "We start a two-week patrol tomorrow. After that, patrols will be a month or longer, so don't worry if you don't hear from me." Andy looked up at the night sky. Growing up, he and Nettie had spent hours lying in the grass on Allen's Hill watching the stars and dreaming about life. Now, separated or not, they could still be together. "Meet me in the stars. I love you. Andy."

IN THE PREDAWN HOURS, AN M35 cargo truck nicknamed "A Deuce and a Half" transported the two squads ten miles north along Road 546, stopping near a teepee-shaped out-cropping of rocks. From this point on, the two squads would separate and travel north by foot and off-road to begin reconnaissance of the villages in the lower part of the Vinh Lee District. He and Gus had split the district in half. Andy and his squad would recon to the west while Gus and his squad went east. The two squads would meet back at the teepee rocks in two weeks.

Andy adjusted his ruck higher on his shoulders and scanned the surrounding terrain while the rest of his squad finished darkening their faces and hands with camo, the experienced soldiers covering every inch of exposed skin except for their trigger finger. The hilly terrain and dense vegetation would make hiking harder, but the elevation would give them a better line of sight and the undergrowth would provide cover.

"Any last-minute advice, Sergeant?"

"I think you're good to go, Lieutenant. You have good instincts. Trust them."

Andy glanced over at his squad. "Question is, will they?"

"They've been evaluating you as much as you've been evaluating them, sir. You've listened to those with in-country experience, and you didn't care who was watching when you did. They noticed. They also didn't question your position assignments this morning, which says a lot. They'll trust a leader who trusts them."

"And frag those they don't?"

Gus laughed. "I don't think that will be an issue, sir. Just don't underestimate yourself or them."

"Well, let's hope that's enough." Andy took a deep breath. "I'll radio you every morning at 0500 and you radio me at 1900 hours unless we need to go silent. If that's the case, radio when you can."

"And meet back here two weeks from today."

"Right. Good luck, Sergeant," Andy said, shaking Gus's hand.

"Good luck to you, too, sir." Gus signaled his squad to head out in staggered formation.

Andy walked over to his squad, hoping his qualms weren't evident. The experienced soldiers had their jaws set, resolved to do what they had to do. The new ones were wide-eyed and nervous. Quy had traded his ARVN uniform for a dark gray, commoner's tunic with baggy pants and a conical, palm leaf hat. If he had to mingle with the villagers, he needed to look the part.

Andy spoke with a confidence he didn't feel. "Stay low, stay quiet. Don't engage unless it's to save lives. If you have the option, use your knife. If you have to fire, make it count, then everyone backtracks a klick and regroups. If a klick isn't secure, go back two. Running password as you come in is your last name and the number of men approaching. If at any point you are unsure about what to do, follow the guys who've been in-country. Under no circumstances do you ever forget where you are, what our mission is, and that there are people out there willing to kill us to stop us. Stay focused. Understood?"

The experienced GIs kept their eyes on the new guys until every one of them nodded.

"Okay. Stagger the line. Strawberry, take us out."

Chapter 3

NETTIE

In the ER break room, Nettie poured two cups of coffee and stirred dried creamer into both. Life had already settled into an uncomfortable pattern in the few weeks Andy had been gone. He'd said letters from Vietnam take a long time to arrive and not to worry if she didn't hear from him, but she did anyway. Worry, school, worry, study, worry, work, worry, sleep restlessly, repeat. No matter how she tried, his being in harm's way overshadowed everything. "Worry spins us in circles, fear motivates us to act," she'd told him the day he left. *Follow your own advice, silly. Stay busy.*

"There you are." TK's voice interrupted Nettie's thoughts.

"Hey." Nettie handed her a cup of coffee.

"Ahh, just what I need." She took a long sip. "CCU just called. Remember the man who collapsed in the doorway and coded here a while back? The angry one?"

"Mr. Pepper?"

"That's the one. They said he finally woke from his coma, and they were able to wean him off the ventilator this week. He's asking to see you."

"Wonder why?"

"They didn't say. The ER's quiet, so go on up. I'll call you if things get busy."

The electric double doors into the CCU clicked opened just in time for Nettie to see a dinner tray fly from behind a striped curtain, leaving a trail of roast, potatoes, green beans, iced tea, clanging utensils, and shattering glass sliding across the floor.

"Mr. Pepper, what the heck are you doing?" an exasperated voice asked from behind the curtain.

"I didn't stutter," he yelled. "I told you to get out!"

"Just wait a—"

"Get out!" Mr. Pepper bellowed.

A nurse with bits of green beans and splashes of gravy splattered across her white scrub dress came from behind the curtain and closed the glass door. Wiping the tea off her glasses with the hem of her dress, she looked at Nettie. "Are you the intern from the ER? The one who took care of 'that'?" She pointed to the curtain behind her.

"Yes, ma'am."

"Well, 'that' wants to see you."

"Maybe I should wait. He sounded pretty angry."

"Are you kidding? He's been angry since he woke up and realized he wasn't dead. He's been giving us a fit ever since. He won't eat. He won't get out of bed, or even bathe. He refuses to take his pills, so we have to sneak his meds into his IV line. He even told the hospital chaplain to take a hike. No one wants to take care of him. Today was my turn."

"Why does he want to see me?"

"No clue."

"How's his heart?"

The nurse's expression softened. "Not good. There's nothing acute going on right now, but his EKG shows a lot of damage. This wasn't his first heart attack, but it was his biggest. He lost a lot of left ventricle this time, which put him into congestive failure. I doubt he'll ever work again, and he may not make it home to Hawaii. I think he knows it, which may explain his behavior. There's not a lot more we can do for him here since he's off the ventilator, so he's being transferred to the step-down unit in the morning. If they're successful in getting him up and moving, he'll probably be sent to the Godfrey Center to begin cardiac rehab in a week or two."

Nettie had rotated through the Godfrey Center, the nursing home side of the hospital, as part of her school clinicals and knew it well. Most patients there were old and confused, and many were grumpy like Mr. Pepper. She admired and emulated Mrs. Henry, the ancient evening charge nurse who worked there. Nurses on that unit called her The Whisperer because she could calm the most agitated patients by talking softly to them.

"Old folks often have high-frequency hearing loss," she'd explained. "They get frustrated when they are not being understood. I get close to their best ear and talk in a low tone, so they understand me. Even unconscious patients can sometimes hear what you're saying. Never underestimate the power of human contact and what it means to someone who feels isolated and alone."

Nettie had also watched Mrs. Henry befriend the unfriendly, read with the intonation of a Broadway actor to patients who could not see, and embrace those who were upset or dying with a level of empathy that couldn't be taught in a classroom. If anyone could help Mr. Pepper, it would be Mrs. Henry.

Nettie took a step toward Mr. Pepper's room and jumped as a cup of water slammed into the closed door, soaking the curtain, glass, and floor.

"There he goes again," the CCU nurse said weakly. "Even the supervisor won't go near him."

"Mrs. Woods?"

The nurse nodded. "I think she's afraid of getting her uniform dirty and hair mussed if he throws something." The nurse began picking up the dinner debris scattered across the floor. "If you're going in there, go. It's not going to get any better."

Nettie stared at Mr. Pepper's room. "Lord, guide me," she whispered. Taking a deep breath, she slid the door open, stepped in, and closed it with an intentional bang. In the bed lay a man with little resemblance to the gentleman who'd walked into the ER and collapsed. His bed-hair went in all directions, as did his unplanned beard. His bare chest still carried remnants of the circular scorch marks caused by multiple defibrillations, and the bed linens, which were bunched up all around him, held remnants of food, various colored liquids, and pieces of pills.

"What the heck do you think you're doing, throwing things around like a crazy person?" Nettie asked.

Mr. Pepper's lost look turned defensive. "Who the hell do you think you are?" His eyes widened. "Oh, I remember. You're the little twit who called me a jackass in the emergency room."

"Okay, we're even with the name-calling," Nettie replied. "Now, you want to tell me what's eating at you to make you behave this way?"

"I don't have to tell you a damn thing."

"No, you don't. But you're the one who wanted to talk with me, remember?"

Mr. Pepper stared at her for a full minute. When he didn't speak, Nettie turned to leave.

"Wait," he said, looking at her name badge. "So, your name is Nettie, huh?"

"Yes."

"Silly name."

Nettie grinned. "And Pepper's not?"

"Touché," he mumbled. "Thank you for getting my ring back." He raised his hand for her to see. "It hadn't been off my finger in over thirty years until that night."

Nettie walked to his bedside. "You are most welcome. I have a ring that's important to me, too. I'd be sick if I lost it."

He looked at her ringless fingers. "Well, where is it?"

"At home. Interns aren't allowed to wear jewelry on duty."

"What kind of ring is it?"

"An engagement ring."

Mr. Pepper laid his head back and smirked. "Well, well, so you're in love."

"Yes, I am."

"If you're a nursing student, I suppose it's some arrogant resident."

"No. He's a lieutenant in the army. I've known him since kindergarten."

"What's his name?"

"Andy."

"No, that's what you call him. What is his name?"

"Andrew Stephen Stockton."

"Where is Andrew stationed?"

"Vietnam."

"Some cozy, behind-the-lines desk job?"

"No, sir. Long-range reconnaissance along the DMZ."

Mr. Pepper's eyes softened and his voice lost its sharp edge. "In harm's way, huh?"

"Yes, sir."

"When does he come home?"

"In the spring. I'm counting down the days on a big calendar."

"When I was in the navy, I used to count down the days until I could come home to Virginia, too."

"World War II?"

He nodded. "Pearl Harbor. One of the lucky ones—kind of."

"Did you have someone waiting for you? Is that why you were counting down the days?"

"Boy, you're nosy."

"So are you," Nettie replied. "We have to be if we're going to get to know each other."

He gave her a sideways glance, then looked out the window. "No. No one was waiting for me. I just wanted the war to be over."

Nettie's gut told her to move on. "Your nurse said you'd be moving to the step-down unit soon. That's good news."

"They're just trying to get rid of me."

Nettie laughed. "If you were throwing things at me, I'd want to get rid of you, too. But that's not why you're moving."

"The cardiologist has been very clear about my long-term prognosis. They're sending me somewhere else to die a slow death."

"Funny. I didn't take you for a 'glass half empty' kind of guy."

"Spoken like someone at the beginning of life as opposed to the end of it."

Nettie nodded. "Maybe. But you're still one of the lucky ones."

"Lucky?"

"Yes, lucky. You get a second chance to live as well as a second chance to die. Those are gifts."

Mr. Pepper squinted at her. "A second chance to die is a gift?"

"The way I see it, yes. You weren't ready to die in the ER that night."

"And next time, I will be?"

"I suppose that's up to you. But at least you have the gift of time to figure it out."

"Thanks to God, I suppose."

"Well, God and some really good nurses and doctors."

"Humpf."

"I think you'll like the step-down unit. You'll have

your own bathroom and shower, and there's more room to move around."

"Are you saying I need a bath?"

"Well, you do smell a little gamey."

Mr. Pepper threw back his head and laughed. "Oh, so the pessimistic jackass stinks, huh? At least you're honest."

"Yes, sir. I try to be."

"I'll bet it causes you problems, this tendency to speak the truth."

"Sometimes."

"Well, don't change. The only people who have a problem with the truth are those hiding a lie."

"Does that mean your half-empty glass is filling up?"

"Don't push your luck, young lady."

The glass door slid open and his CCU nurse stuck her head in hesitantly as if expecting to duck. She looked at Nettie. "TK called from the ER. There's a multivehicle accident on the way in. She needs you downstairs."

"Okay, thanks." Nettie headed for the door. "Sorry, Mr. Pepper, I have to go."

"Wait."

She turned around.

"I didn't want to come home like this. Angry, I mean. I didn't plan it this way."

"I didn't think so," Nettie replied. "You didn't seem like the type."

"And what type is that?"

"The type who cares a lot about a special ring."

"I know you have to go. Will you come back?"

"Sure, under one condition."

Mr. Pepper raised his eyebrows. "And what pray tell is that?"

"No more flying food. Deal?"

"Deal."

Nettie winked and closed the door.

"Did I hear him laughing?" his battle-worn nurse asked from behind the counter.

Nettie nodded. "It's supposed to be the best medicine." Waving goodbye, she pushed through the CCU door and came face-to-face with Mrs. Woods.

"What are you doing up here," the stone-faced supervisor asked.

Nettie calmed her racing heart. "Visiting a patient."

"Interns are here to work, not make social calls."

"Yes, ma'am."

"First, you're not where you need to be, now you're someplace you shouldn't be."

Nettie didn't respond.

"Who were you visiting?"

A bell dinged as nearby elevator doors opened. Two nurses backed out pulling IV poles with multiple bags and pumps, and a stretcher containing a large, moaning man.

Nettie used the distraction to slip through the exit. She wasn't about to subject Mr. Pepper to one of Mrs. Woods's caustic inquisitions if she could help it.

Controlled chaos greeted her as she entered the ER. All three trauma rooms were bustling. Hoping Mrs. Woods hadn't followed her, Nettie found TK and jumped in to help.

Later that evening, the ER secretary called Nettie to the phone. "CCU for you."

"Hello, this is Nettie."

"Nettie, this is the nurse taking care of Mr. Pepper, the one he was throwing food at earlier. He's been a lot easier to deal with since your visit. He took a sponge bath, let me change his sheets, and hasn't thrown a thing since you left. Whatever you said to him worked. Thanks."

"That's great."

"You should visit him again once he gets settled in the step-down unit. He needs to talk, and he needs to laugh."

"I will."

"Good, but don't let the evening supervisor, Mrs. Woods, know."

"Why?"

"After you left, she wanted to know who you'd visited. She said you were being paid to work, not socialize, and that you were not to visit patients anymore. She wasn't even impressed when I told her how well Mr. Pepper responded to you. I don't know what her issue is, but she has one."

"Thanks. I'll be sure to visit him on my own time."

NETTIE WAITED FOR TK AT THE END of the food counter in the cafeteria. The peanut butter and jelly sandwich and carrot sticks she brought from home looked better than most of the items left over from the dinner rush.

TK selected one of the least wilted salads, then sniffed a tuna fish sandwich and put it on her tray. "It's hard to mess up tuna," she muttered, filling a glass with ice and pushing the button on the tea dispenser.

Just as they were settling in at a corner table, Dougie stopped by. Dressed in the laundry department's uniform of white pants and ice-blue tunic, his prematurely wrinkled face looked worried.

"Hi, Miss TK. Hi, Miss Nettie."

"Hey Dougie, where've you been?" TK asked. "We haven't seen you in a while."

He sat down, his mouth drooping. "I got switched to the day shift, seven a.m. to seven p.m., so I don't get a dinner break anymore. I have to take a lunch one."

"I thought you liked working nights."

"I do. It's quiet and nobody's around to make me nervous."

"Then why change?"

"I didn't want to. My boss reassigned me."

"Well, for heaven's sakes, why?"

"He said one of the evening nursing supervisors complained that I'd left a bunch of stretchers and linens messed up in the recovery room one night. She said she knew it was me because she saw me leaving."

"Were you in the recovery room?"

"No, Miss TK. The day shift restocks the units that close at five, including the recovery room. And you know I never leave things messed up, Miss TK. Ever."

"I know you don't."

"I told my boss I didn't do it, and he believed me, but this supervisor lady wanted him to fire me. He moved me to the day shift instead. He said maybe she'll cool off or realize she made a mistake."

"Dougie, when did she say she saw you leaving the recovery room?" Nettie asked.

"A few weeks ago."

"Was it the same night I saw you in ICU?"

"I think so. She came out of the recovery room as I was waiting for the elevator."

"Which nursing supervisor was it?" TK asked.

"The one who smells good."

"Smells good, huh?" TK glanced at Nettie. "Was it Mrs. Woods?"

"Yeah, that's her name, Mrs. Woods."

"I'm really sorry, Dougie," TK said. "Hopefully, your manager will put you back on nights soon."

"I hope so. You all have a good shift." Dougie shuffled down the hall, his hands deep in his pockets.

TK's brow creased. "I've known Dougie since my first day here. He's a hard worker and always does his job well. He's being railroaded. The question is why? Why is she going after Dougie, and why is she going after you?" TK looked at Nettie. "Care to tell me what's going on?"

Though tempted, Nettie couldn't prove anything, and to imply otherwise would be wrong. Plus, if TK got involved, Mrs. Woods could potentially go after her. "TK, I don't know anything for sure."

TK stirred her tea slowly. "You realize the time may come when you'll have to tell someone, whether you're sure or not."

NETTIE ARRIVED HOME AT MIDNIGHT to find another letter from Andy propped against his framed picture on the bookcase. His first letter had been about the flight over and his arrival at Camp Eagle. The thickness of this envelope promised a lot more information. She sank into a chair as Andy's warm voice resonated from the page.

"Camp Eagle is lot like Fort Benning," he wrote, "except hotter, wetter, and buggier. We have a great view of the mountains, and the sunsets are beautiful. My platoon sergeant, Gus, is a good guy. He's been in-country for three tours and knows a lot. Today, we divided the platoon into two squads. Gus will lead one and I'll lead the other."

Andy described the men in his squad as if trying to learn as much about them as possible—their in-country experience, their abilities, and even unique aspects of their personalities. Men with nicknames like Strawberry, Doc, and Cowboy, and call names like Chase, Hollis, Sirocco, Rawlin, and Quy were becoming the most important people in his life.

"I'm listening to the guys who've been in-country for a while. They know things you can't learn in the pines around Fort Benning, such as which animals and birds serve as the best lookouts, how to use shadow variations to set a safer perimeter, which plants and bugs to avoid, how to use bamboo to collect rainwater, how to sleep sitting up, and how to stay focused in a jungle filled with distractions. Gus says once your mind is off the enemy, he's got you, so focus means everything."

Nettie closed her eyes against the words. Once Andy walked away from Camp Eagle, his risk of being killed or wounded skyrocketed. Pushing on, she continued reading as his thoughts turned to her.

"How are your classes going? Are you still enjoying your internship? Do you have enough money? Would you call Mom and make sure she got my letter? Did you remember to get the oil changed in the Oldsmobile when you got back from Georgia?"

Nettie smiled at his practical reminder, but it faded with his next words.

"We start a two-week patrol tomorrow. After that, patrols will be a month or longer, so don't worry if you don't hear from me." His last line read, "Meet me in the stars. I love you. Andy."

Nettie went outside and looked up. Just twelve hours ago the same stars were over Vietnam.

When getting ready for bed, Nettie traded her pajamas for the button-down collar shirt Andy had left at her apartment. Rolling up the sleeves, she propped pillows behind her and read his letter again, searching between the lines for anything she might have missed the first time.

Taking a box of stationery from her bedside stand, Nettie answered all of Andy's questions and asked dozens of her own. She didn't mention the situation with Mrs. Woods. Any trouble the supervisor might cause was miniscule compared to what Andy faced minute-by-minute. She wasn't about to distract him with unnecessary drama.

Turning out the light, she closed her eyes and steadied her thoughts. She had lots of things to talk about with God.

Chapter 4

ANDY

Much of the vegetation in the jungle had thorns of various shapes and sizes, which when combined with chest-high, razor-sharp elephant grass, made the squad's forward movement challenging and painful. The varying density of the brush often required walking ten yards to the side to move five yards ahead. When they stopped longer than a minute, insects swarmed, flying into their faces and crawling up their arms, legs, and backs. Lemongrass, basil, camouflage cream, and mud were the only things keeping the bloodsuckers from feasting on exposed skin. Staying focused took a lot of effort.

As they moved deeper into the jungle, sounds and activity in the treetop canopy increased. Lemurs flew from tree to tree, gibbons and colorful doucs jabbered and bounced around, and exotic birds called and flitted restlessly at a time of day when treetop activity usually began to slow. Andy signaled the squad to take a knee and went forward to talk with his front three. He pointed to the treetops. "Is the wildlife up there reacting to us or is something else stirring them up?"

"It may be us, but predators will get them going, too, sir," Strawberry said.

"Do they get this active when natives come and go?"

"Not usually."

"Then most likely the VC don't stir them up, either, which means they could follow the canopy noise right to us."

"Yes, sir," Strawberry replied.

"Is there any way to keep the canopy calm when we're around?"

"Minimal noise and movement until they learn we don't pose a threat."

"Plus, the longer we're out, the more we look and smell like the natural habitat, the less they'll react," Rawlin added.

"Okay, let's move out." As Andy turned and started back to the cradle, Rawlin grabbed his arm.

"Don't move, sir," he said, pointing at the ground.

Andy's boot sat on the back of a black-and-white banded viper, commonly known as the two-step snake. The ends of the angry serpent alternately writhed and coiled as it tried to strike. "Son of a bitch," Andy muttered.

Rawlin stepped on the snake's head and then used a quick stroke of his knife to separate it from the rest of the body.

"Good catch, Rawlin. Thanks."

"You're welcome, sir."

"Don't worry, Lieutenant," Strawberry teased, "a two-step viper bite doesn't really kill you in two steps. It usually takes ten unless you try to run."

Andy grinned and put his hand on his chest. "The heart attack caused by stepping on it in the first place almost took me out." He kicked the two halves of the snake into the brush, then covered the remaining blood with dirt. "Let's get out of here."

By noon, Andy's greatest leadership challenge had been trying to keep Cowboy's curiosity from pulling him too far out of the staggered formation. Andy had reeled him in twice already and warned him to watch his position. One more time and he'd be Andy's first disciplinary action.

By midafternoon, Strawberry found a wildlife trail heading north, which made walking easier but presented additional hazards. The path wasn't wide enough for staggering, so Andy put more distance between each man. The risk of booby traps also increased. The VC loved to weaponize any path they found, even if it meant killing innocent civilians and wildlife as a consequence. Wading into a stand of bamboo, Strawberry cut off a long stem and stripped the leaves, making sure to hide them in the undergrowth. Moving slowly down the path, he used the thin, curved end of the bamboo as a divining rod to detect tripwires for grenades and triggers for punji spears.

They were making decent time when Strawberry stopped suddenly and lifted his arm at a right angle. The squad froze as he dropped the bamboo and slowly raised his rifle. Rawlin and Chase followed suit, all aiming in the same direction. Thirty seconds later, a massive, nine-foot tiger sauntered out of the brush. No one moved, except Cowboy who stepped off the path to get a better look.

"Freeze, soldier!" Andy hissed.

The huge cat swung his wide head their way and stared as if trying to figure out if they were food or an enemy.

Staring eye to eye with the tiger, Strawberry pulled his shoulders back, puffed out his chest, and slowly raised his arms, followed by Rawlin and the rest of the squad, except for Chase who kept his rifle pointed at the big animal's neck.

When the tiger still didn't move, Strawberry took a grenade, left the safety on and the pin in, and hurled it at the cat's head. Taking a startled jump sideways as the grenade landed, the tiger hesitated then trotted off into the jungle.

Andy spun on Cowboy. "What part of that freeze signal did you not understand?"

"I just wanted to get a better look, sir."

"I don't give a fat rat's ass what you wanted, soldier. Freeze means freeze. Is that understood?"

"Yes, sir."

"And," continued Andy, "if I have to correct your line position one more time, you'll spend the rest of this patrol in front of me. Then, as soon as we get back to Eagle you're going to the stockade for disobeying orders. Is *that* understood?"

"Yes, sir." Cowboy raised his eyebrows in surprise at the rebuke.

Andy went forward to join Strawberry, Rawlin, and Chase as the rest of the squad scanned the jungle around them. "Strawberry, how did you know that damn cat was coming?"

"Brush was moving down low but not on top, sir. Plus, I got a whiff of buttered popcorn."

"What?"

Strawberry nodded. "That's right, sir, buttered popcorn. I don't know why, but it's true. A few months back, a tiger killed a recon soldier out of Camp Carroll. Drug him off while he slept. His squad heard the man scream but they couldn't locate him in the dark. They found what was left of him the next morning. During the debriefing, the squad said they smelled buttered popcorn during the attack."

Andy refused to show the shock he felt. "What are the chances that beast will come back or wait to ambush us?"

"It's always possible, but they tend to attack single prey not groups. Plus, I think he'd eaten recently."

"How could you tell?"

"His belly was hanging low. If he's not hungry, he's not likely to bother us."

"Or maybe he's really a she and she's pregnant and starving," Andy said. "Could you tell?"

"No, sir, too far away."

"Give it another minute, then let's get going."

"Yes, sir, and I'll pick up my grenade on the way."

"Good work, Strawberry."

"Thank you, sir."

Walking back along the line, Andy warned the rest of the

squad to watch for low brush movement and the smell of buttered popcorn. "Sirocco, increase your 360s. Make sure that damn thing doesn't sneak up behind us."

"Already on it, sir."

THUNDER RUMBLED OVER THE DISTANT mountains as they headed out. Gus had said afternoon temperatures could top a 120°F and trigger suffocating downpours. With salty sweat running in his eyes, filling his ears, and puddling in his boots, Andy welcomed the idea of cool rain, but not a mission-slowing monsoon. According to his map, they were still two klicks from the best position to recon night activities at the first village.

A short distance later, Strawberry raised his arm again and motioned Andy forward. A stream with deep, jagged banks lay before them. On the other side sat a fifty-yard clearing before the jungle began again. To cross, they had to spread out, negotiate both banks and the water, then hope they could get across the clearing without being seen.

Andy studied the massive, gray-black wave of clouds pushing in from the north, lying as low as fog. With luck, they could make it across and into the jungle before the rain hit. Checking the clearing once more, he signaled Strawberry to cross while the rest of the squad covered him and prepared to follow. Strawberry carefully descended the soft-pitted bank, crossed the shin-deep creek, and scrambled up the other side. Positioning his M16 in front of him as he reached the top, he scanned the clearing before signaling Rawlin and Chase to cross. Joining Strawberry, Rawlin helped cover the clearing while Chase turned his eyes and rifle toward their rear. Doc, Quy, Andy, and Moretti waded in at thirty-second intervals, while Hollis, Cowboy, and Sirocco guarded their flank.

The surprisingly cool water felt good as Andy negotiated the rocky stream. He'd almost made it across when Chase jumped up and yelled. "Out of the water! Now!"

An eight-foot-high wall of white water barreled toward them, runoff from the approaching monsoon. Hollis, Cowboy, and Sirocco scrambled back to where they'd started as Andy and the others rushed to scale the opposite bank. Andy reached the top just as the angry water surged under his boots.

"Count heads!" Andy yelled. He turned to grab the radio but Moretti wasn't there. Racing back to the creek, Andy saw Moretti on his back, clinging to the limb of a nearby tree and struggling to keep his face out of the raging water. The weight of his ruck and the top-heavy radio prevented him from flipping to his stomach. Luckily, the force of the water had released the radio's strapped-down antennae, which now bobbed above the surface about an arm's length from shore. Andy tossed his rifle to Rawlin as he made a running dive to grab the antenna. Gripping the end of the slippery rod with both hands, he tried to pull Moretti to shore, but Moretti couldn't see or hear him and wouldn't let go of the lifesaving tree limb. As the rising torrent softened the bank, Andy started to slide. Strawberry dropped next to him and got another hand on the antenna as Doc and Quy grabbed their legs.

Rawlin ran downstream, frantically waving his arms to get Moretti's attention over the deafening roar. "Let go! We've got you! Let go!"

Wild-eyed, Moretti turned his head enough to see Rawlin and reluctantly let go of the limb.

Dragging him to dry ground, Doc and Quy quickly unsnapped the radio and ruck and rolled Moretti onto his stomach as he coughed up dirty water and gasped for air. Andy grabbed the radio, praying it still worked. When it buzzed on, he warned troops to the south of the flash flood headed their way. Signaling Hollis, Cowboy, and Sirocco on the opposite bank to take cover, he handed Moretti's ruck to Quy and slung the radio over his own shoulder.

Andy lifted Moretti's chin. "Sorry, buddy, you can rest later. Right now, we need to get the hell out of here. We've made enough noise to wake the dead. Doc, Quy, get him up. Chase, cover our rear. Strawberry, get us into the jungle now!"

The torrential rain following the flood hit hard and fast as they reached the camouflaging brush. Strawberry found an area with a canopy thick enough to divert some of the downpour and signaled the group to stop.

Andy draped his poncho over a couple of bushes to form a makeshift tent for Moretti, who still appeared pale and shaken. "Strawberry, Rawlin, Chase, and Quy, set up a perimeter. Doc, stay with Moretti. I'm going back to help the others cross as soon as the storm passes." Andy grabbed his rifle and retraced their path to the edge of the clearing. He tried to see his men through the rain and across the flooding creek but couldn't. Taking a knee, he waited and watched. The storm moved out quickly, but the receding water did not. Two hours later, Andy darted across the clearing and knelt in soggy brush along the bank. Scanning up and down the stream, he signaled Hollis, Cowboy, and Sirocco to cross one at a time, raising his rifle to cover. Hollis crossed first, climbed the muddy bank, and tucked in near Andy to cover their flank. Cowboy followed, then Sirocco. In staggered formation, the four of them ran across the clearing, pausing at the jungle's edge to make sure they weren't followed.

"Stockton plus three," Andy said in a low voice to alert the perimeter.

"Roger that, Lieutenant," Rawlin responded.

Andy dropped to his knees next to Moretti's makeshift tent. "Luca, look at me. Are you okay?"

Moretti stared straight ahead.

"Answer me, soldier."

"I couldn't breathe," Moretti whispered.

Andy dropped his ruck, removed his helmet, and sat down.

"I couldn't get my ruck off. The water kept pulling me down. I knew I was going to die. I knew it. All I could think of was my mom. She'd be all alone." Moretti's voice caught in his throat. "And I knew I was going to die alone."

Andy wanted to comfort Moretti, but they didn't have time. "Luca, you weren't alone then and you're not alone now. I'm sorry it happened, but we have a job to do. You have five minutes to pull yourself together. Then we need to move, someone could have seen us, plus we have three villages to scout and less than two weeks to do it. The squad's best chance of accomplishing our mission and getting back in one piece is if everyone is operating at a hundred percent. Understand? We need you."

Moretti rubbed his face and took a deep breath. "Roger that, Lieutenant."

"Good." Andy pulled the boonie hat from Moretti's ruck and tossed it to him. "Your helmet is long gone, so this will have to do until we get back to Eagle."

Moretti ran his fingers along the soft rim of the hat. "Lieutenant? Thank you for saving my life."

Andy squeezed his shoulder. "Not me. We."

"You're a Christian, right, Lieutenant?"

Andy nodded. He'd seen Moretti crossing himself at times and figured he was Catholic. "I'm a Protestant. Baptist to be specific."

"Protestants are allowed to talk directly with God, I mean without a priest? Right?"

"Everyone is allowed to talk with God, Moretti. I talk with him every day. Sometimes, several times a day. Human beings created denominations, not God. He wants you to call upon him." Andy pulled the New Testament out of his breast pocket. Keeping the picture, he handed the Book to Moretti. "This says so."

Moretti rubbed his thumb over the worn, crinkled cover. Sliding it into his ruck, he got up and thanked each man who helped save his life.

TWILIGHT HAD SETTLED IN BY THE TIME the squad reached the outskirts of the first village. From the jungle's edge, Andy and Quy used binoculars to study the village's layout, looking for anything unusual: sentries, people in uniforms, black tunics, brown belts, guarded storage huts, motorized vehicles, or villagers behaving oddly. Deep ruts and scattered patties of animal dung marked the one dirt road leading in and out of the village, most likely created by wagons and the water buffalos pulling them. These massive animals grazed silently in a half dozen split-rail pens scattered along the edge of the quiet village.

"I see nothing unusual, Lieutenant. Typical village," Quy said.

"Good. Tomorrow we'll get a look at the other side."

Andy motioned his men to come close. "Set up a dark camp and four-point, doubled-up perimeter, one man sleeping while the other stands watch. We'll rotate the extra men in so once every five days you can sleep through the night. Moretti, tonight's your night to sleep."

Sirocco did the math. "Lieutenant, you're putting yourself in the rotation?"

"Yes." He scanned the faces of his surprised men. "Sleep is sleep and we're all going to need it. Now, you all set up and get something to eat."

Just after dark, Andy saw lanterns moving along the road. Using night-vision binoculars, he watched as women carried small cloth sacks toward the pond that lay between the village and the jungle. Reaching the water, they mounted their lanterns on the sides of small, disc-shaped boats made of woven reeds. Pushing off, each women paddled and swirled toward clusters of flowers scattered around the water's edge. Lowering the color-distorting binoculars, Andy stared at the mesmerizing dance of lights.

"They're seeding the lotus flowers, Lieutenant," Moretti whispered, sliding next to Andy. "Women in the villages place fresh tea leaves in the center of the blossom, then tie the petals closed with thin strips of silk. The tea steeps in the flower overnight, absorbing the nectar. At sunrise, the women come back to collect it."

Andy cocked his head at Moretti, surprised at the fighter's softer side. "You did your homework."

"Actually, my mom did. When I joined the army, she figured I'd be sent to Vietnam, so she bought a book about the country and the culture. She liked the part about the tea ceremony. The post exchange at Camp Eagle sells lotus tea, so I sent her some."

"Where does your mom live?"

"Brooklyn. She's lived in the same apartment for thirty years. Sixth-floor walk-up."

"You walked up and down six floors every day?"

"Multiple times a day."

"No wonder you're so strong," Andy said. "We'll need to remember to locate the lakes and ponds first when we scope out the other villages. We don't want to get caught in the middle of this nightly ritual."

"It is more than a ritual, Lieutenant," Quy said, joining them. "The lotus flower is sacred in our culture. It can live thousands of years and even come back to life after being dormant for decades. To us, the lotus represents a divine eternity. To make and drink tea nurtured in its blossoms is a spiritual experience as well as a tradition."

"Do the VC share this belief?" Andy asked.

"The VC believe in nothing but their own power," Quy replied. "But they like the taste of the tea."

Andy looked back at the dancing lights, wishing he could share the beautiful scene with Nettie. The words he'd write later wouldn't capture the magic. He made a mental note to send Nettie and his mom some lotus tea when he returned to Camp Eagle.

It started drizzling as Andy made rounds on the perimeter one last time. During the day the rain brought some relief from the heat, but at night it promised nothing but misery. Arranging his ruck as a lumpy pillow, he pulled his poncho over his already soaked, dirty uniform, tucked his rifle close to his chest, and tried in vain to get comfortable, the sloppy ground puddling beneath him. Despite exhaustion, Andy's eyes wouldn't stay closed. Human forms appeared everywhere in the dripping shadows. His muscles ached and the freeze-dried stew he'd choked down for dinner sat in an indigestible lump in his stomach. The surreal noises of the jungle assaulted his ears—siren cicadas, bass-blowing frogs, *faaaa-cue* geckos, *reeee-up* birds, screeching crickets the size of his hand, and countless grotesque bugs emanating sounds to match. Even when he managed to push the barrage to the back of his mind, he couldn't let go of the day. In less than twenty-four hours he'd stepped on a poisonous snake, encountered a man-eating but thankfully uninterested tiger, and nearly lost a man to drowning. *How in the world will we survive two weeks of these lethal surprises, much less a whole year?* A little voice in the back of his mind refused to allow him another second of self-pity. *Look at the bright side, silly. Poisonous or not, your size eleven boot and a knife bested that tiny snake. You got to see a real tiger up close and personal, your men are still in one piece, and no one shot at you. Right? You led your first surveillance mission without getting caught, and you got to witness an unbelievable light show. Not bad for a first day. So, suck it up buttercup, count your blessings, and remember I love you more than you'll ever know.* Andy drifted off to sleep with Nettie's voice in his head.

Before sunup, Andy and his men were in recon positions on the far side of the village. Lanterns flickered on hut by hut, then swung gently as the women went back to the pond to collect the lotus-infused tea. At sunrise, they returned to the village and poured the tea into a burlap bag sitting on the back of a rickety, old wagon. Tying the bag closed, a young woman pushed it close to other bags in the center, then joined a gray-haired woman on the driver's seat. Slapping the reins on the back of their water buffalo, the young woman guided the wagon down the rutted road and away from the village.

Remembering the VC often forced old people, women, and children to deliver supplies, Andy eased closer to Strawberry. "Where do you suppose they are taking those bags?"

"Probably to an open-air market."

"I think we need to find out for sure." Andy made coded notes on his map, checked in with Gus, then signaled Strawberry. "Keep that wagon in view."

As the women traveled, they stopped to trade scoops of tea for food and other items with people living along the dirt road. By midmorning, they arrived at a large intersection. Angling the wagon so the back faced both roads, the women climbed down. The younger one put a wooden bucket of water under the buffalo's nose, while the older one pulled the bags to the rear of the wagon so they could be seen. Over the next few hours, travelers going in all directions stopped to smell the tea and check the quality of the rice. Most treated the women with respect and either bartered or paid for their supplies, but some took what they wanted and walked away.

By midafternoon, the women moved their few remaining bags toward the front of the wagon and turned the water buffalo toward home.

Andy pulled his squad deeper into the jungle and took a knee. "This doesn't make sense. Why risk coming to an intersection like this? They've had as much stolen as they've sold."

"Could be a matter of survival," Chase replied. "I imagine they make more money here than going hut to hut."

"They could also be bartering for things that are hard to come by like medicine," Doc added.

"Maybe." Andy couldn't shake the feeling that they were missing something. "But two women out there alone? Remember what Gus said about the VC? Those women could have been seriously hurt or worse—"

By the next week, Andy's squad had finished reconning the second village, found nothing suspicious, and were heading to the third. As a squad, they were developing a rhythm that made their work easier and more efficient. The one exception was Cowboy. He seemed to be trying harder to follow the rules of reconnaissance, but Andy still had to watch him more closely than all the others combined.

"Looks like the next village is about four klicks away as the crow flies," Andy said, studying the map, "which means we're not going to get there before dark."

"There's some dense jungle and a big rice paddy between here and there, but no one should be in the fields right now. Crops are young and at least two to three months away from being harvested." Strawberry pointed to a stream near the halfway point. "This might be a good place for us to overnight."

"I agree," Andy said. "Let's go."

While the jungle had its own unique dangers, it at least offered the squad some camouflage. The rice paddy stretching before them offered no protection at all. Lined with raised dikes of young, bright green rice alternating with ditches filled with brackish, animal dung-filled water, the two-acre paddy had to be crossed to get to the protection of the jungle on the other side. The only discernable movement anywhere in the paddy were ducks swimming in the filthy water and weeding the dikes for free.

"We'll cross here," Andy said, pointing to the two closest dikes. "Strawberry, Chase, Cowboy, Moretti, and I will go to the left. The rest of you go to the right. If anyone is watching, we're going to be sitting ducks, so distance your stagger, move fast, and keep your eyes open. Strawberry and Rawlin lead off."

Halfway across the narrow dike, Cowboy came to an abrupt stop. "What the hell—RATS!" High stepping as if his feet were touching hot coals, he landed on the soft edge of the dike and teetered back and forth. Dropping his rifle, he windmilled his arms in a desperate attempt to keep his balance, but his ruck shifted and he went head-first into the dung-filled irrigation ditch.

Buried upside down and waist-deep, Cowboy kicked helplessly. Strawberry and Chase rushed back, and Andy and Moretti ran forward to help. Grabbing at Cowboy's flailing legs, they tried to pull him out, but were laughing too hard at the cartoon-like image.

"He's going to suffocate if we don't get him out of there," Andy said. "Strawberry, Chase, grab the bottom of his ruck. Moretti and I will get his legs. Everyone pulls on the count of three. One, two, three!"

Cowboy came out of the black, watery muck with a long, loud slurp, and landed on the dike with a dung-flinging plop. Looking like a tarry goblin with bulging white eyes, he snorted and spit over and over trying to clear the muck from his mouth and nose. Those who pulled him from the water backed away from the nauseating outhouse smell.

"Lieutenant," Cowboy sputtered, looking around the dike. "Did you see them? Those rats were a foot long!"

"They're just rice rats, moron," Chase said. "We all saw them. What'd you think they were going to do, eat you?"

"Shut up, you son of a—"

"Quiet!" Andy hissed. He quickly checked the field's perimeter to make sure no one else was around. "Get him up. We've got to get across this thing."

Strawberry and Chase half-carried, half-dragged Cowboy off the dike and into the dense jungle. Once there, they dropped him like a hot rock, then rushed to clean the foul-smelling muck off their hands.

Landing on his knees, Cowboy retched repeatedly as Andy tried to clean the muck from his face and ears with canteen water.

"What about the rest of me?" Cowboy complained when Andy stopped.

"We can't waste any more drinking water. You'll have to live with the smell until we get to the next stream."

"But, Lieutenant—"

"Enough," Andy snapped. "You could have gotten us killed with that loud-mouthed, rookie stunt back there, and we're not in the clear yet. Get on your feet."

Andy unrolled the map. They had at least a klick to go to reach the stream. With luck, they could make it before dark. He signaled Strawberry to go.

THE MEANDERING STREAM CUT THROUGH an unusually dense section of jungle, away from any roads and villages. For now, the extra foliage offered protection, and the canopy wildlife didn't seem bothered by their presence or Cowboy's stench.

"Hollis, Doc, Rawlin, and Chase set up a four-point," Andy said. Once they were in place, he gave Cowboy the all-clear to get into the stream.

Dropping his ruck in the water, Cowboy quickly submerged himself and began using sand from the bottom to scrub himself. After giving the same attention to his shirt and ruck, he waded to shore and hung both in the brush to dry.

"Lieutenant," Cowboy said sheepishly. "Did you see all the fish in that stream? I think they're some kind of catfish. Can we catch a few?"

"With what?" Chase asked, as he guarded the streamside perimeter. "You have a fishing hook on you?"

The thought of eating something other than LURPs pulled Andy in. Remembering the Native American fish-trap he and Nettie had seen in the Chattahoochee River, he motioned to Cowboy. "Come with me and do exactly what I tell you to do."

They separated four logs from a decaying tree trunk and dragged them to the bank. Removing their boots and socks, they pulled the logs into the water and placed them in the shape of a W, the open side facing the current. Backing up, they waited to see if any fish would find their way into the trap.

"Lieutenant," Cowboy whispered, "I know I'm screwing up, but I'm trying."

"No, you're not."

"Sir?"

"You're making stupid mistakes because you keep putting yourself ahead of the squad. Remember what Gus said? It's about being part of a team that is only as good as its weakest link. Right now, you're it. Our best chance of getting through this alive is if everyone focuses on the mission and the well-being of the squad. Understand?"

"Yes, sir. Are you going to report me?"

"Not yet."

"How come?"

"Because I'm betting you'll figure it out. Hopefully, sooner rather than later."

"I'll try, sir."

Andy shook his head. "Not good enough. You just gave yourself permission to fail."

"What?"

"Just trying will get us killed. Don't try. Do it. Plain and simple. That's an order."

"Yes, sir."

Surprised at the number of fish finding their way into the coves of the W, Andy motioned to Quy and Sirocco. "Bring your knives and come here."

The two men waded out, speared two of the scrumming fish, then carried them to the bank. They kept going until ten fish were ready to be scaled, gutted, and beheaded.

Dismantling their trap, Andy and Cowboy returned the logs to the bank, then put their socks and boots back on.

"How's it going?" Andy asked the men cleaning, deboning, and cutting up the fish.

"Just what I always never wanted, sir, sushi," Sirocco joked as he and Quy threw the fish guts into the water.

"I don't eat raw fish," Moretti said. "I'm cooking them, but I'll need to borrow a couple of helmets to do it."

"Helmets? Why?" Sirocco asked.

"We're going to use them as pots to cook in."

"Are you kidding?"

"No. We'll just clean them really well before and after."

Sirocco looked skeptical. "Right."

"Trust me," Moretti said as he dug to the bottom of his ruck. Pulling out two small tins of spices, he added, "My mom taught me to cook. She gave these to me before I left in case the LURPs needed fixing up."

"So, my helmet is going to smell like oregano for the rest of the tour?"

"Beats sweat and buffalo dung, doesn't it?" Moretti replied, matter-of-factly.

"Good point," Sirocco laughed.

Andy unfolded his small entrenching shovel. "Come on, Strawberry, help me."

"To do what, sir?"

"We're going to build a Dakota firepit," Andy replied. "It's something my dad taught me to do when I was a kid. The pit hides the flames and makes the fire burn hotter, which produces almost no smoke."

When the pit was finished, they lined the bottom with smooth river rocks.

"What are we going to burn, sir? All the wood around here is wet."

Andy dug the block of C4 explosive out of his ruck and shaved some into the pit. "Remember, C4 only explodes when ignited with a blasting cap. Igniting small amounts with a simple flame does nothing but provide a long, low, smokeless burn. Should be great for cooking in secret." Lighting a match, he tossed it into the pit.

"Perfect," Moretti said as he cleaned Sirocco and Quy's helmets with sand from the bottom of the stream. Filling them with clear water, he lowered the makeshift pots onto the low flames and added the fish, vegetables from donated LURPs, and some of his spices. Twenty minutes later, the first half of the squad filled their canteen cups with a thick stew. Tasting it hesitantly at first, they finished it with gusto.

Accolades for Moretti's cooking echoed around the camp as the first group finished eating.

Moretti grinned, reveling in the praise and comradery. "After the war, you all can come eat at my restaurant in Brooklyn."

"You have a restaurant?" Cowboy asked.

"Not yet, but I will one day." He put his hands up as if to frame the name. "Moretti's Fine Italian Dining. I'll cook and my mom will be the hostess." Laughing, he added, "My famous fish stew will be the first thing on the menu."

"Okay, fellows," Andy said, "rinse your cups with canteen water then relieve the perimeter so they can eat." For the first time since leaving Camp Eagle, his squad would face the night with satisfied bellies.

At dusk, Andy gave orders to button up the camp. "Doc, you and Hollis kill the fire and fill the hole. Rawlin and Chase, wash the helmets and get them back to their owners. Then you all double up the perimeter and get some rest. We're out of here at 0500."

Later, Andy watched as Hollis joined Cowboy on the perimeter, Hollis talking slow and easy and Cowboy listening intently and nodding. *Good. Maybe the philosopher can help the cowboy get his act together.*

A pesky monkey shook the leaves above Andy's head as he pulled an ongoing letter to Nettie out of his ruck, each entry dated as if he were writing in a diary. He'd mail it as soon as they got back to Eagle. Being careful not to include anything that would give away their position or mission, he described Cowboy's swim in the muck, Moretti's gourmet helmet stew, Sirocco's teasing, and Hollis's big brothering. As the nighttime sky took over, he ended the entry with "Meet me in the stars. I love you."

Chapter 5

NETTIE

To avoid the ire of Mrs. Woods, Nettie visited Mr. Pepper in the step-down unit an hour before her shift began. Pushing the door open, she was surprised by the silence. No yelling, no flying food, no beeping monitors, just a quiet calm. She approached the nurse sitting at the counter. "Is it okay if I visit Mr. Pepper?"

The nurse glanced at Nettie's name badge. "He's been hoping you'd show up."

"He has, huh?"

She nodded. "He said we were to let you in even if he was sleeping. It's kind of sad. The only visitor he's had is his lawyer."

"He told us in the ER he didn't have any family," Nettie said.

"Could be. Or he has them and just doesn't want them to know."

That would explain a lot. "Is he better?"

"His congestive failure is under better control, but his heart suffered a lot of damage."

"Do you think he'll ever go home?"

"Maybe. He's supposed to move to the Godfrey Center next week to begin cardiac rehab."

"Thanks." Nettie knocked on Mr. Pepper's door and went in. The closed shades made the room gray and shadowy, but it still presented a sharp contrast to what she'd seen in CCU. Here the bed linens were clean and straight, items on the bedside stand were neat and organized, and the room spotless. Mr. Pepper, clean-shaven and dressed in navy-blue pajamas with red piping and matching robe, lay on top of the covers like a corpse in a casket.

"Mr. Pepper?"

His eyes popped open. "There you are." He fumbled to find the remote control so he could raise the head of his bed. "I thought you'd forgotten about me."

"Not a chance," Nettie said as she crossed the room and opened the blinds.

"What are you doing?" he asked, blinking.

"Letting some light in. It's beautiful outside."

"I prefer the dark."

Nettie laughed. "You lived in Hawaii for thirty-plus years and you expect me to believe you don't like sunlight?"

"Well—" Mr. Pepper smiled.

"Yeah, that's what I thought. Would you like to get out of here for a while?"

"What do you mean?"

"Just a minute and I'll show you." Nettie checked with the nurse, found a wheelchair, and rolled it into Mr. Pepper's room. "You ride. I'll push."

"Where are we going?"

"To find the sun."

As he got out of bed and pivoted into the wheelchair, Nettie couldn't help but notice that his slippers were nicer than most men's Sunday shoes. "I'm glad to see someone brought your things. I'm sure wearing hospital gowns and tube sock slippers were getting old."

"I had a few things sent from home. And yes, silk feels much nicer than cotton washed in hard soap."

When the elevator doors opened, Nettie turned the wheelchair around.

"Why are you backing in?"

"Well, for starters, it's safer. The little wheels in the front can turn sideways and drop into the open slots in the frame, which would likely dump you in the middle of the floor. It also allows you to look forward instead of back."

"Sometimes it's good to look back," Mr. Pepper mumbled.

"Only if you're a mirror."

"Where did you get such a smart mouth?"

"Same place I got the rest of me—Mom, Dad, and God."

Reaching the top floor, they followed a narrow hall to an old rooftop sitting area. She parked Mr. Pepper in the shade of a scraggly potted tree, then sat on a nearby bench.

"Not exactly an English garden, is it?" Mr. Pepper said, looking around with distaste.

"No, but the air's fresh and the view is incredible."

"I had gardens at my home in Hawaii. A tropical garden with a beautiful waterfall, a butterfly garden, an English boxwood garden complete with a three-tier fountain, and a vegetable and herb garden. They're located on the bluffs overlooking Hanauma Bay, one of the most scenic places in the islands."

"Blue Pacific. Beautiful gardens. It sounds like paradise."

"It is. My company raises exotic flowers and exports them all over the world. Lotus, ilima, orchids, gardenias, hibiscus, royal jasmine, bird of paradise, and plumeria, among others. We sell live plants to other gardens and nurseries, and ship cut flowers to distributors who supply shops, perfumeries, and apothecaries all over the world."

"It must have been hard to leave your work and beautiful gardens. I'll bet you'll be glad when you can go home."

"It was easier to leave paradise than you think. And I won't be returning to Hawaii." Mr. Pepper pointed toward the distant Blue Ridge Mountains. "The Northern Shenandoah Valley of Virginia is my home. I was born in Winchester."

"Do you have family there?"

He shook his head. "I was an only child, as were my parents. They died long ago and are buried in the Valley." Mr. Pepper rubbed his signet ring. "When it looks like your life is coming to an end, your priorities change. Enough about me. How is Andrew Stephen Stockton doing?"

"You have a good memory."

"It's my heart that's not working well," he said with a wink. "My hearing and memory work just fine."

"He's okay—as far as I know. I haven't heard from him in a while."

"Is Andrew a smart man?"

"Very."

"Observant and detail-oriented?"

"Very."

"Respected by his men?"

"I don't know his new squad, but the men at Fort Benning respected him a lot. He's a fair and honest guy."

"Then his odds of coming home alive are much higher."

Hearing reference to Andy's survival phrased in the terms of statistical odds sent a chill through Nettie. Taking a deep breath, she pushed the thought away. "So, when did you move back to Virginia?"

"My jet landed at Dulles Airport the evening I came to the emergency room."

Nettie sat back. "You were having chest pain at thirty thousand feet?"

"A little. The severe pain didn't start until later."

"You could have died up there."

"That much closer to heaven," he quipped. "Plus, I had aspirin and nitroglycerin with me." His eyes followed the skyline. "I didn't come home to live, Nettie. I came home to die."

"Did your cardiologist in Hawaii say you were dying?"

"He said I was running out of heart muscle and consequently, time. He gave me a year, maybe two. And that was before the last attack."

"Well, you're still here, so I guess that achy heart of yours has a mind of its own, huh?"

Mr. Pepper gave her a rare smile. "Indeed, it does."

"You'll start cardiac rehab when you get to the Godfrey Center, that might buy you more time than you think."

"Maybe."

Nettie glanced at her watch. "I hate to do this, but my shift begins in a few minutes. I need to get you back to the step-down unit."

"You'll come see me again?"

"Of course."

"They're remodeling a room for me in the Godfrey Center. It will be ready soon."

"Remodeling?"

"Taking down a couple of walls, adding some decent furniture, rugs, a private phone line, and a television." He chuckled. "All the things the hospital allows when they want your money."

Nettie caught movement out of the corner of her eye. Mrs. Woods stood in the glass door, her mouth in a straight line. Nettie looked for another way into the building but saw none. Bracing herself, she unlocked Mr. Pepper's wheelchair. Maybe the woman would allow her to get him back to his room before opening fire.

By the time they reached the door, Mrs. Woods had disappeared. Scanning the empty halls, Nettie returned Mr. Pepper to his room and helped him back to bed.

"Thank you for the company and the nice ride, Nettie."

"You are most welcome. I enjoyed it, too. I'll come again once you're settled at the Godfrey Center."

Waving goodbye, she hurried from the unit and down the back stairs. At the bottom of the first flight stood Mrs. Woods, arms folded, gaze hard. Nettie froze for a moment, then went down the last few steps.

"I told you visiting patients wasn't allowed."

"Beg your pardon, ma'am, you told me interns were here to work, not socialize. I came to visit on my own time."

"That's not what I said."

"Yes, ma'am, it is." Nettie replied, wishing they were not alone in the stairwell.

"Well, let me make myself perfectly clear now. You are not to visit patients while serving as an intern here."

Intern or not, she'd just promised to visit Mr. Pepper again. "All due respect, ma'am, I checked the policy manual, and it doesn't say we're not allowed to visit patients."

"You're being impertinent. You heard what I said."

Nettie refused to look away under Mrs. Woods's withering stare. "I have to go. My shift begins in a few minutes."

Her heart racing, Nettie cut around the angry supervisor and walked away. Mrs. Woods's footsteps followed her at a distance. Reaching the entrance to the ER, Nettie glanced at her watch. She had less than ten minutes to pull herself together. She heard the door to the stairs open and close but refused to look back.

SATURDAY MORNING, A LONG LETTER arrived from Andy, instantly making Nettie's day better. He'd returned from his squad's first solo recon mission and had a few days in camp before he had to go out again. She took the letter to her room and closed the door. As usual, he wrote about the oppressive heat and constant rain. He also described the interesting things he'd observed about the South Vietnamese people, their dedication to family, their work ethic, and ready smiles. And he shared more about his men—Strawberry's uncanny jungle skills, Rawlin's quiet steadiness, Chase's icy focus, Cowboy's immaturity, Hollis's mentoring, Sirocco's sense of humor, Doc's obsession with dry feet, and of course, Moretti who had become everyone's friend and confidant.

A lump formed in Nettie's throat when she got to the last page and he talked about the patrols getting longer and the challenges they faced, the lack of food and sleep, being dirty and wet most of the time, and the incessant bugs. He didn't mention the constant threat of being killed or wounded. She paced in frustration. *There's nothing I can do to help him.*

Win called from the hallway, "Nettie, are you ready to go?"

"Coming." She kissed Andy's signature, said a quick prayer for his safety, and laid the letter on her pillow. She'd read it again before going to sleep. Grabbing her shoulder bag, she joined Win. Their budget didn't allow for eating out very often, but on Saturdays, Bob's Big Boy Restaurant had sandwiches and french fries for a dollar fifty. The rest of the week they lived on cereal, Campbell's soup, peanut butter and jelly sandwiches, and whatever their families sent in care packages.

"How's Andy?" asked Win as they walked downtown.

"Okay. He's having to do longer patrols. I can't imagine what he's going through—living in a dangerous jungle, knowing there are people and things just waiting to kill him." Nettie's stomach churned as her imagination created one nightmarish scenario after another.

"Andy's sharp as a tack," Win said. "He's been a hunter all his life and knows how to disappear in the woods. Plus, the army trained him to do what he's doing."

"I know."

"He wouldn't want you dwelling on it."

"No, he wouldn't, but my mind keeps going there."

"Then let's talk about something else. How are things going with that wacky supervisor?"

"Still wacky." Nettie had shared everything about Mrs. Woods's behavior with Win except what she'd witnessed in the recovery room. *Without proof, it's just hearsay.* "TK says to stay out of her way, but it's not in me to run."

"If the woman has some kind of axe to grind, she may not let you stay out of her way."

A fleeting "Why me?" gave way to thoughts of Andy. *Do your job and keep moving forward, just like he's doing. One step at a time, one day at a time.*

"Just be smart and be careful," Win added.

At the restaurant, their favorite waitress seated them. The motherly woman knew they were in nursing school and on a tight budget, so she'd bring them extra fruit slices and packs of crackers. In return, they'd drink water instead of tea or soda so they'd have money for a bigger tip.

"How's your internship on the surgical unit going?" Nettie asked Win.

"I'm enjoying it. The pace is steady but not as busy as the ER. There's a new batch of surgical residents coming from George Washington University next week that I've been asked to show around. They'll have a hundred questions, just like we did when we started."

"Maybe one of those residents will catch your eye."

Win shook her head as she swallowed a bite of her Slim Jim. "Not interested. I just want to finish school."

"Famous last words," Nettie teased.

As they finished eating, a half-dozen tired-looking women walked in and sat at a long table close to Nettie and Win's booth. Dressed in suits, pumps, and pearls, the women wore black armbands with POW-MIA arched across the top, a silhouette of a soldier in the middle, and the words "You Are Not Forgotten" written underneath. Nettie shivered at the implications.

Living close to Washington, DC, she and Win had grown accustomed to the almost weekly marches for and against different causes. Seeing large numbers of protestors with peace symbols or ERA NOW stamped on their T-shirts was an everyday occurrence, especially in the subway and on the weekends. These women were a different type of protestor, likely championing their cause in the halls of Congress, not on the National Mall. There wasn't a face among them that didn't have worry lines, but Nettie also sensed unrelenting determination. Given the message on their sleeves, she understood why.

"You're staring," Win whispered.

Nettie nodded but kept her eyes on the table as a petite black woman spoke.

"Betty, the publication of these *Pentagon Papers* has the President, Congress, and the military scrambling to explain why they've allowed the war to drag on for so many years. Won't this help us in the long run?"

"The papers have certainly increased public awareness of the politics surrounding the war," replied the tall brunette sitting at the head of the table. "But it's too early to tell if the Pentagon will respond by increasing their efforts to bring the POWs home or by becoming more entrenched. The fact they cancelled today's meeting with us at the last minute isn't a good sign."

"All the more reason to increase our political action committee fundraising efforts," a feisty, older blonde said, "especially if we expect to influence the presidential and congressional elections next fall. The PAC is going to need more money and volunteers soon."

"You're right, Ann," Betty replied.

At the word volunteer, Nettie found a solution to her sense of helplessness. Day and night, she prayed for Andy not to be hurt, captured, or killed. Maybe she could do something to help the families of those soldiers who had been.

"You're going to volunteer, aren't you?" Win whispered.

"It could be Andy they're trying to help."

Win looked at the ladies and then back at Nettie. "Sleeping in on Saturday mornings is overrated. I'm in, too."

They slid from the booth and approached Betty at the head of the table.

"Excuse me," Nettie said, "we couldn't help but overhear your conversation about helping the POWs and MIAs."

"We're doing our best." Betty motioned around the table. "Officially, we're the officers and committee chairs of the National Alliance of Families of Prisoners and Missing in Southeast Asia or the NAF for short. Our husbands have been POWs or MIAs for several years. We come to Washington from all over the country once a month to lobby congress and military leaders to do more to bring them home."

"I'm Nettie, and this is Win. We'd like to volunteer. We're in nursing school but have some free time on the weekends."

"That's wonderful," the feisty blonde replied. She handed Nettie her business card. "My name is Ann Anderson. This has the address and phone number of our Alexandria office. I'll be there next Saturday if you two want to come by about nine."

"Great. We'll be there. Thank you."

"No, my dear. Thank *you*."

THE FOLLOWING SATURDAY MORNING, Nettie and Win drove to the NAF office in Alexandria.

Steps away from the easy-flowing Potomac River, the old brick storefront had a swinging sign above the door and a bowed window with posters and bumper stickers taped to the inside of the curved glass. T-shirts, flags, and other paraphernalia sat on the wide inside sill. A bell tinkled above the door as they entered a small, bare-bones waiting area.

"Be right with you," a pleasant voice called from the back.

On the wall to the right hung a large bulletin board with hundreds of pictures of soldiers pinned to it. Printed at the bottom were the words "MIAs and POWs." The opposite wall held a horizontal poster with the words, "The mission of the NAF is to obtain the return of all prisoners of war, the fullest possible accounting of the missing, and the repatriation of remains of those not yet recovered who died while serving our nation." Under the poster hung a framed picture of several women. The insert at the bottom said, "Founders of the NAF." Several of the women had been at the restaurant. On the counter sat a framed picture of Mrs. Anderson and a tall, handsome man. The names Steve and Ann were scripted across the bottom.

Mrs. Anderson came out of the backroom brushing stray strands of hair out of her eyes. "Good morning, girls. We're so glad you've come to help us!"

"Hi, Mrs. Anderson. We're happy to be here."

"Let's get started." Mrs. Anderson gestured around the room. "The NAF originated in the late 1960s and was formally incorporated in 1970, which is when this office opened. We coordinate fundraising efforts to bring attention to the plight of prisoners of war and those missing in action. Most of our support comes through direct donations from their families, friends, and communities. We also earn money from the sale of POW/MIA flags, bumper stickers, bracelets, T-shirts, and such." She showed them into a windowless room with an old conference table, mismatched chairs, and a large map of Southeast Asia on the wall. Pinned to the map were several slips of paper with names printed on them. "This room is where the officers and committee chairs meet the first weekend of every month. They drive or fly in from all over the country, work for two or three days, and then go home. The rest of the month we work by phone and mail." She motioned to the map. "The pins mark where our husbands were first reported missing."

Mrs. Anderson ushered them back to the reception area and through a breezeway on the back wall. Entering a large storage room cluttered with boxes, Nettie noted a wall of bins labeled alphabetically by state to the left. Each bin held stacks of papers of variable heights. In front of the bins were two wide rectangular worktables, one tall and one waist high. To the right of the breezeway was a small kitchen area with a sink, old coffee pot, and well-worn mugs. A folding table stacked with black and white T-shirts sat in the opposite corner.

"This is our workroom," Mrs. Anderson said.

A dark-haired guy with gray eyes stood at the tall table counting POW/MIA bumper stickers and putting them in crisscrossed stacks. A petite girl with long dark hair, the same gray eyes, and a prominent pout sat at the shorter table surrounded by envelopes and mailing labels.

"This is my daughter, Laura, and my son, Paul. Laura is a senior at Fairfax High School, and Paul is in med school at George Washington University. Laura, Paul, this is Nettie and Win. They're nursing students at George Mason and are new volunteers. Show them the ropes, would you?"

"Sure," Paul replied, sliding over to make room for Nettie.

Win pulled a chair over to the shorter table. "Want some help?" she asked Laura.

"Suit yourself," Laura replied flatly, pushing supplies toward Win.

"Ignore her," Paul laughed. "She's in a perpetual bad mood."

Laura gave him the finger without bothering to look up. "Those working at the tall table put the orders together, then bring them here. We match the name and address with the package, seal it, and fill out the mailing label. We also add the name and address to the NAF mailing list." Laura pointed to an old Pitney Bowes postage machine sitting at the end of her table. "It's clunky, but it was free and it works. Put the package or envelope in the tray at the top, hit the button on the side, and the postage label comes out at the bottom. Make sure the label sticks, then put the package in the cart by the back door. Envelopes go in the bag hanging on the side. Once the cart is full, we take it to the post office down the street."

Paul patted the big box on his table. "These are customized silver bracelets for soldiers who've been reported as MIA, POW, or killed in action."

Paul and Laura had on bracelets.

"Each bracelet has a soldier's full name, state, and the date the military reported his or her status," Paul said. "We make sure the engraving is correct. If it is, the bracelet goes back in its case and we package it to go to the family." He pointed to the bins on the wall. "Each package or envelope we send out also includes NAF talking points, phone numbers and addresses for the recipient's congressional representatives, and a sample letter to use when they contact them about helping the NAF." Paul handed Nettie a bracelet. "Would you like to start checking these while I finish packaging the bumper stickers?"

"Sure." Nettie opened the velvet-lined case. "William Allen Thomas, Mississippi, May 1, 1971." Andy's name flashed across the metal. Inhaling sharply, Nettie steadied herself against the table.

"Are you all right?" Paul asked.

Nettie nodded. *Stop it. Andy's fine.* Looking at the order, she double-checked the name and spelling, confirmed the date, then used a polishing cloth to remove her prints. Placing the bracelet back in its case, she put it in a shipping box, added a packet of papers for Mississippi, and taped the box closed.

"So, why do you two want to spend your Saturdays doing this?" Laura asked.

Nettie reached for another bracelet to check. "My fiancé's in Vietnam. He'll be gone a year. I want to help—somehow."

"What's his name?"

"Andy. Andy Stockton."

Laura looked at Win. "What about you?"

"Nettie and Andy are my friends."

"Oh, a tagalong," Laura said.

Paul shot her a hard look. "Behave, Laura. Nobody's interested in your bad attitude."

She shot him the finger again.

"Is your father a POW or MIA?" Win asked Laura.

"He's been missing in action for four years," Laura replied, her voice flat.

"Or at least that's what the army says," Paul added. "They can't confirm anything."

"I'm so sorry," Nettie said. *Four years! How in heaven's name do they keep going?*

"That's an awfully long time," Win added gently.

"There are families who've been waiting a lot longer. Don't you read the papers?" Laura asked, her tone condescending.

"That's enough, Laura," Paul said firmly. "You're being rude just because you can. Apologize."

She looked at her brother, the suffering evident in her eyes.

"No," Win said, "she's right. I should have done my homework. This is serious work." Laura had a friend in Win whether she knew it or not. Win understood the pain of not knowing. Her beloved grandmother, Nibi, had been missing since 1969, lost in the flooding caused by Hurricane Camille.

By lunchtime, the bumper stickers and bracelets were packaged and ready to mail. "Come on, Win," Laura said. "You can help me take the cart to the post office."

As they left, Paul opened a case of T-shirts. Pulling out two bundles, he cut the ties and pushed one toward Nettie. "We check the print on each one to make sure it's not blurred, then refold them and put them in stacks on the table in the corner according to size." As they worked, he glanced at her ring finger. "How long have you been engaged?"

"Since Valentine's Day."

"Romantic," he said, grinning.

"It was."

"Known Andy long?

"Since kindergarten."

"Wow. That's amazing. What's he like?"

Thoughts of Andy wrapped Nettie like a blanket. "He's smart, kind, funny, but serious when he has to be. Loves to hunt and fish, anything outdoors."

"What does he look like?"

"Tall, about your height. Athletic. Brown hair, hazel eyes, great smile, and a heart as big as Texas."

"He must be something. You've been smiling the whole time you were describing him."

"He is." Nettie carried a stack of small T-shirts to the corner table. "I don't see a ring on your finger, are you dating anyone?"

Paul shook his head. "Not for a while now. Too much school, too much work, and too little money."

"Boy, do I understand that."

"I need to hold onto my scholarships. With Dad missing, there's not a lot of money coming in. Military benefits are minimal. Mom works here full-time but doesn't make much. Laura and I work a few hours a week at the drug store around the corner to help make ends meet."

"You're right. That schedule doesn't leave a lot of time for a relationship, does it?"

"It might for the right one." Paul grinned. "Is Win seeing anyone?

Nettie smiled. "No, she's not."

"She's beautiful."

"Yes, she is, in more ways than one." Nettie wasn't sure if Win would be interested in getting to know Paul better or not, but he might be good for her serious-minded friend. "How much longer do you have in med school?"

"Another year. I'm getting ready to start a general surgery rotation at Northern Virginia Hospital."

"We have internships there. I'm in the ER and Win's on the surgical unit."

"That's good to know."

Nettie studied the order list for the T-shirts. "These are going to just about every state in the union. That's a lot of support."

"We need it. Public support is about the only thing the NAF can count on these days."

"You must miss your dad so much. I can't imagine what it feels like."

"Yes, you can, otherwise you wouldn't be here. The only difference between us is you're worried about your fiancé ending up in a bad place and my father is already there."

Chapter 6

ANDY

Reconnaissance of the second village had been relatively easy for Andy and his squad. It differed little in terrain, size, characteristics, and patterns of behavior from the first village, and there had been no sign of a cadre or the NVA in either. However, just getting to the third village posed a challenge. A wide, squat mountain stood in their way, and a well-traveled path snaked around it.

"This is no game trail," Strawberry said, studying the path. "It's too wide. People made it."

"So, to avoid them we either have to go over the mountain or lose extra days cutting a wider path around it." Andy frowned.

"We can get a bird's eye view of the village from the top," Strawberry said.

"It's going to be hard to climb with rucks and cover ourselves at the same time," Chase cautioned.

"I agree with both of you." Gritty sweat took its usual path down Andy's neck and back. "We'll climb in pairs, one climbs while the other covers, then switch. Chase, push up with Strawberry on point. Cowboy and I will be behind you in slack."

"Are you sure you want to do that, sir? Cowboy in slack I mean?" Chase asked in a low tone.

"Yeah, I'm sure." *I need to know what the man is capable of.* Since the incident with the rats, Cowboy had stayed in formation, kept his curiosity in check, and readily volunteered for first watch so his perimeter partner could sleep, but the squad still did not trust him.

"Let me talk with him before we head out," Chase said. "If he's never walked slack on a mountain. I want to make sure he knows to aim low and shoot high."

Andy nodded. "Good point. Remind him and the others, then we'll move out."

Two by two, the squad positioned their rucks high and began the slow, exacting climb. The steepness and pebbly terrain worsened the farther up they went. Being careful with their footing, they had to lean into the mountain to keep from pitching backward.

About a third of the way up, Strawberry motioned to Andy. They'd reached an overhanging ledge that rimmed the mountain like a fedora.

"Now we know why there were no paths up," Andy said wryly, scanning the ledge in both directions. "It's not that big, but we have to go up and lean out to get over it."

"At least there's vegetation in the cracks and crevices to hold on to," Strawberry said.

"Cowboy and I are the tallest, so we'll give each man a leg up, then send their rucks. We'll have to string gun straps together to hoist the last man over."

Dropping his ruck, Strawberry positioned his rifle on his back, used dirt as a resin for his sweaty hands, and held on as Andy and Cowboy hoisted him up and out. Grabbing the heavy brush, Strawberry pulled himself over. After a moment, his face appeared above the ledge, "Coast is clear. Send my ruck."

After Chase made it up, Andy waved the rest of the squad forward in twos. When only he and Cowboy were left, Cowboy bent his knees, put his hands together, and motioned for Andy to climb. "I'm taller, sir, I should go last."

Unable to argue the logic, Andy took off his ruck, passed it up to Moretti, and positioned his rifle. "When I'm up, hand me your ruck, then I'll lower one end of the gun straps. Hook it to your utility belt and we'll pull you up." Using Cowboy's shoulder for balance, Andy stepped into his cupped hands, stood, and reached for the brush. As he swung out, the roots of the brush pulled loose.

Making a diving grab for Andy's arm, Cowboy jerked him to safety, but in the process, propelled himself into a ruck-first slide down the mountain.

Andy watched helplessly as Cowboy made blind grabs for anything to break his slide, never uttering a sound as he disappeared.

Scrambling to his feet, Andy strapped his ruck on, and grabbed his rifle. Moretti's face appeared at the top of the ledge. "Did you see where Cowboy landed?"

"No, sir. He went out of sight fast."

"I'm going after him. You all follow the ledge and see if you can find a safe way down." Fearing Cowboy might be hurt or dead, Andy didn't wait for a reply. He headed down the mountain as fast as he could, climbing when he had to and doing a controlled, feet-first slide when able. Leaves and branches slapped him all along the way, and unstable rocks threatened to catapult him to the bottom. Reaching the base of the mountain, he oriented himself, then began a methodical search for his missing man. Looking among the thick brush, he called "Cowboy" in soft whispers. Finally, he heard a reply coming from a nearby tree.

"I'm up here, sir."

Getting close to the tree's trunk, Andy studied the canopy.

Hanging upside down, his ruck wedged among lifesaving branches, Cowboy waved. Andy quickly hid his ruck in the bushes, moved his rifle to his back, and climbed up.

"Hi, Lieutenant," Cowboy said with almost normal clarity.

"Are you okay?" Andy asked, studying Cowboy's scratched up face and hands.

"Yep, just hanging around."

"Smart-ass." Andy grinned. "How the hell did you end up here?"

"Don't really know. Somewhere near the bottom of the mountain, I went airborne. Thought I was a goner for sure, but I landed in the top of this tree."

"What hurts?"

"My ego for sure. I'm sore, but I can feel my fingers and toes and everything still works. My ruck is wedged, which is good because it's the only thing keeping me in the tree. When I tried to pull myself upright, branches started cracking."

Leaving Cowboy's helmet in place, Andy studied the wedged ruck.

"Where's the rest of the squad?" Cowboy asked.

"On their way down the mountain."

Both men froze as they heard voices in the distance that were not speaking English.

Andy quietly eased his rifle to the front and put his finger on the trigger, waiting as the voices approached, then moved past the tree.

When the sound had disappeared, Cowboy whispered, "Black tunics?"

"I don't know. I couldn't see them, and thankfully they couldn't see us. We need to get the hell out of this tree." Andy anchored one knee under Cowboy's shoulder and grabbed his belt. "Hold on to my thigh. When I unbuckle your ruck, swing your legs to the left. There's a branch you can put your feet on. Ready?"

"Ready."

When the ruck released, Cowboy's shoulder dropped heavily on Andy's knee. Swinging his legs around and finding the branch under his feet, Cowboy pulled himself upright.

"Hold tight and stay still until your head clears," Andy said. "You were upside down a long time."

Climbing higher, Andy untangled the ruck and strapped it to his back. Positioning Cowboy in front of him, Andy slowly backed down the tree. Making sure no one was around, he dropped to the ground and motioned for Cowboy to follow.

Despite his best effort, Cowboy stumbled and moaned when he landed. Andy helped him into the thick brush then hurried back to the tree. Breaking one of the smaller limbs, he left the tip dangling and swaying in the breeze. A sign the average person wouldn't notice, but Strawberry, Chase, and the rest of his squad would. He quickly ducked back into the brush.

"I think I met every rock on that mountain and every branch in the top of that tree," Cowboy whispered as he took his helmet off.

Andy unscrewed the cap on his canteen and handed it to Cowboy. "When the squad gets here, we'll get you on your feet and see what you can do."

"Yes, sir."

"Cowboy, I appreciate what you did up there."

Cowboy returned a half-smile. "You're welcome, Lieutenant. The squad needs you, and I'm pretty sure the girl in that picture you carry wants you back in one piece."

Andy nodded. "Get some rest."

"Roger that." Cowboy closed his eyes while Andy kept watch.

Evening had muted the shadows before Andy finally heard the whisper he'd been waiting for.

"Mays and seven," Strawberry whispered.

"Roger that," Andy replied, sliding out of the brush.

Chase, Rawlin, Sirocco, and Hollis instinctively set up a close four-point perimeter around them.

"Boy, are we glad to see you," Strawberry said, breaking the end of the limb completely off and hiding it in the brush.

"Ditto," Andy said.

"Did you find him?"

Andy nodded. Waving Doc forward, he led them to Cowboy.

Doc quickly went back and forth, whispering questions to Cowboy, and palpating his legs, arms, joints, back, and neck. "He's lucky. I don't think anything is broken, but he's banged up. Are we here for the night, Lieutenant?"

Andy shook his head. "Too dangerous. As soon as you say Cowboy can move, we're out of here."

"Okay. Roll up his sleeve. I'll give him some Demerol, and we'll get him up." Doc pulled a small, prefilled syringe from his ruck.

"No pain med," Cowboy said. "We need to move, and I need to be clear headed."

Doc glanced at Andy.

"Okay." Andy turned to Strawberry. "How did you all get down the mountain? Did you find a trail we can follow back up?"

"No trail, but we did find a partial break in the ledge about a quarter mile away that we were able to climb through. We can go back that way. I marked the map. We also recovered Cowboy's gun before we came down."

"Good work. We'll find a spot to set a dark camp on the mountain, then try to get over the top tomorrow."

Cowboy wobbled as Strawberry and Doc pulled him to his feet. They grabbed for him again, but he waved them off.

"Just a little sore, fellows," he said, stepping out of the brush. "Give me my stuff and let's get going."

Moretti helped Cowboy get his ruck on, then whispered, "Saving the lieutenant like that—bravest thing I've ever seen, man."

THE VIEW OF THE THIRD VILLAGE from the top of the mountain raised Andy's concern. Using binoculars, he studied it again. Larger than the first two, this village also had a second road. He watched as the women returned from gathering the morning tea and instead of bagging it to sell along the road, they took it to a large hut where a man stood guard. The guard took each woman's bag, poured all but a little into a larger bag inside the door, then sent the women on their way. He did the same thing as the men brought crops in from the fields throughout the day.

"Maybe this village is rich enough they don't need to sell crops to survive," Rawlin said.

"But why keep most of the supplies in a central place and guarded?" Andy asked.

"Are you thinking the guard is part of a cadre?"

"It's possible," Andy replied. "This village could be part of a VC and NVA supply chain."

Andy checked in with Gus, who agreed the pattern change was significant. "We've got a village on this side doing the same thing."

"I'm calling it in," Andy said.

Moretti turned so Andy could reach the radio. "Alpha One, this is Bravo One. Over."

"Bravo One, this is Alpha One. Go ahead. Over."

Andy quickly and quietly explained the pattern change he and Gus noted. "Over."

"Roger that. Hold, Bravo One." After a minute the voice returned. "Bravo One, Major Smith doesn't think the findings are significant, but says for you to stay with that village until you head south for your stand-down in two days. Over."

"Roger that Alpha One. Bravo One out."
Not significant? Right.

GUS AND HIS MEN HADN'T MADE it back to the teepee rocks
when Andy's squad arrived, so he ordered a four-point
perimeter. "This is supposed to be a safe zone, but things could
have changed. Be careful about friendly fire," he warned.

Finding a little bit of shaded rock, Andy leaned against
the stone, grateful to have survived his first mission and to
be going back to Camp Eagle. Their first extended patrol
had involved long days of boring misery and worry injected
with frequent episodes of sheer terror. The boring misery
involved lugging an eighty-pound ruck in soul-sucking heat
and humidity through miles of jungle, trying to sleep back to
back because the ground is ankle-deep in rolling mud, eating
food that looked and tasted like anything but, and going
day after day without washing your face or brushing your
teeth. Constantly having to defend against painful red ants,
flying snakes, cigar-size centipedes, and other bizarre, biting
bugs that viewed your body as their food supply intensified
the misery. Leeches bothered Andy the most. Every night,
dozens of them, living in the puddles and wet soil of the
jungle, used his exhausted sleep as an opportunity to latch
on. Scalp, lips, eyelids, and ears, no exposed skin was safe.
Even protected areas were vulnerable if his pant legs happened to escape his socks. Almost daily, someone needed
help pulling the bloodsuckers off unreachable body parts.
The bloody trails left by the leeches mixed with camo paint
and dirt to give their faces a horror movie look.

These nuisances, combined with the constant fear of VC
ambushes, tripwires, punji stakes, and nature's predators
exacted a toll on the whole squad. *How do men go on patrols
like this for months at a time and not come back raving lunatics?*
Nettie's words echoed in his head. "Worry spins us in circles

while fear motivates us to act, to prepare for the unknown." *Focus, Stockton. Focus. Stay alert. Otherwise, you'll never get back to her.*

Out of the corner of his eye, Andy saw Chase raise his rifle. Dropping low, he pointed his in the same direction.

Gus's voice came through the brush loud and clear. "Griffin and nine coming in."

Andy shook Gus's hand as he and the rest of his squad emerged from the dense jungle. "Good to see you, Sergeant."

"Likewise, Lieutenant. Looks like you all made it through in good shape."

"We did, all things considered." Andy and his men had decided what happened in their squad, stayed in their squad unless it was germane to their mission. "Glad this round is over."

Gus motioned four of his men to help with backup perimeter security. "Me, too."

Andy radioed for a truck from Camp Eagle to pick them up, then he and Gus sat down to compare notes.

"Villages keeping supplies in a common storage area also had the best ingress and egress with road conditions that would support trucks," Andy said. "These villagers also seemed subdued, which may mean the presence of a cadre whether we can identify them or not."

"I agree. The younger and meaner the cadre, the better the VC likes them. We're likely to see more black tunics and brown belts as we move farther north, especially if our suspicions about a pattern developing pan out."

Andy rerolled his map. "I'd like a shower and a hot meal before I think about doing this again."

"Me too, sir." Gus grinned as the truck from Camp Eagle pulled up. "I think these guys may have something to make our day a little better."

Gus gave a thumbs-up to the driver who hopped out of

the cab with a CO2 fire extinguisher. Walking to the back, he lowered the tailgate and aimed the nozzle at a washtub full of beer, instantly turning the cans frosty cold.

Gus pulled the tab on the first can and handed it to Andy. "Enjoy, sir." He then handed each man a can as they climbed aboard.

Sharpshooters from both squads were the last to load. Two sat in front with the driver and two next to the tailgate, their eyes and rifles aimed outward.

Once back at Eagle, Andy took a long, hot shower, donned new fatigues, then found his way to the camp's Central Communication Center. According to Gus, the Comm Center had a MARS or Military Affiliate Two-Way Radio Station that combined shortwave radio capability with a basic phone system, making it possible to call the United States. Gus also said while calls were not allowed unless approved by the officer in charge, occasionally you could slip one through if he wasn't around.

The round-faced private manning the counter snapped to attention as Andy came through the door. The stamp on his uniform said O'Riley.

"What can I do for you, sir?"

"What are the chances I can make a call to the states?" Andy asked.

The private glanced over his shoulder at the droopy-eyed major sitting at a desk in the office behind him.

"No outgoing calls, Jimmy," the major said.

"Sorry, Lieutenant. Stateside calls are off-limits for now."

Disappointed, Andy gave Jimmy a half-smile and left. After picking up and reading his mail, he wrote long letters to Nettie and his mom, then went to the PX to buy them tins of lotus tea. After arranging to have the letters and gifts sent home, he started to go to the mess tent for dinner, but decided he wanted sleep more. Laying down on his bunk, he had just enough time to thank God for beds and soft pillows before his eyes closed.

Andy clenched his jaw as he and Gus met with Major Smith, their company commander, the next morning. They'd been sitting at a conference table reviewing maps and detailed notes for over an hour, yet the snarky major with the weak handshake still insisted their squads had brought back little valuable information.

"Other than the two villages using communal storage, your squads found nothing supporting the presence of a cadre or VC."

"Sir," Andy pressed again, "in addition to the communal storage, both villages have two good roads, plentiful water, and large supplies of tea, rice, and vegetables. All of which makes them extremely valuable in a supply chain. Also, based on the subdued behavior of the villagers, we believe there are cadres present in both places. We just haven't spotted the black tunics to confirm it."

Gus nodded. "I agree, Major. Something's going on in these villages."

"Well, then do your jobs and bring me something other than storage sheds to prove it."

Andy picked up a one-page map partially hidden among the major's materials. Multiple villages were circled in red, and some had question marks beside them, including the two they'd just talked about.

"Sir, may I ask what this map indicates?"

"That map has nothing to do with your recon briefing, Lieutenant," the major said, taking the map and laying it to the side.

An aide appeared in the doorway to announce that Major Smith's next appointment had arrived.

Waving the aide out, the major returned to his desk.

"Your squads head back out in forty-eight hours. I suggest you get ready. Dismissed."

Andy and Gus gathered their notes and left the building.

"What was that all about?" Andy asked. "I assumed we'd be staying there long enough to plan the next patrol."

"We should be. The man's a moron," Gus replied, ignoring the military's unwritten rule to keep your opinions to yourself. "A Peter Principle commander and brown-nosing REMF. Always has been."

Andy looked at Gus sideways, the outburst taking him by surprise.

"Sorry, Lieutenant."

"Don't be," Andy said. "Explain."

"Major Smith's arrogance, lack of skill, and failure to communicate has gotten men hurt and killed, including one in my last squad. He's not someone you want leading you or guarding your flank. The two villages we presented are heating up and he knows it. They're the canaries in the mine. He just wasn't going to give us the satisfaction of being the ones to confirm it. I can promise when he briefs Colonel Clark, the base commander, later today, he'll use our data but none of the squads will be mentioned. It will be all his intel."

Andy nodded. His first impression of the major had been correct.

"I bet the villages he circled on that map are also heating up and he didn't want us to know," Gus continued. "Did you happen to see which ones they were?"

Andy grinned and pulled the major's map out of his notes. "Accidentally gathered it up with my stuff when the aide came to the door."

Gus let go a belly laugh. "You know he'll have your ass for that."

"I'll return it as soon as we have a good look at it."

They found a quiet corner in the mess tent and studied the map. The two villages they'd just reconned were among a dozen with question marks by them. Other scattered villages, closer to the DMZ were circled in red.

"He must have ARVN intel on the circled villages," Andy said, studying the map's key. "I wonder what it is. Sympathetic villagers? Cadres? VC? Or are they just valuable villages we want to protect? Why wouldn't he tell us what's going on?"

"Either he thinks we can do what we have to do without having the information, a need-to-know situation, or he thinks knowing will taint our objectivity."

Andy angled the map to read a small, handwritten notation in the corner below the key. "Or he's just being a jerk." He turned the map so Gus could see.

"Cadres," Gus read. "Figures."

"I think our squads should spend some time at the firing range before we take off again."

"I couldn't agree more."

Andy made a hand-drawn copy of the map, then returned the original to the major's office. No one was in, so he laid it on the aide's desk and left. Returning to the mess tent, he and Gus spent the afternoon developing strategies for surveilling the next round of villages.

"We have two days to get ready to be on patrol for at least a month, maybe longer," Gus said. "And we're moving far enough north that supply drops will be few and far between if at all. I'd suggest each man get an updated list of jungle edibles and remedies."

"Good idea. Let your guys sleep in tomorrow. We'll meet at the firing range at ten hundred hours and brief them on the next patrol after." Already feeling the hunger, Andy grabbed two apples from a bowl by the door as he left. That night, he lay awake for hours trying to think of ways they could do their jobs better and stay safe at the same time. *Focus Stockton, focus.*

Chapter 7

NETTIE

Nettie shivered as she made her way along the dimly lit underground tunnel connecting the hospital with the Godfrey Center. Even during the day, the painted cinder block walls made it feel dungeon-like, especially when the tunnel angled in the middle making it impossible to see light on either end. The creaking, groaning, and erratic hissing of the old pipes suspended above her head added to the eeriness. *Who in the world thought this was a good idea for a hospital?* She quickened her pace until she saw the light from the Godfrey Center's nurses' station shining at the far end. Inside the glass enclosure stood Mrs. Henry, the wise charge nurse Nettie had worked with before. She waved as Nettie came into view.

"Hey, Mrs. Henry. Nice to see you again."

"Good to see you, too, Nettie. Are you here to visit Mr. Pepper? He's been asking about you."

"Yes, ma'am."

"Interesting fellow, that one. He must have a lot of money and sway. The hospital remodeled the end of the north hall for him, and they did it quickly."

"Is he causing trouble?"

"Not at all. He's been a perfect gentleman. Very quiet. Unusually quiet, actually. And no visitors that I know of."

"Is it okay if I go see him?"

Mrs. Henry opened his chart. "There's a note in here from Genevieve Woods, the evening supervisor. She says you are not to visit Mr. Pepper or any other patient for that matter. What's that all about?"

Nettie sighed. "She told me interns were here to work not visit patients."

"Strange. Why would she do that?"

"I'm not sure," Nettie replied, "but she told the CCU and the step-down nurses the same thing. So, I visit him on my own time."

"Do you know him well?"

"No, ma'am, not really. I helped take care of him in the ER. He was acting out like a lot of people do when they're in pain and afraid they're dying. While he was unconscious, I whispered to him like you taught me to do."

Mrs. Henry smiled. "Good. I can't imagine a better time for him to hear comforting words."

"He asked if I'd keep visiting. As far as I know, he has no family."

"I talked with Mr. Pepper about you visiting after I read this note. He said you were like a tonic for him. CCU and the step-down nurses said the same thing." Mrs. Henry buried Mrs. Woods's note in the back of the thick chart. "I'm not sure what Genevieve's issue is this time, but if Mr. Pepper wants you to visit, it's none of her business. If she says anything, refer her to me. Folks down here don't get many visitors, so I'm not about to turn away a good one."

"Thank you. Need me to take anything to him?"

She handed Nettie a copy of the *Wall Street Journal*. "He waits for this to come every day. You might see if you can get him up and walking a little. It would be good for him as long as he doesn't get short of breath."

"Yes, ma'am."

The north wing of the Godfrey Center had twenty

rooms, the last one being Mr. Pepper's. Nettie knocked on the door. "Mr. Pepper, it's Nettie. May I come in?"

"Yes, of course. I'm glad you came."

Nettie stopped just inside the door. Walls dividing three rooms had been replaced with wide archways, giving the space the appearance of a suite. Subtle navy and gold wallpaper, with accent painting, crown molding, and chair railing added an air of elegance. Jewel-toned rugs covered the hardwood floors in each section. Tie-back drapes in coordinating colors covered the suite's three windows. Mr. Pepper's electric poster bed, located in the first section, had an intricately carved mahogany headboard and footboard with a matching bedside stand and chest of drawers. The silk bed linens matched the fluffed goose down coverlet.

Just past the first archway to the right were two brocade wing chairs with matching ottomans. The end table between them held a Tiffany lamp and a Bible with a thin red ribbon marking a point near the front. A combined television and stereo cabinet had been placed under the window on the opposite wall. Beyond the second archway sat a small dining room set with a colorful bouquet of flowers in a Waterford vase. Scenic pictures of Hawaii were scattered throughout the suite. Near the door hung a stunning picture of a cliff overlooking a brilliant, blue-green ocean bay. Written across the matting at the bottom in beautiful calligraphy were the phrases, "*I'm sorry. Forgive me. Thank you, I love you.*"

"It's the Hawaiian *Ho'oponopono Prayer for Forgiveness and Healing*," Mr. Pepper said, raising the head of his bed. The side of his face looked wrinkled as if he'd been napping. His emerald-colored robe and pajamas matched perfectly.

"It's beautiful." Nettie motioned to the suite.

"Thank you. The hospital administrator allowed me to remodel. For a hefty price, of course, as well as a promise of more to come."

Nettie laid the *Wall Street Journal* on the bedside stand next to a framed photo of a couple sitting under an arched trellis near a pond filled with lotus blossoms. The faces of the couple were somewhat blurred, but the man, dressed in a navy uniform, resembled Mr. Pepper. A vase of colorful tropical flowers stood behind the picture. "The flowers smell wonderful."

"My company sends me fresh arrangements every three to four days. The scent you're noticing in this one is the peach gardenia. It's a hybrid my business partner, Mr. Keona Kalua, has been working on. Isn't it captivating?"

"Yes, sir."

"The gardenia plants won't be ready to ship for two to three months, but when they're ready, I'll have one sent to you. This far north, you'll have to leave it inside or plant it in a protected place outside. Make sure the soil stays mildly acidic."

"Thanks anyway, Mr. Pepper. Neither of my thumbs is green," Nettie confessed, reluctant to be responsible for killing such a beautiful flower.

"Nonsense. I'll teach you what you need to know. Have a seat."

She pulled a small, upholstered chair closer to the bed. "How are you feeling?"

"Better than I did in the units with bright lights, beeping monitors, annoying alarms, and loud voices. Here, it's blissfully quiet, and people leave me alone."

"You like being alone?"

"I've spent most of my adult life alone. There's a difference between being alone and being lonely, you know."

"Which are you?" Nettie asked, calling his bluff.

"There you go being nosy again."

She laughed. "Still trying to get to know you better."

Mr. Pepper's expression turned solemn. "Even desired solitude can get lonely at times. Speaking of lonely, how are you doing with Andrew being gone?"

"Turning the tables, huh?"

"Astute of you to notice."

"I'm trying to stay busy. He doesn't seem so far away when I have things to do."

Mr. Pepper nodded as if he knew how she felt.

"You said your company sells tropical flowers commercially. Do you sell to tea shops?"

"We sell to distributors who sell to all kinds of shops. Why?"

"Andy sent me a decorative tin of lotus blossom tea. He said women in the Vietnamese villages float out on the lakes and ponds at sunset and put raw tea into the lotus blossoms. They tie the petals together so the tea can soak up the nectar, then return at sunrise to gather it." Nettie's voice turned wistful. "He said the swirling lights on the water at night are one of the most beautiful things he's ever seen."

"It is a beautiful sight. I've seen the ceremony many times during my travels," Mr. Pepper said. "In fact, there's a lotus pond near one of the nurseries Mr. Kalua and I own. We sponsor a nighttime garden tour that includes the tea ceremony every Friday. The women who seed the flowers are children and grandchildren of Asian Americans killed during the attack on Pearl Harbor. The women even weave the little disc-shaped, reed boats and make the traditional lanterns used in the ceremony. Proceeds from the tours go to an education fund set up for the descendants of those who died in the attack."

Nettie pointed to the picture on his bedside stand. "Is that the lotus pond you're referring to?"

Mr. Pepper glanced at the photo. "Yes, it is."

"Is that you on the bench?

He nodded.

"The girl beside you is very pretty."

"Yes, she is. I knew her a long time ago."

"She must be special if you kept the picture all these years. Do you still see her?"

"Nettie, you may ask questions, but that doesn't mean I have to answer them."

"Sorry." She gave him a weak smile, before changing the subject. "How are the cardiac rehab sessions going?"

"Incredibly boring, but I'm getting stronger, so I shouldn't complain."

"Would you like to go for a walk now? A short one."

He hesitated, a hint of uncertainty in his eyes.

"I'll take a wheelchair with us, so if you get tired or short of breath, you can ride."

"That works." Mr. Pepper swung his legs over the side of the bed and pulled his pajama legs down to cover his swollen ankles. His support socks were folded and sitting at the bottom of the bed.

"Those are supposed to be on your feet," Nettie said.

"Maybe. After our walk."

Guiding the wheelchair ahead of them, Nettie let Mr. Pepper set the pace as they strolled down the hall.

"This place isn't much to look at, is it?"

"Not really. Guess it's pretty typical for a hospital."

"How do sick people get better surrounded by this?" he asked, waving his hand at the plain, aged surroundings.

"Good question. I guess they get better despite it, not because of it."

Mr. Pepper stopped at the nurses' station. "And how are you this afternoon, Mrs. Henry?"

"I'm very well, thank you, Mr. Pepper." The lines deepened in the old nurse's face as she smiled. "It's good to see you up and about."

He pointed at Nettie, then winked at Mrs. Henry. "She's persistent."

"That's a good thing, isn't it?"

"Time will tell."

"Funny thing about time," Mrs. Henry replied. "It has a way of getting us where we need to be, doesn't it?"

"Let's hope." He turned toward the south hall. "Where does this go?"

"To more patient rooms," replied Mrs. Henry. "At the end of the hall is an exit to an old garden, and beyond that is a parking lot."

"Okay if we take a look?" Mr. Pepper asked.

"Of course."

At the end of the hall, Mr. Pepper peered out the double glass doors. Studying the scraggly shrubs, unpruned trees, and crumbling sidewalk, he shook his head. "It's a pity people who run hospitals know so little about healing." He took a deep breath. "But, no winter lasts forever and no spring skips its turn."

"I didn't realize you were such a poet."

"I'm not. I read it in the *New York Times* years ago." He patted Nettie's hand and sat in the wheelchair. "I'm ready to go back to my room."

Mr. Pepper stayed unusually quiet during the return trip and insisted on getting himself back in bed. "Independence is as important as any medication, Nettie. Remember that."

"I will." She handed him is support socks.

"I hate those things," he complained. "I can't get them on."

"Independence is a good thing," she teased. "So is a little bit of help now and then."

"Okay, okay." He stuck his foot up. "Help."

"Watch how I do it, then you'll know how." Nettie turned one of the socks inside out down past the ankle, put his toes in, pulled the heel over the back of his foot, then telescoped the fabric up his leg. "Now, you do the other one."

"We've put a man on the moon but can't figure out how to mend broken hearts or make compression socks that are easy to get on," Mr. Pepper said, huffing and puffing as he pulled the sock up to his knee.

Nettie set his slippers on the floor by the bed so he could slide into them easily when getting up. "Want to take a quick nap before dinner?"

"Good idea." He lowered the head of the bed, his eyes heavy.

She eased toward the door.

"Nettie?"

"Yes, sir."

"You'll come back?"

"Of course."

"Thank you."

His persistent worry about her not coming back puzzled Nettie. *Maybe that's his story. Maybe people leave him and don't come back.* Mr. Pepper had an eccentric side for sure, but she enjoyed his company and his insight. "No need to thank me, Mr. Pepper. It's what friends do."

NETTIE PEEKED BOTH WAYS TO make sure Mrs. Woods wasn't around as she exited the tunnel and hurried toward the ER. She hadn't seen the supervisor since that awful day in the stairwell, but it was time for the shifts to change, so the woman had to be lurking somewhere.

"Hey, Nettie, wait up."

Startled, Nettie stumbled and almost fell as Paul Anderson ran to catch up with her.

"Whoa," he said, steadying her, his arm around her shoulders.

As Nettie and Paul separated, two nursing supervisors came out of a nearby administrative office. The women's expressions jumped from surprise to disapproval in a split second.

Damnation! So much for staying under the radar. At least Mrs. Woods isn't with them.

"Sorry about that," Paul said, watching the two women whisper and glance back as they went down the hall. "I didn't mean to scare you or cause those two such consternation."

"No worries, I'm just clumsy." Nettie motioned to his green OR scrubs and white lab coat. "Win told me you'd started your surgical rotation."

"I did, just this week."

"How's it going?"

"Busy. We've done three cases today and may be doing a fourth. There's a possible appendicitis in the ER I'm supposed to evaluate. Show me the way there?"

"Sure," Nettie replied. She led him through a maze of halls and doorways.

"Okay," Paul laughed. "I'll never remember how we got here."

"Sure, you will. And, if all else fails, remember the tiles on the floor, lines on the wall, and buttons on the elevator are color-coded directions. Green is for the ER and blue is for the OR." Going in the back entrance to the ER, she gave him a quick tour, introducing him to the nurses and doctors along the way.

"Welcome aboard," TK said, offering Paul a welcoming hand. "Let me know if I can be of help."

"Thanks. Nettie says you're an exceptional nurse."

"I try," TK replied.

"Well, I look forward to working with you."

"Same here."

Nettie checked the patient assignment board and showed Paul to the exam room where the appendicitis patient waited. "Good luck on the case."

"Thanks. I really appreciate your help. See you Saturday?"

"Yep. Win and I are bringing bagels."

As the door closed behind Paul, Nettie turned to go back to the nurses' station just as Mrs. Woods appeared.

"What's the meaning of that disgusting public display I just heard about."

"What?"

"You heard me. And don't deny it. My colleagues saw you and that surgical resident pawing each other in the middle of the hall."

"Mrs. Woods, what your colleagues saw was a nice guy keeping me from falling. There was nothing disgusting about it."

"That is not what they said."

"I can't control what they said or what they think they saw, ma'am, but I'm telling you what happened."

"Given your history of scandalous behavior, I have no reason to believe you over them. I'm reporting you and that ridiculous resident."

Injustice sparked the fire that had been building in Nettie for weeks. Enough was enough. First her, then Dougie, now Paul. Standing straight, she fired back. "Funny thing about scandals. The more you attempt to cover them up, the bigger they get."

Mrs. Woods eyes turned to slits. "What do you mean?"

Paul exited his patient's room and came to stand next to Nettie. "Mrs. Woods, is it? You're a supervisor, right?"

"Yes," she replied through gritted teeth.

"I'm Paul Anderson, the ridiculous resident you just referred to. You might want to lower your voice. The patient in that room and I heard every ugly word you said."

Mrs. Woods never blinked. "You two should be ashamed."

"Ashamed? Us? Sounds like you might have that backward. Nettie is telling the truth. I suggest you listen."

"My colleagues—"

"Give me the names of your—colleagues," Paul said. "I'll be happy to talk with them."

"That won't be necessary," she replied, leaving in a huff.

Whatever clout Paul had as a resident he just spent pushing Mrs. Woods's hostility back into the shadows.

He turned to Nettie. "Will you help me take this man to the OR? It's time to separate him from his appendix."

Nettie guided the stretcher as Paul pushed. Neither spoke until the appendicitis patient had been handed off to the OR staff and they were alone in the hall.

"Obviously, there's a backstory to what happened down there," Paul said. "Want to fill me in?"

Nettie shook her head. "It's better if you don't know."

"You're sure?"

"I'm sure."

"Okay, just let me know if she keeps going with those crazy accusations."

"Will do. Thanks."

"By the way," Paul said with a wink as he turned for the OR, "if I'm ever in a fight, I want you on my side. See you Saturday." He slipped into the bowels of the OR as Nettie hurried back downstairs. Keeping herself together, she and TK stayed busy until the end of their shift. Mrs. Woods didn't show up again, but it was just a matter of time.

Reaching her apartment, Nettie sat on the steps outside the building and watched the stars kaleidoscope. "Andy, I miss you so much."

PARKING THE CAR ALONG THE SHADED Potomac riverfront, Nettie and Win strolled the cobblestoned streets of Alexandria toward the NAF office. They had come to enjoy their Saturday mornings with Paul, Laura, and Mrs. Anderson. The conversations were lively, the work productive, and it offered a respite from the hospital and school.

"Any word from Andy lately?" Win asked.

Nettie shook her head. "His squad is doing extended patrols now, which means no mail pick up or delivery. So, he writes a little each day, then sends me a long letter when he gets back to Camp Eagle."

"Did you tell him about volunteering at the NAF?"

Nettie nodded. "I wasn't sure I wanted him thinking about MIAs, POWs, and KIAs but they're part of the world he's living in now, and I want him comfortable talking about it with me."

"Good point."

"Before this is over, I imagine he and his squad will know soldiers in all three categories." Nettie stopped walking. "I can't imagine the mental and physical stamina it takes to survive over there."

"Andy has plenty of both," Win said giving Nettie a hug.

"Yes, he does."

The aroma of freshly brewed coffee filled the NAF office as they arrived. "Good morning, Mrs. Anderson."

"Good morning, girls. Good week at school and work?"

"Yes, ma'am. Did you all have a good week?" Win asked.

She grimaced. "The Pentagon chiefs turned down our latest request for a meeting, as did a half-dozen senators. But we had a good fundraising week."

"It still blows my mind that the military and politicians have to be forced to do the right thing," Nettie said.

"The politicians will listen when their reelection campaigns gear up, and the Pentagon will listen when a new president is elected. Our PAC is going to influence both. I just hope our POWs can hold on that long."

Paul and Laura were already at work in the backroom as Nettie and Win delivered bagels and cream cheese. Biting into one, Win moaned in satisfaction.

Laura looked up, grinning. "You sound like you're starving."

"Not starving, just really tired of corn flakes."

"Then next time bring doughnuts, big fat, sugary ones. Paul seems to think they're bad for me." Laura laughed and stuck her tongue out at her brother.

It took time, but Laura had warmed up to Nettie and Win. The thaw started when they'd kept their word about showing up every Saturday and stayed until the day's work was done. Apparently, NAF volunteers came and went often. "They come when their loved ones go missing, then disappear when they have answers," Paul had said.

The four of them were well into the morning's activities when the bell over the front door tinkled. They could hear Mrs. Anderson talking with someone, followed by the sound of crying. Rushing to the breezeway, they watched a woman take the picture of a young soldier off the bulletin board. Tears and the loss of hope tore at the woman's face as Mrs. Anderson wrapped her in compassion.

Nettie closed her eyes and leaned against the wall.

"Don't go there," Laura whispered. "You'll drive yourself crazy."

"How do you all keep going day in and day out?"

"Because Dad's still out there. There's a lot of fathers, sons, brothers, husbands, and fiancés still out there. So, we keep going, one step at a time, one day at a time."

Pushing their angst to the background, they all went back to work.

Hours later, Paul placed the last box in the cart. "Come on, Win, help me roll this to the post office."

Laura watched them leave with a slight grin. "I bet he's finally going to ask her out. They've been flirting with each other for weeks."

"I'm okay with that, are you?"

"I'd be thrilled. Paul hasn't dated anyone seriously since Dad went missing."

"Win's a slow mover, so keep your fingers crossed." Nettie washed the coffee pot and mugs, then put them on the drainboard to dry. "What about you, Laura? Are you seeing anyone?" She shook her head. "A few dates here and there, but no one seriously. I'm trying to stay focused on keeping my grades up and helping Mom."

"I understand."

"What made you decide to go to nursing school?" Laura asked. "Was it something you always wanted to do?"

"I started thinking about it after reading the Cherry Ames book series as a kid. Then, in 1969, during the emergency response to Hurricane Camille, I met a national guard nurse named Linda Howard. It was amazing to watch her work. She made such a difference. I knew I wanted to do the same thing. She's active-duty army now and is stationed with the Mobile Army Surgical Hospital at Camp Eagle. The same camp where Andy's stationed."

"I have to start applying to colleges soon," Laura said. "I'm thinking about George Mason's nursing program. If I'm accepted, I can live at home and still help Mom."

"It's a good program."

"That's what I hear. Do you suppose I could go to work with you sometime, to see what it's like?"

"Of course. I'd love to have you. I'll bet Win would, too."

"I'm not sure I can handle the blood and guts."

"You'd be amazed at what you can handle when people are suffering."

Chapter 8

ANDY

Andy looked around the quiet camp. Everyone had eaten, a double perimeter had been set, and he was out of the rotation for the night. He could sleep until predawn if sleep cooperated. He settled on the damp ground and pulled out his ongoing letter to Nettie. Knocking a furry, six-inch centipede off his forearm, he wrote about the funny-looking bug keeping him company, the scent of the angel trumpet flowers next to him, and the shades of twilight he could see through the jungle canopy.

"Overall, the squad is doing well. Strawberry spotted a rare silver-back deer hiding under a bush, and Doc found a plant the leeches don't like. He gave the entire squad leaves to tuck into their socks. Quy taught Chase and Rawlin how to find duck eggs and Moretti figured out how to cook them in split pieces of bamboo. Sirocco and Hollis made a fish trap out of river rocks and sticks, and Cowboy has finally settled down."

Andy ended the entry with a touch of homesickness. "I can't wait to picnic at River's Rest, drink all the ice water I want, go to a softball game, and stargaze on Allen's Hill with you."

THE NEXT MORNING, ANDY'S SQUAD dropped to the ground as the rapid, blunted popping of AK47s echoed in the distance, something his squad had become used to hearing during their long deployments. Counting Mississippis from the echo of the last shot, he figured the shooter to be at least a mile away, which gave his men breathing room. Even at a hundred yards with line of sight, it would be unlikely the VC could make the shot. Their lack of training on the old Russian rifle negated its well-known accuracy at long distances. However, in close proximity, the VC's point-and-spray firing technique killed everything in sight.

No other US or ARVN units were reported to be in the area to draw fire, which meant the shots were likely coming from the village Andy and his men had surveilled the night before. They'd counted six black tunics with brown belts and witnessed the harassment and beating of several villagers who resisted. Watching VC brutality without the ability to intervene frustrated everyone in the squad. Counting fresh graves covered in white flowers and burned-out buildings as part of their recon statistics only added to their discontent. The VC rarely buried their dead, and if the villagers buried them, there were no white flowers of mourning.

Andy motioned his men to come closer. Taking a knee, they grabbed canteens as Andy talked. "We need to circle back to that village and see what those shots were about. I'm guessing the VC are getting tired of waiting for those villagers to welcome a cadre."

"This is getting old," Strawberry said. "That's the third village those bastards have terrorized during this patrol. I'd like to give them a dose of their own medicine."

"Major Smith will have a conniption if we blow our recon cover," Rawlin countered.

"I agree with both of you," Andy said, pulling out his map. "In case the VC are headed this way, we need to drop down and circle back to the village from the south." He traced the proposed route with his finger. "Questions?"

No one spoke.

"Okay, stay low, and head out."

It took the better part of two hours to circle down and back to the village. Andy smelled the acrid smoke long before he focused his binoculars on the smoldering huts. His stomach churned at the sight of bodies lying in the dirt, five men, three women, and a young girl. Some survivors walked around shell-shocked, while others openly grieved. Andy waved Quy forward. The young interpreter would enter the village and talk with those who were willing.

"You know what we need, Quy," Andy said. "Who, what, when—"

"—and how many of them carried real weapons."

"Do you still have money?" As was the army's custom with friendly villages raided by the VC, Quy would leave money with the elders to buy supplies until they could get back on their feet.

Quy patted the pocket hidden in his tunic and nodded. "A little."

Andy studied the rutted, dirt road running straight through the middle of the village. "Strawberry, Rawlin, and Hollis, you three cover Quy as he goes in. Chase, Cowboy, and Sirocco, you all cover him as he leaves. The rest of us will cover what happens in the middle. Everyone comes back here after." Andy put his hand on Quy's arm. "Be careful. The VC may be watching the village. If you sense they are still around, keep walking." Scanning the village one more time, Andy gave his squad a thumbs-up. "Go."

Quy handed his M16 to Moretti and gave Doc his ruck. Straightening his palm-leaf hat, he fell in behind Strawberry. Once near the road, he would break off and enter the village on his own.

Fifteen minutes later, Andy found Quy with the binoculars as he intersected the road and headed for the village. Once in the common area, Quy approached a small group of people standing and kneeling near the bodies. He spoke to an elderly, stooped man.

"The old guy must be a village elder," Moretti whispered.

Gesturing toward the bodies and the burned-out parts of the village, the old man started talking, stopping frequently to dry his eyes. Quy eased him down to a frayed bamboo bench, then sat on the ground close by. They talked for a long time as the remaining villagers mourned and prepared the dead for burial. When Quy rose to leave, he took money out of his pocket and gave it to the elder. Struggling to get to his feet, the old man took Quy's hand in both of his. Bowing, Quy continued his walk through the village.

Once back with the squad, Quy sank to his knees and took a long drink from the canteen Moretti handed him.

Andy knelt as others set a four-point perimeter without being asked. "Let's hear it."

"Six brown belts raided the village this morning. The old man is the lead elder. Until now, he's resisted their attempts to form a cadre in the village. So, the bastards decided to teach him a lesson. They shot and killed his wife and son. They raped and murdered his daughter-in-law and eleven-year-old granddaughter and conscripted his two grandsons for the NVA as they left the village. The youngest boy is seven."

Andy swallowed the bile rising in the back of his throat.

"When they were done raping, torturing, and murdering, they plundered the victims' homes and storage huts, then burned them to the ground." Quy's voice broke. "They told the old man if he did not welcome the cadre by the time they returned, the rest of his village would suffer the same fate. When they left, they took most of the village's water buffalos."

Determination replaced Andy's rage. "Strawberry, the road heading west out of the village intersects with one going north in about five klicks, doesn't it?"

"Yes."

"That's where they're headed, and those buffalo don't travel fast," Andy murmured to himself. He waved his men in. "If we can catch up to those VC before they reach the DMZ, we might be able to rescue the boys before they are turned over to the NVA. It's not our mission, but I think we need to try. And, if at all possible, do it without giving ourselves away, which means leaving no enemy witnesses." Andy looked at each of his men. "Volunteers only. The rest will wait here."

"Are you sure about this, Lieutenant?" Moretti asked. "If Major Smith finds out, he's going to make a boatload of trouble for you. He may even take your bars and break up the squad."

"Trouble's relative, Moretti. I couldn't live with myself if I didn't try." Andy looked around again. "Who's in?"

Everyone raised their hands.

"Moretti, turn off the radio. We're going to be tracking close to these guys, and I don't want it giving us away. If we're going to catch them, we need to move fast and stay close to the road. Strawberry you're on point, Rawlin slack, Chase sharpshooter."

"Rear security," Cowboy volunteered.

"Okay. The rest of you are in the middle. Let's go."

It didn't take long to catch up with the marauding VC. They had indeed stayed on the road to keep the dozen slow-walking water buffalos moving. Their rifles were slung obliquely across their backs signaling little concern about encountering trouble. Three VC walked in front of the buffalos and three walked behind. The two bruised and battered boys, their hands bound, were tethered to the horns of the last trailing animal.

The VC's lack of military training and general carelessness gave Andy and his men the advantage. The murderers would need several seconds and both hands to get the rifles off their backs and into firing position. With their hands occupied, the knives hidden in their brown belts became less of a threat.

Stopping out of ear shot, Andy pulled out his map, as his squad gathered around. Thankfully, the closest village was friendly and still over two miles away. Clearing a spot in the dirt, he diagrammed his plan. "The only way to do this," he whispered, "is to take them all down at once so they don't have time to get to their weapons or escape. He pointed to Strawberry, Rawlin, and Sirocco. "About a half-mile ahead is a rice paddy. Cut through the jungle and get in front of them. Take position on this side of the paddy. Be ready to come in behind the three VC in the front as soon as they reach the first irrigation ditch. Left to right, mark your man, and use your knives to take them out. Back of the neck if you can, throats if you can't. Hollis, you go with them to cover. If any of the VC gets the upper hand, take them out. Cowboy, Moretti, and I will come in behind the last three and do the same. Chase, you'll cover us. If anyone tries to escape, catch them. If you can't, shoot them. When these scumbags are down, tie their rifles and ammo bands to their belts, then roll the bodies into the irrigation ditch. Doc, you and Quy free the boys. Bring them to this spot and wait. If this thing goes south, the goal is to get them back to their grandfather. Everyone understand?"

"Thank you for doing this, Lieutenant," Quy said.

Andy gave Quy a thumbs-up, erased the diagram, and nodded to Strawberry. "You four leave your rucks here and take off. Stay out of sight until the VC are in position. When you see me and the others go, you all follow hard and fast."

Dropping their rucks, Andy, Cowboy, Moretti, and Chase inched closer to the VC and crouched in the dense brush. Andy signaled for Cowboy to take the man on the left, Moretti the one in the middle, and he'd take the man farthest away on the right.

When the VC reached the irrigation ditch, Andy signaled his group and they took off running. A second later, Strawberry and his group burst out of the brush and ambushed the first three from behind. Seeing what was happening, the rear VC tried frantically to get the straps of their rifles over their heads but it was too late. Cowboy and Moretti quickly dropped their targets, but Andy's target had seen them coming and took off into the jungle. Andy stayed tight on his heels, knife in hand. He'd almost caught the man when the surrounding foliage disappeared, and they were running on a narrow path. Andy made a grab for the man's black tunic just as he veered off the path and back into the brush. As Andy followed, he heard a ping. *Ping*? He hit the ground a split second before the tripwire grenade went off, the blast so close and loud it imprinted his skin and clothes with shards of debris and caused painful ringing in his ears. Rattled, but conscious, Andy slid the blade of his knife under his leg, then lay motionless. His barely open, grit-filled eyes burned as he watched the VC's sandals move back down the path toward him, slowly, deliberately. Andy could smell the man's sweat as he knelt and reached for the M16. Rolling sideways, Andy shoved his knife into the man's heart and jumped up. Grabbing his rifle, he aimed at the man's head but didn't need to fire. Blood stopped spurting from the murderer's chest the moment his heart stopped and he fell over.

Chase hurried cautiously down the path, his rifle up and finger on the trigger, his head scanning left and right. Spotting Andy, he pointed his rifle at the ground, obviously relieved. "Boy, am I glad to see you!"

Grabbing a canteen off his belt, Andy washed the grit from his eyes. "Everything on the road taken care of?"

"Yeah," Chase replied. "They'll be fish food in short order. Quy and Doc are freeing the boys."

Andy picked up his aviator sunglasses, which now had a crack in the bottom of the right lens. Putting them on, the crack disappeared from his line of sight unless he looked for it. *Good*. Returning them to his pocket, he pulled the dead man into the debris field. "Help me stage this guy."

Chase bent the VC's arms and legs into positions consistent with an explosion, while Andy found a sharp stick among the debris and shoved it into the stab wound. Rubbing dirt and debris on the dead man's exposed skin, hair, and clothes, they finished by throwing his hat into the brush as if it had been blown off. As they turned to leave, Andy noticed something trailing from the VC's pocket. A little girl's heart necklace. The chain had blood and skin on it, as if ripped from the neck of its owner. Andy pocketed the necklace as he and Chase backed down the path toward the road, using leaves and brush to cover their boot tracks while leaving the imprints of the VC's sandals.

By the time they reached the road, the rest of the squad had submerged the remaining bodies, covered the blood with dirt, erased the boot tracks, and were letting the water buffalo track up the scene.

"Do you want to keep the buffalo going north so the tracks are consistent?" Strawberry asked.

Andy nodded. "Hopefully, whoever finds them will be more interested in keeping them than knowing where they came from." Using his canteen, Andy cleaned the little girl's necklace.

Joining Quy, Doc, and the rescued boys in the shadows of the jungle's edge, Andy showed the necklace to Quy. "Ask the boys if this belonged to their sister."

The boys started nodding before Quy finished speaking, their faces pale, their wide-eyed expressions lost.

"Please take this to your grandfather," Quy told the oldest boy, as Andy handed him the necklace.

Andy gave the signal to head out. "Let's get these boys home."

BY DARK, THE BOYS HAD BEEN RETURNED to their grandfather and the squad had disappeared back into the recesses of the jungle to set up camp. Moretti turned the radio on to report in. It immediately blared, "Whiskey, Tango, Foxtrot!"

Major Smith's intense delivery of the military's version of an expletive made Moretti hold the receiver away from his ear. "Bravo One, I said come in. Over." The cadence of his words reflected anger as opposed to concern.

Andy took the receiver. "Alpha One, this is Bravo One. Over," he said with steely calm.

"Well, it's about damn time," the major responded testily. "Why haven't you been responding, Bravo One? Was your radio off? Over."

"Alpha One, this is Lieutenant Stockton. I ordered radio silence, sir. Over."

"Why? What the hell's going on? You were supposed to check in from your next site hours ago. Over."

Bracing for what was to come, Andy explained his decision to break reconnaissance protocol to rescue the two little boys.

"You did what? Over."

Andy didn't have time to reply as the major expressed his displeasure.

"You are positive no witnesses escaped?" the major snapped, ending his tirade. "Over."

"Affirmative," Andy replied. "We covered our tracks and we've had no additional encounters or visuals. Over."

"What a stupid stunt," the major continued. "How can you be sure the VC will not hold those boys, their grandfather, and other villagers accountable for the disappearance of their men? Over."

"Because the village is abandoned, sir. Everyone left after the attack. The boys and their grandfather are already on their way South to Hue. They have extended family there. Over."

"Where the hell are you now, Bravo One? Over."

"Heading to our next recon site. Over."

"Why did it take so long for you to notify me, Lieutenant? Over."

"Because I needed to get my men out of there—sir. Over."

Andy's squad snickered.

"Did your second agree with this harebrained stunt? Over."

"It was my call, Major. Over."

"I'm sure it was, Lieutenant." Sarcasm dripped from each word the major uttered. "If you were here, I'd pull your bars. Over."

Andy'd had enough. "I'll be glad to bring them to you—sir. I could use a shower. Over." Everyone snickered again, except for Moretti.

"You have a job to do, Lieutenant. And just to make sure it gets done, we'll give your squad plenty of extra patrol time. Alpha One out."

"Roger that, Alpha One. Thank you for your concern about the squad's well-being—sir. Out."

Andy tossed the receiver to Moretti.

"He could make real trouble for you, Lieutenant."

"He may be an ass, Moretti, but he's not stupid. He just lost sight of what we're fighting for, if he ever had it to begin with. Plus, he's not going to break up a seasoned recon squad operating at the edge of the DMZ."

Andy looked at the faces of his squad. "Sorry, fellows. Looks like our stand-down is going to be delayed again."

"Those little boys were worth it," Strawberry said. The others nodded in agreement.

Quy's eyes glistened. "We just gave their grandfather a reason to keep living. They have each other. They're still a family."

"Would you do it again?" Moretti asked Andy.

"If I had to do it over? I'd be waiting for those bastards as they came into the village."

Later that night, Andy allowed himself to think about how close he'd come to dying. Ceasing to exist at the hands of a man who raped and murdered innocent people. He didn't regret killing the man. There'd likely be more innocent victims if he hadn't. But there is always a price to be paid, always questions to be asked when a moral person kills. He knew the answers would be found over time and in long conversations with God. Until then, he prayed that walking the gray line between killing and murder was forgivable. As he slipped into sleep, he hoped Nettie looked up when the stars above him reached her side of the world.

ANDY SAT IN THE OPEN DOOR of the vibrating Huey, one leg propped against the mounted machine gun, the other anchored around a strut. Even with the hot wind in his face, he couldn't escape the smell of old blood, ammunition, spent shells, and his own stink. It felt good to sit on something other than the ground and even better to be above the jungle and not in it. His squad had paid a high price for detouring to save the little boys and for his mouthing off to Major Smith. The stand-down they'd anticipated after their last long patrol had been canceled, as had their detour south to a safe drop zone to pick up supplies. To date, his squad had been on patrol over sixty days, the last thirty with significantly lighter rucks. Two months of being in the same clothes and sleeping with one eye open had taken its toll. They needed uninterrupted sleep, food, baths, and a trip to the infirmary to address various bites and persistent rashes. Even their toothbrushes were worn down to the plastic as they tried to remove the taste of what they had to eat.

Thanks to Quy's knowledge of the jungle and Moretti's ability to disguise food, the squad had learned to live on beetles and other dull-colored, non-smelling bugs, hairless worms, bananas and their blossoms, coconuts, mangos, fruits they didn't know the name of, and fish when they had water and time. Appetizing or not, it kept them going. They'd learned to stay away from plants smelling like almonds, those with white or yellow berries, and those producing seeds inside pods. And while white water lilies were edible, white umbrella-shaped flowers were not. When the chlorine tablets ran out, they filled their canteens with rainwater captured in their ponchos and helmets or with stream water that had been boiled over their dwindling supply of C4. When they ran out of camo paint, they used mud. Lemongrass and basil were the only bug repellants available, and those plants were hard to find.

The helicopter ride to Camp Eagle had been the only support they'd received, and Major Smith hadn't authorized that until the squad had already hiked to within ten miles of the base.

Next time, Andy, keep your mouth shut.

The chopper sprinted over the treetops at two miles a minute, a hundred and twenty times faster than his squad could travel on foot. *Why didn't I become a pilot?* To date, the monitoring of the northern Quaing Tri Provence had been inhumanely hot and humid, slow and boring most of the time, and heart-pounding fast and terrifying at others. Now, high above the jungle and its hidden dangers, Andy allowed himself to be distracted by thoughts of home, his mother's cooking, a soft bed, a good night's sleep, a day without fear of dying or being seriously hurt, and the feel of snowflakes. He yearned for Nettie. He'd run out of paper to write her weeks ago and resorted to writing in the margins of other entries.

He touched his breast pocket where their picture stayed protected.

"Maybe they'll let you call her this time," Moretti said.

Andy gave him a thumbs-up, then turned his gaze out the door. After a moment, he realized Moretti's eyes were still on him, not teasing, just empathetic.

"Only a few months to go, sir. Maybe when this is over you and your girl can come to Brooklyn to meet my mom. She's a great cook."

Andy nodded. Moretti was gold. He'd become an expert at finding food when there was none and improvising to make things tastier when the spices ran out. He listened when the men wanted to talk. He told them about his home in Brooklyn and what it was like to live in New York when they needed to think about something other than the enemy, the mission, and themselves. He hadn't been in a fistfight since the squad formed.

Andy studied his men as they reclined in the belly of the Huey. They'd become a cohesive team, even to the point of finishing each other's sentences. Everyone had gained competency at walking point, slack, and rear security, and had cross-trained on the radio, even though Moretti made his ownership of the device clear. They'd grown accustomed to biting bugs, rain, hiking through tangled brush without leaving a trail, operating on little or no sleep, and minimal food. They moved from one village to another with a calmer approach to surprises the jungle threw at them and with significantly fewer mishaps. They'd become exceptionally skilled at assessing characteristics of villages and projecting where and when they would see cadres, but they'd yet to see any obvious NVA activity.

"We'll be on the ground in two minutes, Lieutenant!" yelled the copilot.

Andy gave him a thumbs-up and signaled his men with two fingers. He looked forward to seeing Gus when they got in. He hadn't seen him since their last stand-down two months ago, and their radio conversations could only go so far. Not only did they need to compare intel before briefing Major Smith in the morning, but Andy wanted Gus's thoughts on a pattern he'd noticed. Some villages sent men to sell tea and rice along busy roads and markets, while other villages sent women. Sometimes, the men returned with residual bags of tea and rice, while the women seldom did. He wasn't sure it meant anything, but it was unusual and recurrent.

Once Andy's squad had boots on the tarmac, he called them together. "Enjoy your stand-down but don't overdo the food or alcohol. You don't want to spend your free time in the infirmary. Meet me at the mess hall at noon tomorrow, and I'll fill you in on the briefing with Major Smith."

"Let's hope he's forgotten about our detour to rescue those kids," Moretti said.

"Where's the fun in that?" Andy asked with a wink.

"Yeah, we just don't want to break in a new lieutenant," Moretti teased.

Leaving the airfield, the squad headed straight to the supply tent, then to their barracks and showers.

Standing in the steady flow of clean, warm water, Andy swore he'd never take soap, shampoo, toothpaste, and a sharp razor for granted again. Dressed in fresh fatigues and new socks and boots, he headed to the Comm Center. As usual, Jimmy, the private at the counter asked the droopy-eyed major behind the desk for permission to make the call, and as usual, he refused.

"Thanks anyway," Andy said. Leaving the center, he swung by the post office, picked up his mail and a big care package from home, then headed to the mess tent. Claiming a table in the back of the almost deserted space, he set his mail down, grabbed a tray, and loaded it with two bacon, lettuce, and tomato sandwiches, two large cookies, two Pepsis, and two tall cups of ice. With his hunger and thirst subsiding, Andy immersed himself in the words and worlds of those he loved. He would read their letters again and again while in camp, committing them to memory, and then stow most of them in his footlocker to be read again when he returned from the next patrol. He'd keep Nettie's most recent letter in his breast pocket with their picture.

Delicious scents floated up as Andy unpacked his box of goodies—a container of his favorite homemade cookies, hard candy, mixed nuts, tins of seasoning for Moretti, and dozens of Kool Aid packets. It didn't take much of the colored powder to hide the taste of chlorine tablets. Andy would share the more perishable treats with his squad while in camp. The more durable ones would be unwrapped and stored in the small, waterproof pockets of his ruck before he headed out again. The box also contained notebooks, pens, several pairs of thick, water-wicking green socks, shoelaces, and tubes of antifungal cream to treat the jungle rot that kept popping up on his constantly damp feet.

After penning return letters to Nettie and his mom, Andy dropped his care package off at the barracks, then headed to the PX. He wanted to send something home that spoke to the beauty of the besieged country, and not its sorrow. In the native arts section of the store, he found intricately coiled paper figures. He selected a lotus flower for Nettie and a dove for his mom.

"Looks like it's time for a new pair of aviators, Lieutenant," the clerk said, pointing to the cracked lens.

Andy's thoughts flashed to the moment the grenade exploded above him, the small crack in his glasses a constant reminder that being focused had saved his life. "No, thanks," he replied. "These work just fine." Adding the return letters to each gift box, Andy arranged to have the packages shipped home, then headed to the landing field to see if Gus's squad had arrived.

"Yes, sir. They're back," the signalman said. "But it's not good. They were ambushed on the way in. Two dead, one of ours and their ARVN interpreter, and the sergeant is in bad shape. They took him to the hospital."

Stunned, Andy turned to leave.

"Lieutenant, if Gus is alive, ask him about the chopper."

"Why? What happened?"

The signalman looked around to make sure they were alone. "Just ask him, sir."

Andy hurried to the hospital only to wait for hours on a bench near the entrance. He'd found a corpsman who relayed a message to Linda Howard, the head surgical nurse and Nettie's friend. She sent word back that Gus was in the OR and she'd be out when they moved him to recovery.

It was late afternoon before Linda exited the tent, her face mask dangling around her neck, her blood splattered scrubs covered with a clean lab coat. "It's good to see you again, Andy," she said giving him a hug. "Sorry it has to be under these circumstances. How do you know Gus?"

"He's my platoon sergeant and headed up my second squad. How's he doing?"

"He's in recovery now and is stable."

"Thank God," Andy said, sighing with relief.

"You should wait until tomorrow to visit him. He's pretty groggy."

"Sure."

"There's more," Linda added, grimly. "We had to remove most of his left leg. A bullet mangled the femoral artery and nerves. His squad saved his life. They held pressure on the artery and refused to let up until they had him at the hospital and the medical team could take over. Gus still lost a lot of blood. He's getting a third unit of whole blood now."

"But he's alive. That's what matters."

"He has a long way to go, Andy. He lost men. Those wounds are hard to heal."

THE NEXT MORNING, ANDY WENT to see Gus before his briefing with Major Smith. Ushered to the back of a large tent where beds were divided by portable screens, Andy found Gus flat on his back, a clear IV going in one arm and ruby-colored blood dripping slowing into the other. Thick gauze and a wide ACE bandage wrapped what remained of his left leg. Two pillows elevated it above the level of his heart. Gus smiled weakly as Andy came behind the screen and pulled a chair close.

"Hey, Andy. I'm glad to see you." They'd moved past using military titles when they were by themselves long ago. "Glad you're back in one piece. Your squad okay?"

Andy nodded. "I'm so sorry about your men."

Gus clenched his jaw to hold back tears. "They were good soldiers, good men."

"Yes, they were."

"Would you do me a favor?" Gus asked. "I'm going to write letters to their families and want to make sure they get to the post office. Would you take them for me?"

"Of course. I'm going to meet with the rest of your squad as soon as Major Smith lets them go. He's had them sequestered for debriefing since you all got back."

"Good. I know they'll want to talk with you."

Andy motioned to his missing limb. "Good thing you have two."

Gus managed a chuckle. "This isn't exactly how I viewed retirement."

"My guess is you'll be kicking ass with an artificial leg in no time."

"Maybe. I'm being flown to the Army hospital in Japan at the end of the week for rehab. When the stump heals, I go to Walter Reed to get a prosthetic leg. My wife and kids are going to meet me there. I'm not sure how they're going to handle this."

"They'll do fine as long as you do."

"I always knew you were a glass-half-full kind of guy."

Andy grinned. "Who wants to live life from the other half?"

"That's true. At least I get to go home sitting up. And, I have a job waiting for me at my dad's hardware store." Gus's expression changed. "Look, Andy, there's something you need to know before you head back out on patrol. My squad wasn't shot up by enemy sympathizers or even by VC. We were shot by men in enemy camouflage. My point man also saw a radio antenna, and Due Le heard someone shouting military orders in Vietnamese. Both men died before we could get them here. You know as well as I do, the VC and their sympathizers don't have camouflage or radios, and they don't use military language."

"NVA."

Gus nodded. "I think we surprised an NVA recon squad as we were hiking in. They weren't expecting us any more than we were expecting them."

"What makes you think that?"

Gus leaned over and pulled a banana slug bullet out of the drawer of his bedside stand. "They dug this out of my leg during surgery. Looks like a 7.62 millimeter, which is what the NVA uses. Those guys fired a single volley, then disappeared. They weren't looking for a fight, they were looking for information."

"Damn." Andy leaned back and exhaled at the implications. "They were reconning Camp Eagle."

"That's right. You'll need to be extra careful from now on. They know we know they're here, and recon or not, they didn't hesitate to fire."

"We've told Major Smith over and over the VC were coming through the DMZ like a sieve and that the NVA were bound to follow."

"The man hears what he wants to hear," Gus replied wearily.

"Not this time. He may not like it, but he's going to hear it." Andy leaned forward. "The signalman at the airfield said to ask you what happened with the chopper yesterday."

Gus closed his eyes for a moment. "According to the chopper crew, Major Smith refused to give the order to pick us up until he finished breakfast. We were coming in on our own when we were ambushed."

"That son of a bitch," Andy said, fisting his hands. "I'm going to—"

Gus touched Andy's arm. "Don't. You can't go at him head-on, you know that. He'd like nothing better than to take down a lieutenant who challenges him."

"He's going to keep on until he gets someone else killed or injured if I don't." Andy looked Gus in the eye. "I don't know how, but that man's time for controlling soldiers in the field is going to end."

An hour later, Andy stood with Major Smith in front of a map marking where Gus and his squad were attacked.

"Lieutenant, I'm not convinced it was the NVA who attacked Sergeant Griffin's squad. No other recon squads, including yours, have reported any NVA sightings. And the fact it happened this far south makes it likely the attackers were VC sympathizers."

"I disagree, sir. As Gus pointed out, it wasn't a planned attack. His squad surprised those men. Men who were wearing camouflage and carrying a radio. The VC and their sympathizers aren't equipped like that," Andy replied.

"We don't have verification of that information. The two soldiers who allegedly saw them died in the attack."

"Sir, we have the banana slug the surgeon pulled from Sergeant Griffin's leg. It's a 7.62, which the NVA uses in both the AK47s and the SKSs. Plus, the automatic fire came in a short burst, then stopped and the enemy disappeared. Like Gus said, they weren't looking for fight, they were looking for information."

"And like I said, Lieutenant, we don't have verification of that information."

"Sir, we've been reporting for months that VC intrusions are increasing in the Vinh Lee District. And we know the NVA follows the VC whether we have eyes on them or not. That information combined with the circumstances surrounding the attack on Gus and his men is compelling evidence. The NVA is reconning Camp Eagle."

"Well, Lieutenant, if you're so convinced the NVA have breached the DMZ without being seen and have infiltrated spies this far south, why haven't you found them?"

"Sergeant Griffin did find them, sir, and he lost two men and a leg in the process. We're going to lose more men if this intelligence is not reevaluated."

"Lieutenant, did you just imply I'm not taking the attack on this squad seriously?"

"No, sir."

"That's better."

"I'm not implying it; I'm saying outright that an accurate, ongoing analysis of our intelligence might have prevented the attack on Gus and his men in the first place or least gotten a chopper out to them before they got shot up."

The major's eyes narrowed. "Is that so?" He strolled behind his desk, lit a cigarette, and leaned back in his chair.

"Do your job, Lieutenant. Give us some intelligence we can actually use. Your squad goes out again in forty-eight hours. Dismissed."

Andy fought the urge to knock the man out of his chair. Cutting his squad's stand-down by more than half reeked of retaliation.

In the army, every boss had a boss. Major Smith's boss was the base commander, Colonel Clark. The army also never tolerated jumping the chain of command, so getting accurate intelligence information into the base commander's office would be a challenge. However, if Andy could manage to do it, Major Smith's faulty decision-making might become evident as well.

Leaving Major Smith's office, Andy headed back to the hospital. Perhaps Gus's service to the army wasn't over, and perhaps Linda Howard could expand hers.

Chapter 9

NETTIE

Nettie and TK had just finished their first rounds of the evening when Nettie received a page to come to the nurses' station. At the door stood two men with a cart holding a large peach gardenia. Four feet wide and three feet tall, the beautiful blossoms outnumbered the leaves. Holding the gardenia was an exquisite, hand-painted planter with carved onyx legs and a matching, attached drip tray.

"Nettie, this magnificent thing is for you," one of the nurses said.

Nettie pulled the engraved card from its holder, already knowing the sender. "Thanks for being so patient and helpful. We had to wait to send this until the plants were the right size to ship. I hope you enjoy it for years to come. Instructions for its care are enclosed. Sincerely, Mr. Pepper."

"Where would you like for us to put the jardinière?" asked one of the men, looking at Nettie.

"The what?" Nettie asked.

He pointed to the planter.

"I—uh."

"What's the meaning of this?" Mrs. Woods asked, marching down the hall.

Grabbing a piece of paper from her pocket, Nettie scribbled the address of her apartment and handed it to the delivery men. "It needs to be delivered to this address, please. My roommate should be there to accept it." Returning the card to the holder, she turned to face the music.

Mrs. Woods pushed past her and took the card before the men could leave.

"What are you doing?" Nettie said. "That card is addressed to me."

Mrs. Woods face turned dark as she read. She motioned Nettie into an empty office and slammed the door. "You continued a relationship with this man after I told you not to?"

Nettie took a deep breath. "Ma'am, I visit him on my own time, and there is nothing in the intern handbook, the hospital staff's handbook, or the school of nursing's handbook that says I can't or shouldn't."

"I said you can't! I said you shouldn't! You blatantly ignored my directive."

"All due respect, ma'am, you're being unfair. He is my friend—"

"Friend?"

"Yes, ma'am."

Mrs. Woods uttered an ugly laugh. "More like you're taking advantage of a sick old man by soliciting expensive gifts."

"What? I never—"

TK came into the office without knocking, a portable phone in her hand. "Mrs. Woods, Mrs. Henry from the Godfrey Center would like to speak with you."

"Tell her I'll call her back," Mrs. Woods snapped.

TK didn't budge. "It pertains to this conversation."

The irate supervisor stared in disbelief at TK. "You called her?"

"Yes."

Mrs. Woods grabbed the phone. "This is Genevieve."

Nettie couldn't hear Mrs. Henry's side of the conversation, but Mrs. Woods's mouth went rigid as she listened.

"She disobeyed me and continued to see this man."

"You gave her permission? Why?"

"I don't think you considered—"

"Yes, of course I do."

"No, of course, I don't."

"No, I do not."

"I understand." Mrs. Woods hit the off button, slapped the phone in TK's hand, then spun on Nettie.

"You may have manipulated Mrs. Henry in order to keep visiting that rich old man, but soliciting gifts from patients is a serious policy infraction and grounds for dismissal."

"Mrs. Woods, I told you, I didn't ask for the plant. I've never asked him for anything."

"Did you know he was going to send it?"

Nettie remembered the conversation with Mr. Pepper. "He said something about sending me a plant, but I told him—"

"Of course, you knew," Mrs. Woods smirked.

"Mrs. Woods," TK insisted, "If you don't believe Nettie, why not ask Mr. Pepper?"

"I don't need to ask anyone to know what's going on, and I do not need any more interference from you. Heaven knows what else this girl is trying to swindle out of that man."

Nettie opened her mouth to fire back at the ugly accusation but stopped when TK squeezed her arm.

"Nettie, would you go check on our patients, please? I'll join you in a few minutes."

Nettie swallowed hard. She respected TK too much not to do as she asked.

"Don't let the old biddy get you down, Nettie," one of the ER nurses whispered as Nettie left the station.

Hours later, in the cafeteria, TK and Nettie finally had a chance to talk.

"That woman is hell-bent on getting you out of this hospital," TK said. "She might have succeeded tonight if it weren't for Mrs. Henry and this." TK handed Nettie a packet of papers. "It's an evaluation of your performance in the ER, completed by me, the head nurse, and the director of the internship program."

Relief poured over Nettie as she looked over the review of her work—each criteria marked as excellent. "Thank you, TK. Coming from you, this means a lot, especially considering what happened this afternoon."

"You're welcome, but that's not all. The director wants to talk with you about extending your internship next year."

"Does Mrs. Woods have a say in it?"

"No, thank goodness."

"Then, I'd love to."

TK set her glass down. "Don't you think it's about time you told me what's really going on with her?"

Nettie was tempted to enlist the help of her friend and preceptor, but something told her to stay quiet. "I'm not going to drag you into the middle of something I can't prove."

NETTIE PEEKED INTO MR. PEPPER'S room when he didn't respond to her knock.

"Hey, Nettie," Mrs. Henry said as she came out of another patient's room. "Mr. Pepper was hoping you'd stop by. He has something to show you. He's in the old garden."

"Thanks, Mrs. Henry. And thank you for helping with Mrs. Woods the other day."

"I'm glad TK thought to call me. Genevieve's being unreasonable."

"Well, I'm grateful for your help and your trust. How's Mr. Pepper?"

"He's been much more active and happier lately. You'll see why in a minute."

As Nettie walked down the south hall, she saw workmen tilling up the old garden while a front-end loader broke up the asphalt in the small parking lot and loaded it onto a dump truck. A plywood walkway stretched from the door to the middle of the garden where Mr. Pepper sat under a sideless tent, dispatching additional workers.

"Ahh, Nettie, there you are! My company is expanding to the East Coast," Mr. Pepper said with a smile and wide wave of his arms. "Of course, it's just asphalt, poor dirt, and rocks now, but once all of that is dug out and hauled away, a good drainage system will go in, followed by a deep foundation of rich soil. Come spring we'll plant a magnificent healing garden that patients from all over the hospital can visit. What do you think?"

"What a great idea! How did you ever get the hospital to agree to it?"

"Money, my dear. Lots and lots of money. It buys just about everything," he added wryly. "It has taken months for my lawyers to work out the details, but the papers have finally been signed." He motioned to one of the folding chairs under the tent. "Sit. Let's chat."

As Nettie settled in, Mr. Pepper pointed in different directions, his eyes bright. "Just imagine it. Beautiful tall trees interspersed with pink and white dogwoods, redbuds, and miniature maples. Flowering bushes, ferns, medicinal plants here, fragrant herbs there, scattered annuals, perennials, and benches strategically placed along a path leading to a pond with a tiered waterfall."

"It sounds wonderful," Nettie said.

"That's not all," Mr. Pepper continued. "Virginia's winter

climate can be hard on gardens, so we've secured land near the back of the hospital's property to build a nursery, one to support this healing garden. Once it's built, we'll have a place to grow and protect the most vulnerable trees and plants during cold weather, as well as have a beautiful inside garden for people to visit. Of course, the hospital board thinks the nursery will be some type of plastic Quonset hut, but it's not. My partner, Mr. Kalua is bringing a crew from Hawaii to build it and the garden. He will ensure both are beautiful and therapeutic. He's a very talented man."

Nettie marveled at her friend's enthusiasm and resources. She also noticed his breathlessness after talking and his swollen ankles. "I'm sure they will be beautiful, but don't wear yourself out in the process."

He noticed her looking at his ankles. "What a pain in the ass you are." He laughed. "I'm telling you about plans for beautiful gardens, and you're focused on my feet."

"Sorry. The projects sound amazing. I just want you to keep getting better at the same time."

"All right, I'll wear those obnoxious socks and take three walks a day under one condition."

"Which is?"

"That you'll help with the garden and nursery."

Nettie's eyes widened. "Mr. Pepper, as I said before, neither of my thumbs is green."

"Mr. Kalua and I can help you with that. It's a learned skill." He looked out across a garden only he could see. "Gardens are the respite people seldom realize they need, a place where beauty pushes the burdens of life away for a while. My goal is to live long enough to see the healing garden and nursery completed. If that doesn't happen, I'd like for Mr. Kalua to have someone to help him, an assistant who knows the area." He studied Nettie's face as she deliberated, hope driving the intent look in his eyes. "I would consider it a personal favor."

Every time-related commitment Nettie had flashed through her mind—school, internship, volunteer work at the NAF, and her quiet time alone to miss Andy. *How in the world can I carve out time to help build a garden and nursery I know nothing about? How can I not?* Before she responded, there was a question Nettie needed to have answered. "Mr. Pepper?"

"Yes."

"Why me?" She met his eyes. "For this, for everything. Why me?"

"I was wondering when you'd get around to asking that question." Calm smoothed his face as he touched his ring. "I've always been spiritual about the beauty and power of nature but not in the religious sense. My parents raised me in the Presbyterian church but as an adult, I fell away from formalized religion. That night in the ER, when the pain was more intense than any I'd ever known, when I knew I was dying, I was terrified. And I was angry—with myself, with you all, with the way my life turned out, and with the fact I couldn't control what was happening to me.

"Coming to the realization that you are helpless is a humbling thing, especially when you're used to being in control. For some reason, when I arrested that night, you were able to cut through all the noise in my head and throw me a lifeline." He straightened himself in the chair. "You may think what I'm about to tell you is bizarre, and it is actually, but I want you to hear it anyway. When my heart stopped the second time, I felt myself leave this body and float up to a corner of the ceiling. I watched as you pumped my chest and filled my lungs with air over and over. I saw TK and others rush in to help. When you stepped back and closed your eyes, I heard you say, 'Please God, lift him up, ease his pain, and heal his heart.' I felt myself leaving, letting go of life. Then you said something else. Do you remember what it was?"

Nettie didn't realize she'd spoken out loud that night. In fact, she wasn't sure she had. "I said, 'Don't go, Mr. Pepper, not now—'"

"And not like this," he added, finishing her sentence. "The next thing I knew, I was back in this body and I heard you whisper in my ear that my ring was on my finger and God was in my corner. I woke up days later in CCU, confused and both glad and mad that I was still alive. For a long time, I didn't know what to do with myself. It would have been so much easier if I'd died. I wouldn't have had to face the pain in my life again. But then you reminded me I'd been given a second chance to live and a second chance to die. I'd been given the gift of time. Time to figure things out and find a new path." He patted her hand. "You wanted to know why you, dear girl? That's why."

Mrs. Henry always said it was the little things that made the biggest difference in people's lives. Nettie had her answer. "I'll do what I can," she told Mr. Pepper.

"You intuitively know how to care. The rest can be learned."

Later, as Nettie got Mr. Pepper settled in his room, Dougie knocked and came in with an arm load of linens.

"Hey, Mr. Pepper. Hey, Nettie."

Nettie glanced back and forth at the two men. "I didn't realize you two had met."

"Dougie is kind enough to take care of my linens so they don't get torn up in the industrial washing machines."

"And Mr. Pepper tells me stories about Hawaii and all the places he's traveled," Dougie said, pointing to the scenic pictures surrounding them. "He even gave me some plants to start my own flower garden and told me how to take care of them."

Nettie grinned. "I should have known you two would find each other."

THE EVENING SHIFT HAD JUST started when the trauma code sounded on beepers across the ER. Ambulances carrying victims of a car accident were less than five minutes out. As part of team one, TK and Nettie had to prep the trauma room closest to the entrance and take the first high acuity stretcher. Sliding the glass doors open and pushing the curtains back, Nettie spiked two bags of Ringer's lactate solution and one bag of saline and primed the lines. TK opened the trauma cart and began setting up two sterile trays, one a cut-down tray and the other an abdominal tap tray. A respiratory therapist hurried into the room to ready the intubation and Ambu set at the head of the bed.

"Is everything ready?" a male voice snapped.

A tall man in green OR scrubs and matching cap came through the door.

"Just about," TK replied, sliding the tap tray next to Nettie. "It's been a while since you've had trauma call, Dr. Parcel, how've you—"

"Do we have an ETA and injury report yet?" he interrupted.

"ETA is any minute," TK answered, ignoring the surgeon's rudeness. "The injury report isn't in, which means the rescue squad is too busy to send it, which means it's bad."

Paul Anderson followed Dr. Parcel in. Spotting Nettie, he smiled and gave a little wave. She did the same.

"Paul, stand near the wall," Dr. Parcel said as he covered his scrubs with a trauma gown. "I'll let you know if I need you. Who's this?" he asked, pointing at Nettie.

"This is Nettie," TK replied. "She's interning in the ER."

Recognition flashed in Dr. Parcel's eyes. "Stay on the wall and out of the way."

"No," TK countered, her voice firm. "She's part of my team and has things to do."

"Then keep her out of my way."

Nettie had worked with several surgeons, but never one like this.

Ignoring Dr. Parcel's comment, TK went to the large dry-erase board mounted on the wall and recorded the names of the trauma team members in the room. When finished, she discreetly put a small yellow dot in the lower right-hand corner of the board.

"What does the dot mean?" Paul whispered to Nettie as she passed.

"It flags the team to be on their toes."

"For what?"

"Trouble." Nettie cut her eyes toward Dr. Parcel. "Sometimes those on call aren't the best ones to have in the room."

Paul laughed out loud, which earned him a scorching glare from Dr. Parcel. Leaning closer to Nettie, Paul added. "I assume he doesn't know about this color-coding system?"

She shook her head. "The ones who need it never notice."

"You're trusting me with this secret?"

"Yep. You're not the type that needs coding." Nettie winked at him as the silent red light over the emergency entrance started blinking, signaling the arrival of the first ambulance.

The team went to work as the first stretcher rolled through the door. TK stayed by the patient's side while getting report from the rescue squad. The respiratory therapist managed the victim's airway, nurses started IVs and applied blood pressure cuffs and cardiac monitors, and the laboratory and X-ray technicians lined up at the door waiting for the call to do their jobs. TK kept them all moving fluidly and efficiently.

"She's really good," Paul whispered.

"Yes, she is. She's the one you want by your side if you're ever lying on one of these stretchers."

"He's bleeding into his belly," Dr. Parcel said as he palpated the patient's rigid abdomen and studied the downward slope of his blood pressures. "Where's the tap tray?"

"On your left," TK responded. "It's ready to go."

As Dr. Parcel whipped around, his arm hit the sterile tray sending instruments, prep solutions, sutures, and the metal tray clanging to the floor. "Bloody hell!" he shouted.

Nettie froze. She'd heard the same phrase, uttered the same way in the dark corner of the recovery room that night. She stared at Dr. Parcel, grappling with the realization.

"What are you staring at?" Dr. Parcel yelled at Nettie, kicking the tray and sending it sliding across the room.

TK turned, her voice calm, her expression intent on restoring order. "Focus people. Nettie, there's a backup tray on the counter behind you. Set it up, please."

Banishing the imagery of Dr. Parcel and Mrs. Woods, Nettie grabbed the backup tap tray, placed it on the instrument stand, and carefully peeled back the layers of sterile wrapping.

TK motioned to one of the assistants to clear the hazards from the floor as she handed Dr. Parcel a new pair of sterile gloves. "If you'd like some help, we can call the backup surgeon."

Everyone in the room knew TK had just fired a warning shot over Dr. Parcel's bow that said behave yourself or you'll be replaced.

"Don't be absurd. I don't need any help. I just need this clumsy girl out of my way."

Nettie stayed where she was. She knew her job, and it wasn't to enable this surgeon's temper tantrum.

It took the better part of an hour, but once the patient had been stabilized, Dr. Parcel tossed his gown and gloves on the floor and headed to the door without so much as a nod to the team.

"Dr. Parcel," TK called after him. "We need to debrief this case as soon as we get the patient to ICU."

He discarded TK's reminder with a backward, nonchalant wave of his hand and left.

In trauma care, seconds counted. ER protocols, team

member responsibilities and positions, management of equipment and procedures, as well as essential interactions among the team were planned with precision for that very reason. Consequently, each trauma code underwent a thorough debriefing to ensure these criteria had been met and if not, why. Dr. Parcel's self-centered, time-wasting tantrum would have consequences.

Paul handed Nettie a piece of paper with his pager number on it as he followed Dr. Parcel out the door. "Sorry about that guy," he whispered. "Let me know when the debriefing starts and when you all are going to dinner. I'd like to join you."

"Sure."

"Thanks for the good work folks," TK said to those still in the room. "Meet me in the conference room in thirty minutes for the debriefing. We need to see what we can do better next time."

"Get a different surgeon," someone said from the back of the room.

NETTIE, TK, AND PAUL FOUND A table in the corner of the cafeteria and set their trays down.

"That was my first trauma debriefing," Paul said. "I liked the way you all analyzed everything by role and time instead of people."

"It keeps the team's focus where it needs to be," TK replied.

Since Dr. Parcel hadn't bothered to show up for the debriefing, the impact of his behavior on the team's efficiency would take place with TK and the director of the ER. TK didn't fool around when it came to quality control measures that influenced patient's lives. Neither did the ER charge nurses. To eliminate Dr. Parcel's ego-centered type of trouble, they would skip over his name whenever it showed up on the trauma call schedule and the physician referral list until they felt he deserved another chance, if ever.

"I don't understand why he, or anyone for that matter, behaves like that," Paul said.

"Happy, well-adjusted people don't," TK replied.

Nettie wondered if unhappiness is what drove Dr. Parcel to sneak around in the dark with Mrs. Woods. Perhaps it drove them both.

Dougie approached their table, his eyes darting hesitantly toward Paul. "Hi, Miss TK. Hi, Miss Nettie."

"Hey Dougie, good to see you." TK motioned to Paul. "Dougie, this is our friend Paul Anderson. Paul, Dougie."

Paul held out his hand. "Nice to meet you."

Dougie shook hands cautiously, then eased into a chair. "I have good news," he said, turning to TK. "I'm back on the seven p.m. to seven a.m. shift."

"That's wonderful. How? Why?"

"My manager said the overnight linen supplies have been all messed up since they moved me to days. Too much of this, not enough of that, and things being missed altogether, so he moved me back to nights. He told me if that nursing supervisor said anything else, I was to let him know."

"I'm glad for you, Dougie," Nettie said, relieved he didn't have to fear Mrs. Woods anymore.

"Dougie," Paul asked, "since you work in the laundry department perhaps you can tell me where to find tall scrub pants? The standard ones in the OR dressing room are too short, and I hate wearing high riders."

Dougie hesitated, as if deciding whether to allow Paul into his small circle of trust. He looked at TK, then back at Paul. "Do you have a locker in the OR dressing room?"

Paul nodded. "Number 24."

"Leave it unlocked whenever you're done for the day. I'll put some tall scrubs in there for you and lock it back."

Nettie grinned. Paul would never want for tall scrubs again. Her smile faded as Mrs. Woods entered the far side of the cafeteria. Tray in hand, she took note of who was sitting at their table then entered the administrators' private dining room.

NETTIE AND WIN WENT TO THE NAF office earlier than usual on Saturday. The organization's officers had arrived from all over the country for their monthly meeting, so things would be busier than usual. They joined Paul and Laura in the back room. Both worktables were already stacked high with envelopes, mailing labels, rolls of stamps, and reams of letters requesting donations to support the work of the NAF.

Mrs. Anderson appeared in the breezeway dressed in the same suit, pumps, and pearls she'd worn the day they met. "We're going to the White House. Wish us luck and hold down the fort."

"Go get 'em, Mom," Laura said.

"It's a shame the NAF has to use politics to get the POWs home," Nettie said, as Mrs. Anderson left. "You'd think it would be a priority for the military."

"But it's not," Paul replied. "The *Pentagon Papers* gave Mom and the other wives no choice but to become politically active. Three presidents kept us in this war, and the fourth can't seem to get us out. Now that the NAF has a PAC, we might be able to make something happen."

"What was it the newspaper called the NAF? 'Just a bunch of housewives?'" Nettie laughed at the irony.

"Yeah. Housewives who are ignoring pressure from the Pentagon to sit down and shut up," Laura added. "Even the *Washington Post* says the NAF's efforts have resulted in better treatment of the POWs. North Vietnam knows the whole world is watching. If the Paris peace talks are successful, Dad and Andy may be coming home sooner rather than later."

Nettie dared to hope. She managed to keep the heart-pounding fear for Andy's safety at bay by staying busy from dawn until well into the night, but once she laid down in the dark and quiet, the fear almost suffocated her.

After a long day, Nettie and Win returned home to find a thick envelope stuffed in their mailbox.

"It's from Andy." Nettie's hands trembled as she opened it.

Win unlocked the door and took Nettie's bag off her shoulder. "You read. I'll fix dinner."

Chapter 10

ANDY

Andy knelt to study the small area of debris. His squad had been monitoring the roads and villages as close to the DMZ as they could get for the past three months and had not found one shred of evidence of NVA infiltrators until this morning. They'd come across what appeared to be a deserted NVA camp, complete with broken limbs, crushed brush, filtered cigarette butts, and a broken bootlace.

"VC don't wear boots, and they don't smoke filtered cigarettes," Andy said.

"There weren't many and it looks like they've been gone awhile," Moretti added.

"I agree," Andy said. "The question is why were they here in the first place, and there's no good answer." Andy pulled the map from the cargo pocket in his pants. "The closest village is Ru Linh, which we've surveilled a couple of times before and ruled it low risk. It has no strategic military advantages. It's isolated to the west and has one narrow, dirt road. It's not located near any major intersections or anything else for that matter, except the Thanh River, which is too small to be of much value."

"So, what changed?" Strawberry asked. "What's the attraction?"

"I don't know," Andy said, stowing the map. "But if there's something of value there now, we need to find out what it is."

Andy sat on a downed tree trunk, removed his helmet, and ran his fingers through his sweaty hair. If the NVA were in Ru Linh, there would be no stand-down for his squad any time soon. Someone had to stay close to monitor the activity. His squad had been on patrol for ninety days without a break, the fleeting sound of Air Force jets passing overhead their only connection with anything familiar. Their LURPs and other supplies had been exhausted long ago, so they survived on what the jungle provided. Creek baths and rain showers with palm leaves as both soap and washcloth kept them smelling like the jungle, but their uniforms were tattered, their socks threadbare, and their boots wet, worn and cracked. Andy studied his men as they watched their surroundings, rifles in constant readiness, the dark circles under their eyes a ready testament to what they'd already endured. They needed sleep, food, a bath, and a change of clothes, yet never complained.

"Looks like we'll be holding our noses and eating more of Moretti's banana, mango, yucca, wild yam and beetle stew with a side of crickets, ants, and nuts awhile longer, huh?" Strawberry joked.

"Hold on there," Moretti laughed. "No complaining unless you want to take over cooking detail."

"We're long overdue for a stand-down, fellows," Andy said, "but we need to find out what's going on in that village."

"Then let's stay focused and get on it," Rawlin said.

"Right," Chase added. "The sooner we know, the sooner we can get out of here."

"Agree," the others echoed.

Andy nodded, grateful that fate and Gus had blessed him with such a squad. "Thanks, fellows."

"Does this mean the beer is on you when we get back to Eagle?" Sirocco quipped.

"Definitely," Andy replied, grateful for the momentary lightheartedness. "Fifteen-minute break, then we head to Ru Linh." As the squad assumed their resting positions, all looking outward with guns ready, Andy put his helmet on and closed his eyes. If he let it, fatigue would overtake him. He thought of Nettie. She'd be waking up soon, starting her day as the second half of his began. He felt more at peace when he was with her, even if only in his imagination. He longed to read the letters he knew were waiting at Camp Eagle, to know what was going on at home. He had letters to send as well, written in the dark when their overnight camps were secure and quiet.

A twig broke behind him, bringing all rifles to bear on a gibbon trying to sneak close enough to steal food that wasn't there.

"Okay, fellows, let's move out," Andy said. "Leave this camp as we found it."

Just then the radio gave a soft squawk. "Bravo One, this is Alpha One, come in. Over."

Andy took the receiver. "Alpha One, this is Bravo One, go ahead. Over."

"Bravo one, Colonel Clark wants you to re-surveil the village of Ru Linh. Over."

Colonel Clark? Not Major Smith? "Roger that, Alpha One. We're already on it. We just found what looks like a deserted NVA camp about a mile east of the village."

"Roger that, Bravo One. Report back when you have eyes on. Alpha One out."

"What the hell's going on?" Moretti asked.

"I'm not sure," Andy replied. "But something's cooking here and there. Let's go."

THE SOUNDS COMING FROM THE village of Ru Linh confirmed something wasn't right long before Andy had binoculars on it. A thick hedge and small lake separated the jungle from the village, but he could still see NVA uniforms all over the place. Some carried bags and metal ammo boxes while others milled about, talking. Sentries were posted on the road and in front of what appeared to be a command center. Nearby, officers were relaxing around a fire, dipping their evening meal from a common kettle. Andy couldn't see any vehicles or tents but assumed they were on the other side of the village. That many men didn't hike in. Signaling his squad to stay low, they retreated into the jungle. He took a knee as the others gathered around. "Well, now we know," he whispered.

"I counted at least forty men," Sirocco said.

"I agree," Hollis replied. "And it looks like they've been there for some time."

Andy pushed his helmet to the back of his head. "Moretti, hand me the radio."

The squad kept watch as the radio squawked back and forth softly.

"HQ wants you to gather additional intelligence on strength and mobility tonight, as well as anything that would suggest a timeline," the base radioman relayed. "Then they want you back at Eagle on the double. Over."

"Alpha One, are you saying they're ordering us back to Eagle? Over."

"Roger that, Bravo One. Start humping in at first light. We'll send a truck to pick you up when you reach the teepee rocks."

"Roger that, Alpha One. Bravo One out."

Andy handed the receiver back to Moretti. "Why the hell are they ordering us back to Eagle after we just found a village crawling with NVA? What do they know that we don't?"

"Maybe more NVA forces are on the way," Moretti said.

"It's possible," Andy replied. "But that little village has more than it can support now."

"Don't look a gift horse in the mouth, Lieutenant," Cowboy grinned. "By the end of the week, we'll be showering, brushing our teeth, sleeping on a real mattress, and eating as much fried chicken and mashed potatoes as we want."

Andy smiled but couldn't shake the feeling his squad's involvement with Ru Linh was just getting started. "Okay, tonight Strawberry, Hollis, Cowboy, and Moretti will circle wide and come in on the far side of the village. Get a count on uniforms, weapons, ammo, vehicles, tent capacity and anything else that doesn't fit. Chase, Rawlin, Sirocco, and Doc, you four do the same on the nearside. Chase, see if you can get close to the back of that command center. If the flaps are up on the windows, you may be able to get a peek inside. Quy and I will follow the hedgerow to that big wisteria tree near the top of the lake. When the women return to the village from seeding the lotus flowers, we'll use the distraction to move closer to where those officers are hanging out. With luck, we'll hear something. If everything goes well, we meet back here no later than 0100. If anything goes wrong, backtrack a klick from this point, regroup, and Moretti calls it in. If a klick isn't secure, go back two."

Everyone nodded.

"Four-point double perimeter for now. Try to get some rest. We head out at dark."

As the last hint of daylight faded, Andy and Quy darted from the jungle to the thick hedge surrounding the lake. Staying low, they followed it to the wisteria tree and slipped under the heavy, vine-like branches just as the women from the village began their nightly pilgrimage toward the water.

Climbing into their small boats, the women swirled and spun from flower to flower seeding each with tea, the soft glow of their lanterns creating mesmerizing trails of light.

Hearing male voices, Andy and Quy sank low to the ground and pointed their rifles as an NVA officer and a man dressed in a black tunic came down the path from the village and turned toward the wisteria tree. Andy centered his rifle on the officer's chest while Quy targeted the second man, their fingers light on the triggers. The officer's unbuttoned, short-sleeved, safari-like jacket and relaxed walk contrasted sharply with the angry face and stiff posture of the man with a knife and pistol stuck in his brown belt.

Stopping at a bench near the tree, the NVA officer turned to sit just as a breeze swayed the wisteria's branches. For a split second, the officer and Andy locked eyes. Neither reacted. Moving slowly and deliberately, the officer sat, crossed his legs, and relaxed his arm across the back of the bench. The man in the tunic leaned forward, tense yet oblivious of the rifle aimed at him. The officer began speaking in a calm, steady voice loud enough for Andy and Quy to hear. The more he spoke the straighter the man in the black tunic sat. When dismissed, the man stood, gave a slight nod to the officer, then turned for the village, his gait hard and fast. The NVA officer turned his gaze toward the boats on the lake, his shoulders relaxing the longer he watched. He remained seated until after the women had returned to the village and the scattered lights in the huts began to flicker out. Bathed in moonlight, he walked back to the village, gave a half salute to the sentry, then disappeared into the command center having never glanced toward the wisteria tree again.

As soon as the village sentry turned his back, Andy and Quy skirted back along the hedge, darted into the shadows of the jungle, and stopped.

"What were they talking about?" Andy whispered.

"You're not going to believe it. In a nutshell, the NVA officer told that VC that if he or any of his men harmed another child or adult in that village they'd be shot."

"What?"

"You heard right, Lieutenant."

"Not a word about seeing us?"

Quy shook his head.

Nothing about this village is making sense. "Forget the timeline. That officer saw us. As soon as the others are back, we need to get the hell out of here."

Andy didn't wait to hear his men's scouting reports. As soon as everyone returned, the squad backtracked two klicks. Moving through the jungle at night, while unwise, seemed the lesser danger. Calling everyone close, he asked, "What did you see?"

"Vehicles and supplies to support at least sixty men on the far side of the village," Strawberry replied. "Most of their supplies are under bamboo lean-tos making them invisible from the air."

"They also have a sophisticated communication system hidden in the bamboo," Moretti added. "The antennas are long enough to signal across this entire sector."

"I was able to get a glimpse in the back window of the command center with night binoculars," Chase said. "I saw three pretty detailed maps on the wall, similar to the ones we use, only bigger."

"Explain," Andy said.

"They appeared to highlight troop movements, roads, selected villages, water sources, and such. They had keys at the bottom, but I couldn't make them out."

"That's too many maps and too much detail for a run-of-the-mill NVA unit," Andy said. "They sound like recon maps. That combined with a far-range communication system means Ru Linh could be an NVA intelligence center."

"That's not all, Lieutenant," Rawlin said. "Something else is weird. They aren't armed very well."

"What do you mean?"

"They had two types of rifle stands. The smaller ones held what looked like old SKSs. The larger ones didn't hold anything but blocks of wood that have been carved and painted to look like rifles. If my estimates are right, only every third or fourth man has a real rifle. Most of the ammo boxes looked fake as well."

"There's only one reason they'd do that," Strawberry added. "Intimidation. Nothing but a show of force to mislead the ARVNs and us."

Andy rubbed the back of his neck. "If this place is a decoy of some kind, it would explain why that NVA officer saw me under the tree and did nothing. He wants us to go back and report what we saw."

"But why use an intelligence center as a decoy?" Strawberry added. "It doesn't make sense."

"No, it doesn't, but we're not going to figure it out now. I want more distance between us and them. Move out."

Chapter 11

NETTIE

Nettie entered the administrative suite in the school of nursing and nodded at the secretary. "Hey, Maggie." For two years, she'd helped Maggie around the office between classes as part of the school's work-study program. Today was the first time she'd ever been called to the suite for anything else.

"Good morning, Nettie." Maggie smiled and nodded toward the next office. "Go on in, Dean Fraser is waiting for you."

Nettie tapped on the door and peeked in.

"Are you ready for me, ma'am?"

The petite, gray-blond woman motioned to the two chairs in front of her desk. "I am. Have a seat."

Nettie sat, folding her hands in her lap.

"Relax, Nettie. This is a fact-finding meeting, nothing more." She picked up a piece of paper from her desk and moved to the chair next to Nettie. "I received this letter from one of the supervisors at the hospital, a Mrs. Woods. She's questioning your commitment to patient care and safety because of missing time and ignoring directives from her. She also implied that you initiated an inappropriate relationship with an older, wealthy male patient, a Mr. Pepper, in order to solicit gifts." The dean laid the letter back on her desk and turned to Nettie. "So, tell me what's going on."

Nettie fumed at the injustice of Mrs. Woods's manipulative, self-serving accusations and blushed with embarrassment that the dean she respected had to hear them. Over the past quarter-century, Dean Kate Fraser had built the School of Nursing from the ground up, designing a strong program grounded in the sciences while expanding the art of nursing to include the best empowerment trends of the feminist movement. While women around the country were taking off their bras, nurses were taking off their caps, trading their white uniforms in for practical scrubs, and moving their education from hospital to university settings. Dean Fraser's philosophy that nurses and physicians had different but equally important scopes of practice was fueling a new generation of independent nurses. The last thing Nettie wanted was to have this busy, visionary woman drawn into a tawdry soap opera of Mrs. Woods's making.

"Yes, ma'am," Nettie replied. Without mentioning the recovery room incident, she described what had transpired with Mrs. Woods and her relationship with Mr. Pepper. "Ma'am, I didn't ask for the gardenia. In fact, I told him not to send it because I didn't have a green thumb. He said he'd teach me how to take care of it."

"You're sure that's everything that happened with him."

"Yes, ma'am. I would never solicit gifts from him or anyone else. And I don't believe he would have ever sent the planter if he thought it would cause a problem. He's a good person."

Dean Fraser picked up another group of papers from her desk. "This is a copy of your internship evaluation. It's signed by your preceptor, the head nurse, and the director of the internship program. It's an excellent report. I took the liberty of calling these women yesterday to thank them for mentoring you, and to see if they offered any unsolicited information about the situation with Mr. Pepper and Mrs. Woods. They had nothing but positive things to say and never mentioned any problems. And I understand they want to extend your internship another year."

"Yes, ma'am."

"Clearly, this evaluation and the comments from the people you work with are inconsistent with the accusations Mrs. Woods is making. Why would she write such a letter?"

Nettie paused. As much as she wanted to stop the attacks, the long-range consequences of implying that Mrs. Woods committed adultery could be devastating to innocent people. "Ma'am, I can't say for sure why Mrs. Woods wrote that letter."

Dean Fraser paused as if waiting for the rest of the story. When Nettie didn't elaborate, she nodded. "Well, I believe you and I believe the people within the organization who signed this evaluation. Consequently, the veracity of Mrs. Woods's accusations come into question. She's asked me to transfer you to a different hospital. Do you want to move your internship?"

"No, ma'am."

"I was hoping you'd say that. Sometimes the most valuable lessons aren't the ones we learn in a classroom, they're the ones we learn when people abuse power. You might as well learn how to deal with those types of people and situations while we're here to help you."

"Any suggestions on how I do that, ma'am?"

"Keep doing what you're supposed to do, confront conflict in a respectful and professional manner, and when you're right, stand your ground. You may have to wait for it, but the truth will have the last word." She paused. "Remember, this woman wasn't born mean, something made her that way. Leave the door open to reconciliation. She may surprise you."

The dean rose, signaling the end of the meeting. "I assume you intend to continue visiting Mr. Pepper?"

"Yes, ma'am. He's a long way from home and doesn't get many visitors. I check with Mrs. Henry, the charge nurse on his unit, before I visit, and I go on my own time."

"Good. And please make sure this gentleman understands you cannot accept any more gifts."

"Yes, ma'am."

Nettie started for the door but Dean Fraser called her back.

"While it's important you learn how to handle this situation, don't let it get out of hand before you tell me what's really going on."

NETTIE HELD THE DOOR AS Mr. Pepper rose from the wheelchair, pivoted, then eased into the passenger side of her car. Tucking in the hem of his cashmere overcoat, she noticed he had his support socks on. *Progress!* Closing the door, she collapsed the wheelchair, put it in the trunk, then slid behind the wheel. It had taken time, but Mrs. Henry had gained permission for Nettie to take Mr. Pepper on weekly Sunday morning field trips to check on the construction of the nursery firsthand.

As the car glided along the gentle curves and sways of the hospital's service road, Mr. Pepper gazed left and right. "We'll have to do something with the landscaping along this road when the weather breaks. It's quite dull. If we want patients to visit the nursery, the road to it should be inviting. I'll talk with Keona about possibilities."

Rounding the last curve, Nettie stopped the car so Mr. Pepper could study the nursery from a distance, something he liked to do with each visit. Instead of the typical Quonset-type greenhouse covered in plastic, Mr. Kalua's team had built a beautiful round building with more architectural appeal than most houses. Sitting on top of a protected knoll, the story-and-a-half building had walls of teak and reinforced glass, a second-story observation area, and a copper cupola. An arched walkway surrounded the main level and a gently curving sandstone path connected the circular driveway to the front of the building. Sloping away from the building were areas of tilled-up soil that would become terraced flowerbeds in the spring.

Mr. Pepper studied the building and grounds from one end to the other. "Nettie, see the unusual crystal tint of the glass? It's been treated with a glaze that diffuses light and reflects heat." Spreading his hands thumb to thumb, he framed the movement of the sun from dawn to dusk. "The glass panels are designed to slant toward the light and open and close depending on the outside temperature." He motioned for her to continue up the driveway. "It's really coming along nicely, don't you think? Let's take a spin around the outside first, shall we?"

Nettie helped him transfer to the wheelchair, then pushed him along the walkway, enjoying the ambiance as they strolled. Months ago, when Mr. Kalua and his team arrived from Hawaii, he talked about how the designs for the garden and nursery integrated the principles of nature. "Sharp angles are rarely found in the natural world. Curves, smooth lines, rounded edges, diverse colors, and layered context diffuse energy and help nature balance itself," he'd explained. Now that both projects were nearing completion, Nettie could see and feel what he meant.

"What do you think?" Mr. Pepper asked. "Is this a healing place?"

"Well, I feel better just being here."

Mr. Pepper chuckled. "There is little medical evidence that nature's designs heal, because few people actually study it."

"Do you think it works?" Nettie asked.

"Yes, I do. Maybe one day science will figure out how to see the unseen and measure the unmeasurable. Until then, I like the idea that something out there is helping us."

"Me too, Mr. Pepper. Me too." In the months Nettie had been visiting him, she'd watched the ribbon in his Bible move through the Old Testament and into the New. It now marked a place somewhere among the Gospels. Maybe Mr. Pepper would find his something among those pages.

In the back of the building, Nettie stopped long enough for Mr. Pepper to check the blue fluid-in-glass thermometer mounted on an outside support beam. "Our nurseries in Hawaii maintain a comfortable eighty degrees during the day and seventy degrees at night because that's the year-round climate. Virginia has a lot more variation in temperature, so the building's heating and air conditioning system is designed to mimic the region's temperatures and humidity but avoid plant-killing extremes." He sighed. "Like people, plants and trees are happiest in their native environments."

Returning to the retractable glass doors in the front, the sandstone path continued into the building. Nettie felt the gentle breeze of the building's newly installed, low-profile air curtain as they entered.

"The outward flow of air helps maintain a consistent temperature inside. And it will help keep the bugs out during the spring and summer," Mr. Pepper explained. He pointed toward the ceiling. "The good bugs, the pollinators, will enter through those open panels."

"Won't bad bugs come in that way as well?" Nettie asked.

He shook his head. "Not if we strategically place flower beds around the building and grounds that attract the good bugs that eat the bad bugs. Good bugs love flowers like black-eyed Susan, cosmos, dill, Shasta daisies, and mountain mint."

The look and smell of new construction gave way to the heavenly scents of plants and trees as they moved farther into the atrium. In the months since he'd come from Hawaii, Mr. Kalua had guided his team in completing the building and filling it with beautiful displays of small deciduous trees, leafy palms and ferns, soil and air loving plants, perennials, and flowering bushes waiting to bloom in spring. Hanging plants swayed gently above them, and colorful containers of herbs, spices, and whatnots filled the nooks and crannies. Instead of plastic, ceramic, and terra-cotta pots and planters, Mr. Kalua used nature's containers for everything. Hollowed-out tree trunks, bowls made of thick moss or heavy vines, stones with hollows and cracks for drainage, and lots of containers made of coconut fibers called coco.

"We use a lot of coco in our nurseries in Hawaii," Mr. Pepper explained as they moved around the atrium. "They're great for nurturing the roots of plants and trees and are a naturally renewable resource. Most importantly, they don't harm the natural world like plastic."

Nettie guided the wheelchair to the small, lagoon-like area in the center of the atrium, complete with a waterfall and a stone pond. Flanking the waterfall were teak benches under trellises covered with jasmine and hundred-petal rose vines. "This is like another world."

"Yes, it is. It will be even more beautiful and therapeutic when the flowers on these vines and the other plants bloom. Different scents influence the brain in different ways. If we're stressed, some scents relax us. If we're tired, some give us energy, and some lift our spirits when we're sad. Other scents decrease pain and help us think more clearly. The effects of the scents and their beautiful blossoms can be powerful, which is why healing gardens are so important."

Nettie wondered if Mr. Pepper had built a life surrounded by gardens for those very reasons.

They had just reached the back of the atrium when the sun's rays hit the glass roof at the perfect angle to send an array of small prism-like rainbows dancing across the atrium.

"Great timing," Mr. Kalua said in his soft, Hawaiian Pidgin voice as he joined them. "The rainbows only come when the sun is at the right angle and the overhead misters are running." He bowed slightly. "How are you today, Miss Nettie?"

"I'm well, Mr. Kalua. And you?"

"I am blessed another day." Turning to Mr. Pepper, Mr. Kalua bowed again. "Aloha, my friend."

"And aloha to you." Mr. Pepper motioned to their surroundings. "You are an extraordinary artist, Keona. Everything is coming together beautifully."

"Nature seldom disappoints," the Hawaiian replied.

Nettie pushed the wheelchair through a hidden opening created by overlapping walls, transitioning them from the atrium to the back of the building. Mr. Kalua helped Mr. Pepper stand and offered his arm for support as they methodically moved from one platform of gestating plants to the next. The two men discussed strengths, vulnerabilities, growth projections, and best timing for display as only experts could.

Following at a distance with the wheelchair, Nettie had a feeling such rounds had been part of their daily ritual in Hawaii. As the two men talked, she wandered into a cluster of young trees at the back of the room. Weeping cherries, dogwoods, redbuds, miniature maples, and trees she didn't recognize created a wonderful inside forest. Partially hidden in the middle were two small, bushy trees with thick, oval-shaped leaves, and blossoms. Surprised they were blooming this time of year, Nettie stepped closer to study the white, daisy-like flower. Half of each blossom was missing. *That's odd.*

Nettie turned to ask Mr. Pepper and Mr. Kalua about the tree, and they were already standing behind her, smiling.

"I was just going to ask about these blossoms."

"You've managed to find the most unusual trees in the building," Mr. Kalua said. "They were delivered just this week."

"What kind of trees are they?"

"They're called Naupaka trees. They grow abundantly in the mountains, valleys, and along the coastline of the Hawaiian Islands and bloom year round."

"I've never seen blossoms shaped like this."

"The flower's shape is rooted in Hawaiian lore," he explained. "Storytellers speak of a handsome young man named Kaui who lived in the mountains on the Big Island. His parents held great wealth and position in their village and wanted their son to marry someone of the same stature. But Kaui fell in love with a beautiful commoner named Naupaka. Although poor by birth, Naupaka knew with hard work she and Kaui could build a beautiful life together. Kaui's pleading for his parents to accept Naupaka landed on deaf ears. They said if he took her as his wife, they would cast him off from their family's wealth and position forever. Though torn, Kaui chose wealth and position over love. Broken-hearted, Naupaka took the flower from behind her ear, tore it in two, and gave half to Kaui. She left him, her village, and the mountains behind, to build a new life along the beaches of the great water. It is said Kaui mourned for Naupaka all the days of his life."

Nettie fingered one of the half-blossoms, her thoughts going to the picture on Mr. Pepper's bedside stand, the one with him and an unknown woman sitting next to the lotus pond. "Well, I say good riddance to this Kaui."

Mr. Kalua laughed out loud, as Mr. Pepper looked puzzled. "What?"

"You heard me. Good riddance. Better Naupaka finds out what a weak putz Kaui is before she married him. I'm glad she brushed his dust off her feet and moved on." Nettie pressed ahead. "And as for Kaui living a life of longing, who says he did?"

"Pardon?"

"He could have just as easily picked himself up, dusted himself off, learned the lessons he needed to learn, and moved on, just like Naupaka. Either way, it was his choice. If he didn't like his reality, he had the ability to build a new one. Maybe the half-blossom isn't about lost love at all, maybe it's about an unfinished life open to a universe of possibilities."

"Those who wish to sing will always find a song," Mr. Pepper said. "Perhaps you're right, Nettie. Maybe it's time we find a new song for this tree. Keona, what do you think about developing a hybrid Naupaka, one with a different color blossom and new legend? We can name it Hope."

As usual, the tables in the backroom of the NAF office were packed high on Saturday morning, but Paul, Laura, Nettie, and Win had become very efficient at clearing them.

"We're going to the post office," Paul said, as he and Win headed out the door with the cart, a job they'd been readily volunteering to do the last few weeks. Since they'd started dating, Win glowed whenever she talked about Paul and the stress lines around Paul's eyes had almost disappeared.

Nettie and Laura were cleaning up when the bell above the front door jingled. Mrs. Anderson's usually warm tone disappeared as she greeted the visitor, "Good morning, Colonel."

Nettie and Laura peeked through the breezeway to see who had come in.

"Just another Pentagon flunky trying to get the housewives to shut up," Laura whispered.

"This one's a colonel," Nettie replied. "Maybe the message will be different this time."

"It won't. There's always someone higher up giving the orders."

"Good morning, Mrs. Anderson," The distinguished, graying air force officer said as he removed his cap.

"I'm surprised to see you," Mrs. Anderson said, her tone icy. "Especially since the Pentagon has refused to meet with the NAF and ignored our letters for months." Mrs. Anderson came from behind the counter, her back straight as an arrow.

"Well, ma'am, we've been rather busy."

"Yes, so have we," Mrs. Anderson said defiantly. "Since we've received no help from the military and our elected politicians, we're going public with our efforts."

"Yes, ma'am, we noticed," Colonel Bell replied, clearing his throat. "That's why I'm here. We believe television interviews, newspaper and magazine articles, and such are counter-productive to our efforts to bring our soldiers home."

"What efforts?" Mrs. Anderson asked icily. "If you are doing something—anything—please tell me."

"Ma'am, regardless of what you may think, we've been working diligently to bring them home."

"If that's true, then what you've been doing is ineffective at best and it's time for a different strategy," Mrs. Anderson replied, not giving the colonel an inch of wiggle room.

"Ma'am, we believe our shared interests would be better served if the NAF maintained its humanitarian focus."

"And leave our husbands in the hands of the Pentagon, which views them as little more than collateral damage? I don't think so."

The colonel blushed. "There are some at the Pentagon who feel keeping a humanitarian focus would be better for your husbands'—uh—careers."

There it was, the threat Mrs. Anderson and the NAF board had been anticipating for months. To date, visits from Pentagon personnel involved polite requests for them to cease and desist any activities that might embarrass the military. It was only a matter of time before the gloves came off.

Mrs. Anderson stepped closer to the colonel. "Let me get this straight. The Pentagon is threatening our husbands' careers—should they make it back alive—because the NAF is breaking the military's 'keep quiet' rule?"

"No, no threats, ma'am. It's just that some feel—"

"Are you one of those someones?" Mrs. Anderson demanded.

Conflicted feelings flashed in the colonel's eyes, but Pentagon policy won out.

"Ma'am, the 'keep quiet' rule serves a greater purpose."

"Well, Colonel," Mrs. Anderson replied hotly, "your precious rule hasn't served the greater purpose of bringing our husbands home now, has it? So, tell those someones at the Pentagon that the NAF has no intention of bowing down to their 'keep quiet' rule. And if those someones show the first hint of punitiveness toward our husbands and their careers because of it, the NAF will go public with those threats as well."

"Ma'am, perhaps—"

"Save it, Colonel," Mrs. Anderson snapped. "Years of inaction have proven the White House and Pentagon view our soldiers as expendable, regardless of the official hype indicating otherwise. And since both The White House and Pentagon are intended to serve the public, it is only right the public knows exactly what is and is not being done."

"Ma'am, it could harm—"

"Hogwash. The only thing being harmed right now are our soldiers. The NAF is a very patriotic organization, Colonel, so much so that we intend to be involved in the upcoming presidential and congressional elections. We're supporting candidates who give full-throated support to bringing our POWs and MIAs home."

Contrary to the admiration in his eyes, Colonel Bell tried again, this time pointing to the NAF Mission Statement hanging on the wall. "Ma'am, this says your organization's mission is a humanitarian one, not a political or military one."

Flushed with anger, Mrs. Anderson opened the door for him to leave. "And the Pentagon says it doesn't leave any soldier behind."

The colonel nodded at Mrs. Anderson and donned his cap. Pausing at the door, he added, "I'm very sorry about your husband, ma'am. And, no, I'm not one of the someones."

Chapter 12

ANDY

It took five days of hiking for Andy and his men to reach the teepee rocks. Given what happened to Gus's squad, no one relaxed. Exhausted after three months in the jungle, they'd called for a truck to give them a ride in. After an hour of waiting, they gave up and started walking.

They were still two klicks out when a shiny clean jeep with matching driver and passenger approached, slowed, then stopped. According to the numerous stripes on his uniform, the man in the jeep staring at them with disgust held the rank of a CSM or command sergeant major, the highest-ranking enlisted man in the army. Soldiers with this rank were so rare, Andy had only heard tell of them, as if they were some mythical creature.

The tall, broad-shouldered CSM exited the jeep, barely touching the frame. His deep green, freshly starched uniform barely had a wrinkle in it, his mirror-like boots were dust-free, and his face clean-shaven. He presented a powerful contrast to the filthy, worn-torn, falling apart uniforms and boots and scruffy faces of Andy and his men. The CSM's intense blue eyes squinted as he approached the squad. "Who is in charge of—*this*?" he asked, waving two fingers back and forth.

Andy bristled. "I am, Command Sergeant Major. Lieutenant Andy Stockton."

"What is the meaning of this disgraceful show?"

Andy stayed calm despite his higher rank being ignored. "We've been on recon patrol for three months and are on our way to Camp Eagle for a stand-down."

"Humpf. You filthy jungle rats are not coming into my base looking like that. I don't care how you do it but get yourselves cleaned up and presentable. Stay at the gate when you get there. If you have some resemblance to US soldiers by then, I'll consider letting you in." He headed back to the jeep.

Anger surged from Andy's gut to his mouth. He tossed his rifle to Moretti.

"Don't do it, Andy," Moretti whispered, his eyes popping. "Don't do it."

Andy just grinned, slid his cracked aviators down his nose, and propped a hand on his cocked-up hip. Yes, there would be hell to pay but he didn't give a damn. "Command Sergeant Major!" he boomed. "Stand at attention."

The heels of the CSM's boots crunched the gritty dirt as he spun around. "What did you say?"

"You heard me, you pompous blowhard. Stand at attention."

The incensed man took a step toward Andy. "Just who the hell do you think you're talking to?"

Andy grinned. "Last time I checked, lieutenants outrank sergeants, even CSMs." Andy spit the acronym out as if it was sour milk. "So, snap your sorry ass to attention—*sergeant*, and do it *now*."

His eyes shooting sparks, the CSM refused to move, his jaw locked, his mouth a rigid line.

"Last warning, you arrogant rear echelon motherf—"

Moretti coughed loudly, muffling Andy's last word. Snickers resonated through the squad.

Andy wasn't about to use the insult's acronym, REMF. He wanted the man to feel the burn of every disparaging word.

The CSM's face turned an ugly shade of purple. His power and position within the US army might be legendary but the technicality of his rank wasn't. He clicked his heels, straightened his back, and tilted his chin up.

Andy stepped closer, going nose-to-nose with the man. "Just so we understand each other, *Sergeant*. You are refusing to let these brave, hard-working soldiers onto a base that is not yours because they're—*dirty*?" Andy circled the man so tightly he smelled his shaving cream. "Tell me, *Sergeant*, when was the last time you washed those pretty little manicured hands of yours or shaved that pansy-ass face with clean water? Because for ninety days these soldiers haven't had decent water to drink, much less to wash and shave in. They haven't been able to brush their teeth, eat anything except stale LURPs and jungle food, had a change of clothes, or even been able to relax out of fear that some VC had a bullet, grenade, or tripwire waiting to blow them to pieces. We've reconned that damn region you REMFs said you wanted and now you're going to stand here like some kind of despot and deny us access to *our* camp?" Andy went nose-to-nose with the man again. "I'll be dammed. Now, get your sorry, fat ass back in that jeep, *Sergeant*. Then hightail it back to Camp Eagle and get everything ready to give these soldiers the warm, hospitable welcome they deserve. Do you understand me, *Sergeant*?"

"Understood." The man hissed back through gritted teeth, the muscles of his face barely moving.

"Louder, *Sergeant*, these brave men didn't hear you."

"Understood," he hissed louder.

"Understood what, *Sergeant*?"

"Understood—sir."

"Glad to see you finally recognize your betters, *Sergeant*. Dis—missed."

The CSM whipped around and headed for his jeep.

Andy pushed his aviators back in place. "You forget something, *Sergeant*?"

Rage emanated from every part of the man's body. He turned, saluted Andy, then spun so hard he crushed the gravel under his heels. Fast walking back to the jeep, he climbed in the front seat, refusing to look at Andy or the squad again.

As the jeep pulled away, the driver put his hand behind the CSM's seat and gave Andy a big thumbs-up.

His squad surrounded Andy with slaps on the back and cheers. Only Moretti looked concerned. "You know they're going to have your ass for that."

"Probably."

"You're not worried?"

"What's the worst they can do? Send me to 'Nam? Send me on patrol for three months without a break? Let's go."

"Shouldn't we try to clean up first?"

"Hell no. We're going in just as we are."

Two klicks later, Andy heard the noise resonating from Camp Eagle before his squad passed the outermost sentries and crested the bald ridge to see it. The sight of the sprawling base brought instant relief. Whatever trouble the CSM could cause paled in comparison to the opportunity to call Nettie and not worry about being shot, blown up, or falling into a punji pit. Even if they put him in the stockade, he'd be able to shower, sleep on something other than the wet, bug- and snake-infested ground, and eat until he was full.

Since the last time they were at Camp Eagle, an additional fifty yards of brush had been burned away from the perimeter and another ring of razor-sharp concertina and foot-tangle wire put in place. The north gate and the two metal guard towers flanking it also had additional sandbag fortifications. Either Major Smith had changed his mind or someone else had finally seen the intelligence reports about the NVA surveilling the camp. Andy and his men pointed their rifles toward the ground as they zigzagged through the wire toward the gate. The military police in the towers swung the gray noses of their 50-caliber machine guns up and away and began whistling, cheering, and giving Andy and his men a victory sign.

Moretti laughed. "Word travels fast. I wonder if the driver of that jeep still has a job?"

Two corporals waited just past the gate as the squad entered. The one resembling the CSM's driver stepped forward. "Lieutenant Stockton, would you come with me, sir? Colonel Clark, the base commander, would like to see you." He pointed to a waiting jeep.

The second corporal addressed Andy's squad. "The rest of you please follow me."

The squad moved behind Andy instead. "Huh-uh," Moretti told the corporal. "We go where the lieutenant goes."

Andy turned to his men. "Thanks, fellows, but not this time. You all go get cleaned up and get some decent food. I'll catch up with you later."

Andy silenced their grumbling with a glance and turned to the driver. "Let's go."

The jeep wound its way through the maze of streets and unmarked tents and buildings, finally stopping in front of a large metal hut, fortified with towers of sandbags and flanked by steps leading underground to a reinforced bunker.

"Keep standing your ground, Lieutenant," the driver whispered as he opened the door to the camp's headquarters. "The big man respects that." He led Andy past a dozen small offices to an area in the rear of the building with a sign that said, "No Entrance."

"Wait here, please," the corporal said. He knocked and went in. A few seconds later he returned and held the door open for Andy.

The anteroom had two desks facing each other across an aisle, a captain on the left and a major on the right. Andy saluted them both.

"Welcome, Lieutenant. I'm Major Loring."

Andy nodded. "Sir."

The major motioned to a corner near his desk. "Put your rifle and ruck here, then follow me. They're waiting for you."

They? Curiosity piqued as Andy stowed his equipment.

The major knocked on the next door and entered without waiting for an answer.

"Colonel, Lieutenant Stockton is here."

"Show him in," a strong voice responded.

Major Loring opened the door wide and stepped aside as Andy entered the big, yet surprisingly plain office. Color-coded maps of Vietnam and the Vinh Lee District hung on the wall to Andy's right. A large, paper-strewn desk sat in the middle of the back wall, flanked by flags of the United States and the 101st Airborne. A full-bird colonel with the name Clark stitched on his uniform sat behind the desk. Andy knew what the man had to do to earn those silver birds on his collar—graduate from the Army War College and serve with distinction for at least twenty-two years. Andy saluted him.

Sitting in front of the colonel's desk was Major Smith, a satisfied smirk on his face.

A tall, distinguished-looking man dressed in plain fatigues and smoking a cigar lounged on a worn leather sofa sitting along the wall to the left, his name and rank not apparent. Erring on the side of caution, Andy saluted him, too. Smoking a cigar in a colonel's office required a rank higher than his.

"At ease, Lieutenant." Colonel Clark motioned to a chair next to Major Smith. "Have a seat."

Andy strode forward and sat down, aware that these men knew how filthy he was and what three months without soap and a change of clothes smelled like. Sinking into the soft leather, Andy tried to remember the last time he'd sat in a chair.

Major Smith slid his chair away to escape the smell. Andy smiled and leaned his way.

"Been on patrol a while, Lieutenant?" Colonel Clark asked.

"Yes, sir. Three months—straight. No supplies." Andy glanced sideways at Major Smith.

The colonel nodded as if he already knew. "I'm sure you and your men are glad to be back in camp."

"Yes, sir."

"I understand you had an encounter with the command sergeant major on the way in."

"If you mean the insubordinate jackass who insulted and disrespected my men, yes, sir."

"That's enough of your smart mouth, Lieutenant," Major Smith snapped.

The man on the sofa chuckled. "You must have dressed him down pretty good, Lieutenant. I can't remember a time when my CSM was mad enough to talk to himself."

His CSM? Andy looked from the man on the sofa to Colonel Clark for clarification.

"Lieutenant, meet General Abram West, Commander of Military Operations in Southeast Asia."

Andy's stomach lurched, but he refused to let it show. He nodded in the direction of the only four-star general he'd ever seen, much less met. "Sir."

"Sounds like the CSM had it coming," General West said, leaning forward to tap his cigar in an ashtray. "The man can be a pain in the ass for sure, but he serves my command well, Lieutenant, which is why from this point forward you *will* give him the respect he deserves. Understood?"

"Yes, sir. He'll get it as long as he gives my men the respect they deserve. We have enough enemies to deal with out there, General. We don't need our own coming at us from behind."

"That's enough, Lieutenant," Major Smith growled.

Andy's gaze never left the general.

"Major Smith," General West said, "I think Colonel Clark and I can handle it from here. You may go."

The major shot Andy a nasty look.

To add insult to his injury, Andy grinned back. *This one's for you, Gus.*

When the door closed, General West blew a smoke ring toward the ceiling. "Your point about enemies from within is well-taken, Lieutenant. Right or wrong, not many men have the grit to do what you did on that road today or the character to stand in this office and defend it. And not many squads are willing to stand up and share the consequences of their lieutenant's actions, as I understand yours were."

The CSM's driver certainly hadn't wasted any time in spreading the news. No question had been asked, so Andy stayed quiet, waiting for the punishment he knew had to come.

Instead, Colonel Clark got up and opened the door to the anteroom. "Major Loring, have my driver escort Lieutenant Stockton to the supply tent and then to his quarters to get cleaned up." Turning to Andy, he added, "Lieutenant, get a hot meal and a good night's sleep, then be back here at 0800 tomorrow. We need to discuss Ru Linh."

Andy watched the two officers exchange glances and felt his squad's much-needed stand-down slipping away. "Yes, sir."

Andy left headquarters concerned about what was to come but glad to be within camp walls. "Comm Center first, please," he told the driver.

"Yes, sir."

Andy bounded up the stairs and into the center.

Jimmy stood in his usual place behind the counter. Surprised at Andy's appearance, he almost forgot to salute.

Ignoring protocol, Andy used the private's first name. "Hi, Jimmy, what are the chances I can make a call?"

Jimmy looked over his shoulder at the closed office door behind him and winked. "As long as the major keeps napping back there, chances are good." He handed Andy a notepad and pencil. "Write the number and place you're calling, sir, then have a seat."

After negotiating a half-dozen call relays, Jimmy waved Andy over. "It's ringing." He held the phone so Andy could hear.

Nettie's sleepy voice answered.

"Ma'am, there's a Lieutenant Andy Stockton calling for you. If you accept the call, please say 'Yes,' and when you've finished speaking, please say 'Over.'

"Yes! Yes! Operator, I'll take the call. Oh—Over."

Jimmy handed Andy the phone and stepped away.

"Nettie, can you hear me? Over."

"Yes! I'm so happy to hear your voice! Are you all right? Over."

"I'm fine, honey," Andy replied, closing his eyes and savoring the moment. "It's good to hear your voice, too. Over."

"Your mom and I have been so worried. Over."

"I'm sorry about that. My squad has been on patrol for three months. We couldn't get anything in or out. Over."

"It's crazy that they keep you out that long. Crazy and dangerous. Over."

"Maybe, but that's the army. I'm a lot better now. We're back in camp and get to stand-down for a while. Over."

"Thank God you get to rest. Over."

"How are you, honey? How's school and work going? Over."

"Good, but busy. Did you get my letters? Over."

"Not yet. I'll head to the post office as soon as we hang up." Andy closed his eyes again. "Honey, I miss you so much. Over."

"I miss you, too! More than you'll ever know. It's like part of my heart is missing. I'm counting down the days until you are home. Over."

"I'm counting them down, too, babe. Over."

The droopy-eyed major opened his office door and adjusted his sleep-wrinkled uniform. "Calls are limited to five minutes, Lieutenant. Wrap it up."

Jimmy hustled back to Andy mouthing the word, "Sorry."

"Honey. Would you let Mom know I'm okay and that I'll try to call her before I go back out? Over."

"Of course. I'll call her as soon as we hang up. Over."

The major didn't bother to hide his eavesdropping and his irritation. "I said wrap it up, Lieutenant."

"Nettie, I have to go. I love you. Over."

"Come back to me. Over."

"Count on it. Over."

When the line went dead, Andy handed the receiver back to Jimmy. "Thanks." He gave the major a half salute and left.

"Do you have time to take me a few more places?" Andy asked the driver.

"Sir, since you put that arrogant CSM in his place, I'll drive you anywhere you want to go."

"Then head to the mess hall. I'm starving." As Andy got in line, those in front kept motioning him forward. It was no secret where he'd been and for how long. Reaching the counter, he placed an order for two hamburgers. The cook loaded the burgers with everything and put two big brownies and two small cartons of milk on the tray. Nodding his thanks, Andy finished the hamburgers and a carton of milk before leaving the tent. Wrapping the brownies in a napkin, he put them and the extra milk in his pockets, then climbed back into the jeep. "Post office."

After picking up his stack of envelopes and packages, they went to the supply tent where Andy was given new everything. Once back at his quarters, the driver helped him unload his supplies.

"Thanks for the ride and the help. I really appreciate it," Andy said, shaking the driver's hand.

"Sleep well, Lieutenant."

Andy undressed, bagged everything so it could be burned, then laid the new fatigues on his footlocker. Taking an extra-long hot, soapy shower, he brushed his teeth, shaved his face and head, then laid down to read Nettie's letters. He fell asleep before his eyes closed, Nettie's letters laying on his chest.

HAVING SPENT THE BETTER PART of a year in forced quiet, the noisy walk to headquarters the next morning unnerved Andy. No rifle, no cautionary three-sixties, and no need to look down every third step, but he did anyway. Eleven months in country, one month until he could go home. Maybe, just maybe, what the colonel wanted to discuss would keep him and his squad close to Eagle after their stand-down. Taking the steps two at a time, he headed to the anteroom. Major Loring ushered him into Colonel Clark's office right at 0800. Dressed in fatigues and sipping from large mugs, General West and Colonel Clark were already seated around the coffee table when Andy walked in. The half-empty carafe on the table indicated they'd been there a while. Andy also noted a delicate, flowered tea service with a matching cup and saucer on the table. A woman would be joining them.

Andy saluted both officers, surprised Major Smith wasn't in the room. The major had been unusually quiet the last few weeks of the squad's long patrol and with his abrupt dismissal from the meeting yesterday, Andy felt a change might be coming.

"At ease, Lieutenant," General West said. "Sleep well?"

"Yes, sir, very well."

"Have you eaten?" He motioned to an untouched tray of doughnuts on the table.

"Yes, sir. I ate with my squad."

"Well, let's get to the point of this meeting, shall we?" Colonel Clark rose and motioned for Andy to join him in front of a map of South Vietnam just below the DMZ.

"Is Major Smith joining us?"

"He'll be briefed later," Colonel Clark replied. Turning to the map, he pointed to the Vinh Lee District. "I believe your recon patrols have been monitoring enemy activity in this region."

"Yes, sir. The place is like a sieve. The only ones honoring the DMZ are the ARVNs and us." Andy noted that the codes and colored stick pins scattered across the map reflected the patterns his squad had been reporting. Penciled arrows marked suspected VC movements. Color-coded, arrowed lines reflected supply wagon routes, pink for those driven by women, and blue for those driven by men. Pins also dotted the map. Green ones marked villages his squad said were void of enemy activity and yellow ones marked villages with cadres. A single red pin sat over the village of Ru Linh.

The colonel pointed a finger at the red pin. "I believe this last time out, you found what may be an NVA communication center here."

"Yes, sir. But it's more than just a communication center. We're pretty sure Ru Linh is a forward intelligence center." Andy reiterated what his squad had seen, including maps and markings, hidden antennas, estimated numbers of NVA, and the fake rifles and ammo boxes.

"That's valuable information, Lieutenant. The fact that it's not a well-equipped combat unit might make what we have to do a little easier," Colonel Clark said.

"Sir?"

General West joined them at the map. "Lieutenant, we have reason to believe the NVA officer in command of Ru Linh wants to defect. We want your squad to bring him in."

Red flags flew in a dozen directions as Andy processed what the general had said. "Why would one of their key intelligence officers want to defect, sir?"

"Good question. The ARVNs have a program called Chieu Hoi, which translates as open arms. The program provides a variety of incentives, including money and relocation, for VC and NVA soldiers to defect to the South. However, we believe the commander's reason is more personal. His sister, a woman named Bien Nguyen, approached the ARVNs a couple of weeks ago with the possibility of his defection. They brought her to us. We've been working with them since to develop a plan to bring him in."

"All due respect, sir, why should we believe her any more than we believe him?"

"Because she came forward at great personal risk," General West replied. "She is a long-time freedom fighter, as were her parents and grandparents. She's wanted by the VC, the NVA, as well as Chinese and Russian insurgents because of her long-standing underground activities to undermine their efforts to control South Vietnam. She has endured multiple attempts on her life and bears the scars to prove it."

"If she and her family are long-term freedom fighters, why did her brother join the NVA?" Andy asked.

"Perhaps that question is best answered by Bien." Colonel Clark went to the door. "Major, please show Mrs. Nguyen in."

A diminutive woman dressed in a light-gray, embroidered silk tunic with a mandarin collar over loose white pants entered the room, back ramrod straight, sandals soundless. Her dark hair swirled in a bun at the nape of her neck. Wisps of gray at her temples were the only hint to her age.

Andy noted deep scars on the left side of her face and neck, as well as the long, sharp, ivory hairpin tunneling through her thick bun.

"Gentlemen." The woman shook hands with General West and Colonel Clark, an unusual move for a Vietnamese woman. She then turned to Andy.

"Lieutenant," Colonel Clark said, "This is Bien Nguyen. She serves as a liaison between the South Vietnamese Freedom Fighters and the ARVNs. The Freedom Fighters are a secret, yet widespread group of South Vietnamese patriots who've been helpful in gathering intelligence on communist invaders. Bien, this is Andy Stockton. His squad just finished surveilling the region around your family's village."

Bien's grip was petite but strong, and her smile warm but guarded as she shook Andy's hand.

"Let's sit." General West motioned for Bien to have a seat on the sofa with him as the colonel and Andy pulled chairs closer.

"Bien, would you like tea?" the general asked.

"Please."

The sweet scent of lotus blossoms filled the room as the general poured jade-colored tea into the delicate cup himself, a clear sign he respected this woman.

"Thank you," Bien said as she accepted a small, cloth napkin and the cup and saucer. Closing her eyes, she savored the aroma, then took a gentle sip. "It is delicious." She gave the general an appreciative smile.

Colonel Clark waited until Bien set her cup and saucer on the table before speaking. "Bien, we've shared your request for us to help your brother defect to the South with Lieutenant Stockton. He and his squad will be escorting you to Ru Linh and back. It would be helpful if you explained the events that brought you and your brother to this point."

"Of course." Bien's dark eyes fixed on Andy, her English accented but clear. "Fifteen years ago, a group of VC came to our village to recruit volunteers for the North Vietnamese Army, something our village had resisted for months. They demanded to know how many people lived in the village, which families had boys, who had weapons, who had transportation other than animals, and where we stored our food supplies. When our elders, including my father, refused to say, the VC bound their hands and feet and forced them to watch as their wives and daughters were beaten, raped, and murdered. I was left for dead. My father and other leaders of the resistance were decapitated and their heads placed in a circle in the center of the village as a warning."

Bien's tea quivered as she raised her cup. The quivering had stopped by the time she returned the cup to its saucer.

"My grandfather and fiancé had taken a wagon of vegetables to market when the attack happened. They returned to find my parents dead, me beaten and raped, and my brother, Trai, gone. Trai and other boys from the village had been taken, conscripted by the Viet Cong for service in the NVA."

Andy noted sadness in Bien's eyes but no tears. "Have you seen or heard from your brother since?"

Bien shook her head. "We searched for years, secretly venturing into the north many times. The only thing we found were dead-ends and reports of thousands of missing children." Bien took another sip of tea. "My grandfather never recovered from the loss of my parents and Trai. His dying wish was that I never stop looking for my brother and never stop working for a free Vietnam."

"I understand your grandfather was a freedom fighter, too?" Andy asked, continuing to study Bien's face for any telltale sign that her words were lies. He saw none.

"Yes. He grew up fighting against the French occupation, then against the Russian and Chinese communists who had gained control of North Vietnam. My grandfather fought with words, not weapons, as did my parents. Their courage to speak out cost them their lives."

Andy nodded, acknowledging their sacrifice and Bien's loss.

"After recovering from the attack, I secretly organized women from the village who'd also lost loved ones. We helped other families secure hiding places for their sons and daughters in case the VC returned, and we developed a plan to track VC and NVA movements in the region in hopes of providing our village and others with some warning before future attacks. Within a year, we had developed an effective intelligence network within our district. Eventually, the network spread across this entire end of the DMZ and is still in place."

"What kind of network?" Andy asked.

"Route reconnaissance," Colonel Clark answered, motioning to the color-coded map on the wall. "The reason the supply routes driven by women parallel VC movements is because Bien's female volunteers are tracking them. Bien and ARVN intelligence kept this form of surveillance a secret to reduce the risk for the women. Yours was the first recon squad to pick up the pattern."

Andy turned to Bien, respect in his eyes. "You track them with wagons?"

"We provide female volunteers with wagons and bags of good rice and tea," Bien explained, "then dispatch them as observers along the roads and intersections leading in and out of the DMZ. For the most part, the VC live in the jungle. Consequently, they must forage for what they eat and drink.

The only tea available is a wild, bitter one called shan tuyet. It didn't take long for them to develop a preference for our lotus tea and good rice. When they steal supplies from us, our observers monitor what direction they come from and where they go, how they are dressed, if they have weapons, and how much they steal. If stealing for themselves, they will take what they can carry. If stealing for many, they'll take all of it. From this, we can estimate enemy numbers and travel patterns."

"Do they ever take your wagons?"

Bien chuckled. "Rarely. We purposely use old wagons and sickly water buffalos to pull them. The VC don't like the smell."

Andy marveled at the elegant simplicity of their plan. "Why just women observers?"

"Women do not raise the level of suspicion men do."

"Are you sure it's the VC who are stealing from you? Could it be plain thieves as well?"

"I am sure that happens occasionally. Most South Vietnamese value honesty, politeness, and cleanliness. The VC, as a rule, do not. The VC are also quite proud of their black tunics and brown belts, and often send the same men to steal supplies. All of this makes them easier to identify."

"How do you get the information from the observers to the ARVNs?"

"Have you seen the lotus tea ceremony the village women perform at night?" Bien asked.

Andy nodded.

"During the ceremony, while the boats are in the water, our observers pass coded information to another woman, a runner, who delivers it to an undercover ARVN intelligence officer."

"How do you know the observers and runners are not VC or VC sympathizers?"

Bien pointed to her ivory hairpin. "To the average eye, the pin is unremarkable. However, if you look closely, you'll see that it is a hand-carved dove with blue eyes."

"The color of freedom," Andy said.

Bien nodded. "Observer pins are black. Runner pins are white. Each pin has a hidden number carved among the feathers. We know who has each pin. Information is only passed between women who have these pins.

Andy took a guess. "You make and assign the pins?"

"Yes."

Ingenious. "Do the VC ever hurt your observers?"

"Sometimes. Our women are instructed not to resist thievery, which reduces the attacks against them; however, brown belts will hurt them at times just because they can."

"Then why do they risk it?"

"Because they and their families have been the targets and victims of these ruthless invaders. Our network does not want for volunteers, Lieutenant."

"How many do you have?

"We started with six. We now have over two hundred. Over the years, ten women have been killed, and many others have been attacked. In some cases, observers have had to kill their attackers and hide the bodies. At other times, they'll let the attacker go to protect their cover."

Andy took another guess. "They use the hairpins as weapons?"

"Yes. My grandfather described it as an effective weapon hidden in plain sight."

"Where do you get the tea and rice to sell?"

"Initially, we used our own supplies. When our network started growing, we sent some of the women to cities to find jobs. They sent money back to us to buy rice and tea from farmers who also lost family members to the invaders. Now, ARVN intelligence helps us stay supplied."

"Do you still live in Ru Linh?"

Bien shook her head. "A few months after my fiancé and I married, the VC returned to the village. They accused my husband and me of being anticommunist and, like our parents, they wanted to make examples of us. They tortured and murdered my husband, then turned their knives on me." Bien touched the scars on her neck. "The only reason I survived is that one of my observers who'd killed a VC thief kept his gun. She shot my attackers before they knew she was there. Their bodies were never found."

Colonel Clark gave Bien a respite by refilling her teacup.

"I knew the VC would come for me again," Bien continued, "so I moved south to Saigon. With so many people in the city, I could blend in. Initially, I worked in a garment factory twelve hours a day, six days a week to earn money for the network. Several years ago, ARVN intelligence approached me about expanding the network. They hired me to recruit and coordinate observers and runners and distribute money and supplies."

"How did you hear about your brother?" Andy asked.

"About two weeks ago, Cam, a childhood friend of Trai's and mine, traveled from Ru Linh to Saigon to find me. She endured many hardships during the trip and while searching the city for me. For security reasons, the ARVNs block direct access to anyone associated with the network. Cam finally went to their intelligence headquarters and begged to see the commander. When she was allowed to speak to him privately, she told him about Trai, who he was, and his desire to defect. The commander contacted me, and together we approached American intelligence. They brokered the meeting here with me, General West, and Colonel Clark."

"Meeting here had several advantages," Colonel Clark added. "First, it kept Bien's role and location in Saigon protected. Second, Camp Eagle is closer to Ru Linh. And third, we had a squad with firsthand knowledge of recent NVA activity in the area."

"If Trai's defection is legitimate, it could significantly delay any offensive the NVA are planning," General West added.

"Yes, sir." Andy turned to Bien. "How did Cam know Trai wanted to defect?"

"Cam and Trai had always been close. Until he was conscripted, it was assumed they would marry one day. When Trai returned to Ru Linh, Cam said he was unlike other NVA soldiers. He was kind. He allowed the villagers to live and work in peace. Even resisters were treated humanely instead of beaten and murdered."

Andy remembered what the NVA officer told the cadre leader while he and Quy were hiding under the wisteria tree. "If you or any other member of your cadre harm another child or adult, you'll be shot."

"It didn't take long for Trai and Cam to find each other and fall in love again," Bien continued. "They began meeting secretly at a hidden cave on the Thanh River, which flows near the village. As children, the three of us used to play in the cave. It was there that Trai told Cam he wanted to come home, that he wanted to defect."

"And you believe her?"

"I do. Not only is she Trai's and my friend, but she is an observer, and her father was a freedom fighter. He was killed at the same time as my parents."

"What if this whole thing is a ruse to draw you into the open?" Andy asked.

"That's a possibility we have to consider," Colonel Clark emphasized.

"It is a risk I am willing to take, Lieutenant." Bien pulled a small piece of rosewood from her pocket and handed it to Andy. "I believe Trai is sincere because of this. He asked Cam to bring it to me."

Looking closely at the small, richly hued piece of wood, Andy realized it was carved in the shape of a dove, each feather intricately etched on open wings, the dove's blue eyes focused straight ahead.

"Like my hairpin, our grandfather made this. He gave it to Trai the day before the VC invaded our village and took him. It represents freedom. An ideal your country describes in its Declaration of Independence. My country has yearned for the same freedom for centuries. As a freedom fighter, this dove had great meaning to my grandfather. I believe it has similar meaning to Trai."

"All due respect, ma'am. It could still be a trap. You're a valuable target." Andy returned the dove.

"Yes. It could be a trap."

"Then I suggest my squad goes to Ru Linh while you wait here." Andy looked at General West and Colonel Clark, but their eyes were on Bien.

"No, Lieutenant," Bien replied. "Trai is my brother. I am not going to ask you to do something I am not prepared to do."

"You're prepared to be captured or killed?"

Bien never blinked as she met Andy's eyes. "No. I'm prepared to kill to avoid being captured or killed."

Her voice left no doubt in Andy's mind that she'd be going with them and was prepared to do whatever she had to do.

He turned to Colonel Clark. "When and how are we to take Trai?"

"Your squad will escort Bien to the cave near the river. Bien will determine if his wish to defect is sincere. If it is, your squad will take him at the lake."

"Why the lake and not at the cave?"

Colonel Clark leaned forward, elbows to knees. "Because, if we take him at the lake during the seeding of the lotus, there will be witnesses to his capture. The NVA and VC have publicly tortured and murdered anyone suspected of trying to defect. It's better for Bien and Trai's long-term safety for them to believe that he has been captured or killed. The lake is also far enough from the village that you all will have time to escape before the NVA become aware of the abduction."

"I saw an NVA officer at the lake when we surveilled the village a week ago," Andy said. "It may have been Trai. He was sitting on a bench near a large wisteria tree."

Bien nodded. "Cam said Trai goes there every night to watch the women seed the lotus blossoms. She also said his men are used to him taking walks to the river, so that shouldn't raise suspicion either."

Colonel Clark returned to the map and motioned for Andy and Bien to join him. "Our plan is for your squad to get Bien as close to the cave as possible." He pointed to a clearing south of the village. "This is your LZ, your primary landing zone."

"Choppers? That close to the village? They're too loud," Andy said.

"Not these," Colonel Clark smiled. "We're going to use modified Hughes 500 Penetrator choppers, nicknamed 'The Quiet Ones,' to get you in and out. The CIA has been testing them here for the past few weeks. You can't hear them unless they're right on top of you. Even then, the sound is so distorted it's hard to tell what it is and where it's coming from. They're small, but the engineers who are here testing them said if we strip everything out and pack light, we can squeeze five to six people in each.

Andy studied the distance from the proposed LZ to the lake. The NVA in the village wouldn't hear the choppers, but they weren't the only ones to worry about. There were houses scattered all over the area.

"Once you're on the ground, you'll follow the river to this bend and take cover here." Colonel Clark tapped a forested area close to the water. "According to Cam and Bien, this is a grove of ancient tualang trees. Their large, above-ground roots will provide cover for the first part of the operation but still allow line of sight on the cave's entrance."

"Villagers avoid the tualangs because the canopies are full of giant, aggressive bees," Bien added. "Honey hunters harvest the massive honeycombs once in the spring and once in the fall. Cam said the spring harvest has already taken place, so no one should be there to interfere with our plans."

After living in the jungle for the better part of a year, Andy and his men had seen many tualangs and were well aware of the giant bee's reputation. Luckily, the hives sat high enough in the feathery canopy the squad had been able to avoid trouble.

The colonel pointed to the map again. "The cave lies here, just past the bend in the river and a quarter-mile east of the lake."

"Is there only one entrance?" Andy asked Bien.

"Yes. It's tall, narrow, and camouflaged by overlapping stones."

"We're going to insert you tonight, about eighteen hours ahead of the abduction," Colonel Clark said. "That way you'll be able to assess activity around the cave. If you spot anything suspicious, you'll abort the operation."

Andy flinched. Telling his men they'd be deploying again just thirty-six hours after they arrived was a gut punch.

"If the coast is clear, Bien will enter the cave at 2100 hours."

"And if it's an ambush?" Andy asked.

"If I sense a trap as I approach the cave," Bien replied, "I'll signal you by putting my hand on the side of my neck. You and your men escape to the landing zone. If I can escape, I will go in the opposite direction. I have friends near the village who will hide me until it is safe to leave."

"And if you're already in the cave and can't escape?" Andy asked.

"I am prepared to die by my own hand or theirs to protect what I know."

Not on my watch.

Bien studied Andy's face, as if reading his thoughts. "The decision is mine, Lieutenant. Sometimes we must sacrifice for the greater good."

"Are you prepared to sacrifice your brother? To kill him if necessary?"

"If this is an elaborate trap to capture me, then the brother I love is no more. And, yes, I'm prepared to kill the man who is left."

Colonel Clark cleared his throat. "Let's hope it doesn't come to that. If all goes well, Bien will rejoin you at the tualangs, then two of your men will escort her back to the primary LZ. You and the rest of your squad will follow Trai back to the lake. If he goes to the bench near the wisteria tree and remains standing, it means his troops are close enough to cause a problem, so wait. Your go signal is when he sits on the bench. Approach him from behind and make just enough commotion to be sure the women on the lake take notice."

"If this works as planned and the witnesses report the abduction, it is only a matter of time until the NVA follows us," Andy said.

"With luck, you'll be at the LZ before the NVA troops in the village get their act together and begin searching," Colonel Clark said. "Remember, the witnesses will be on the lake. They'll have to row to shore, then run back to the village to report it. Even then, they'll only know the general direction you left in."

"And remember," General West added, "you're taking the NVA post commander, so it will take time for the remaining officers to get organized. That alone should buy you time."

Andy didn't bother disagreeing. Operations developed in offices like this seldom unfolded as planned. He and his squad would have to figure out what could go wrong and develop contingency plans.

"Once you have Trai and get back to the LZ, the choppers will set down on your signal. If the primary LZ is hot, the choppers will back off until you signal from the secondary LZ which is two klicks southeast of the primary."

Andy studied the two landing areas. The choppers would be on the ground less than a minute, so everyone would need to be in place before he called them in. The squad would divide into two groups. Trai would be placed in one cradle and Bien in the other. Both groups would need to run like hell as soon as the choppers touched down. If the primary LZ turned out to be hot, the squad would not only lose anonymity but they'd have limited time to get Trai and Bien through the dense jungle to the secondary site.

Colonel Clark checked his watch. "We'll brief your squad at 1600 today in the operations building."

"Yes, sir."

"Questions, Lieutenant?"

"A few. But I'll save them for the briefing, sir." This was a high-risk mission under the most ideal circumstances, and theirs were far from ideal. His was a recon squad, not a special ops one. They were used to avoiding the enemy, not wading into them, and his men were bone weary. However, the colonel was right. His squad was the best one for the mission. They knew Ru Linh and the jungle surrounding it. "Colonel, when this is over, my men need a break."

"I've already arranged for a ten-day rest and recuperation period effective the moment you all get back," the colonel replied.

"Thank you, sir." Typically, R & Rs were three to seven days. A ten-day break was rare.

"One more thing, Lieutenant." The Colonel opened the top drawer of his desk and pulled out the banana slug bullet that had been removed from Gus's leg. "I thought you might like to return this to Sergeant Griffin."

Andy fingered the blunted end of the enemy bullet. Gus and Linda had managed to get the telltale piece of evidence to the right people after all. "Yes, sir. I'll see that he gets it." Andy put the bullet in his pocket.

"Get some rest, Lieutenant," General West said.

"Yes, sir."

As Andy left, he stopped at Major Loring's desk. "Sir, we've been out for three months. Would it be possible for me to send a couple of letters home on the next transport?"

Major Loring nodded. "Sure. I'll send them out with the dispatches going to the Pentagon this afternoon. Where do they live?"

"My fiancée lives in Northern Virginia and my mother lives in Central Virginia."

"They'll most likely have them tomorrow."

"Great." Andy hurried to the barracks to add last minute entries to the diary-like letters he'd written Nettie and his mom. Buying envelopes large enough to hold them at the PX, he added the mailing addresses, and delivered them to Major Loring. "I really appreciate this, sir."

"Godspeed tonight, Lieutenant."

"Thank you."

Chapter 13

NETTIE

Nettie navigated the empty stretcher out the ICU door and down the hall past the recovery room. She'd managed to avoid going in the after-hours trysting place for months, and thankfully Mrs. Woods had been keeping her distance since her malevolent letter to the dean had not elicited the desired response. As Nettie pushed the elevator button, a familiar voice rang out from the direction of the operating room.

"Nettie, wait up! I have great news!" Paul Anderson came running up, his OR greens uncovered, his face flushed.

The news had to be important for him to not cover his green scrubs with a lab coat before leaving the OR. The hospital's infection control folks would not be happy if they found out.

"Mom just called, my dad has been moved off the MIA list and onto the POW list. He's alive!"

Paul picked Nettie up and spun her around just as the elevator door opened. A wide-eyed Mrs. Woods stared at them as she stepped out.

"Well, well, you two are at it again?" she smirked.

Paul set Nettie down. "Just celebrating some great news, that's all."

"There is a time and a place for celebrating, and this is neither," Mrs. Woods replied sarcastically. Looking at Nettie, she added, "I'd think you would have learned that lesson by now." She turned to Paul. "I imagine your surgical supervisor will be interested in knowing about your unprofessional behavior." She studied his uncovered green scrubs. "As well as your failure to follow infection control protocol."

Paul's eyes narrowed and his voice hardened. "I'm going off duty, so it doesn't matter that my greens are uncovered, and I don't appreciate being threatened."

"Paul." Nettie touched his arm.

"This is harassment, Nettie, pure and simple."

"Let me handle it. Please."

Paul's mouth went in a straight line as he glared at Mrs. Woods.

Nettie smiled at him. "Go celebrate the good news about your dad with Laura and your mom. Win and I will see you in the morning."

Paul shot Mrs. Woods another glaring look, then as if to spite her, he leaned down and kissed Nettie on the cheek. "See you tomorrow."

When he was out of earshot, Mrs. Woods snapped. "Just what is it that you think you're going to handle, young lady? This is the second time I've caught—"

"Mrs. Woods, we both know what this is about, and it has nothing to do with Paul."

Mrs. Wood straightened her stance. "I'm sure I don't know what you mean."

"And I'm sure you do." Nettie locked eyes with the supervisor. "As you said, there is a time and place for everything, and a hospital isn't the place for inappropriate behavior, is it?"

"What are you implying?"

"I'm not implying anything, ma'am, I'm agreeing with you. Inappropriate behavior does not belong in the hospital.

The thing is, there wasn't anything inappropriate about Paul celebrating good news about his father who was MIA. It's unfair of you to imply otherwise and to threaten him."

"Well, we'll just see what your internship director and his surgical supervisor have to say." She turned to walk away.

Paul's surgical supervisor, Dr. Parcel, was the very "bloody hell" man Nettie suspected of being with Mrs. Woods in the recovery room that night. If he were to follow Mrs. Woods's lead, he'd likely do anything to protect their dirty little secret, even if it meant harming Paul's career. Nettie stepped forward. "Ma'am, if you report Paul for anything, I will tell what I know."

Mrs. Woods spun around, her eyes shooting sparks. "And just what is it you think you know?"

"I know to protect your affair, you've lied, repeatedly, about me, Dougie, and now Paul."

"How dare you. You have no proof of anything."

"Proof? You leave proof everywhere you go. Your Paradise perfume lingers in the air a long time, even in after-hours places like the recovery room."

Mrs. Woods eyes narrowed as she leaned closer to Nettie. "You think anyone's going to believe the accusations of some intern whose been caught twice dallying with a surgical resident and some nobody from the laundry? I hardly think so."

Calm washed over Nettie as she realized the truth behind Mrs. Woods's eyes. "It must be miserable."

"What?" Mrs. Woods hissed.

"Living such an unhappy life."

NETTIE HAD LITTLE TIME TO WORRY about the consequences of her encounter with Mrs. Woods. The ER had stayed so hectic, she and TK didn't finish their notes until midnight. They were on their way out the door when Win called to say a man in an army uniform had just delivered a thick envelope from Andy.

"He was driving a car with the Pentagon emblem on the side."

"What? Did he say anything?"

"Just that he'd been asked to deliver the letter to this address."

"Okay. I'm on my way." Nettie tried to calm her competing thoughts. *I just talked with Andy. He's safe and sound in camp. Since when does the Pentagon hand-deliver personal letters at midnight?*

"Call me when you know something," TK said.

"Will do."

Win had a cup of chamomile tea and Andy's letter waiting on the kitchen table when Nettie arrived home.

Dropping into a chair, she opened the bulging envelope. Each page had dated entries on the front, back, and along the sides. Some were a single sentence, some were long and unhurried, and others had overlapping lines as if written in the dark. Most of the pages were smudged with dirt and rain marks.

Every line pulled her further into Andy's world, the beauty of multicolored sunsets after monsoon rains, the exquisite plants and flowers they were using as nature's medicine cabinet, the taste of the funny-looking, protein-packed bugs Quy and Doc had them eat, and the expertise his squad had gained while living and working in a jungle that never slept.

She felt the warmth of Andy's voice in her head until the last hurried entry, dated the day after his phone call. They were being ordered out again within hours. Reading between the scribbled lines, she sensed the urgency as well as his fatigue. *What in heaven's name could be so important that the army is pushing him and his squad so hard?* Nettie laid the letter in her lap, closed her eyes. *Lord, whatever it is, please keep him and his squad safe.*

The ringer on the telephone startled Nettie's eyes open. Win hurried to answer it. "Hello." Looking relieved, she handed the receiver to Nettie. "For you. It's the hospital."

"Nettie, this is Mrs. Henry in the Godfrey Center. Mr. Pepper has just been transferred back to the CCU. I'm afraid he's gone into pulmonary edema. He's asking for you."

"I'm on my way."

NETTIE SLIPPED THROUGH THE DOOR of the day-bright CCU. This many lights this late at night wasn't a good sign, but you can't save dying people in the dark. Nurses and respiratory therapists were popping in and out of the middle room, their faces concerned, their actions fast and focused. The name beside the door read "Pepper."

"What are you doing here?" Mrs. Woods stood with the oncoming night supervisor behind the counter circling the nurses' station, her expression hard.

Nettie gave her a cursory glance, then turned her attention back to the brightly lit room. "I was asked to come."

The CCU nurse who had worked with Mr. Pepper before spotted Nettie and waved her over. "I'm glad you're here. He keeps asking for you."

Nettie walked to Mr. Pepper's door. The head of his bed had been raised to ease his fast and shallow breathing. His eyes were closed, his skin ashen, and a green-tinted oxygen mask covered his mouth and nose. The EKG monitor above his bed showed the wide complexes of a failing heart. Rotating tourniquets on his extremities cycled every few minutes, temporarily decreasing the amount of blood his weakened heart had to pump. A bulging Foley bag hanging at the foot of the bed showed Lasix was doing the same thing. A central intravenous line with multiple ports placed in his upper chest controlled the infusion of medications, and a ventilator stood ready in the corner.

"How's he doing?" Nettie whispered.

"So, so," the nurse replied. "I just gave him more low-dose morphine, which is reducing his preload, but it's also making him sleepy." She checked the numbers on the monitor and recorded them in the chart. "Feel free to stay awhile. I have another critical patient in the next room, so I'd appreciate an extra set of eyes on this one."

"Of course." Nettie glanced toward the nurses' station. Thankfully, the two supervisors had disappeared. Stepping into Mr. Pepper's room, she found herself wishing he'd sit up and spar with her like he did during his first CCU stay, anything to show a spark of life. Moving to the side of the bed, she picked up his hand. Cool and damp, it sat limply in hers. "Mr. Pepper, it's Nettie," she whispered, touching his forehead.

His eyelids fluttered, struggling to open but not finding the strength. They went smooth and still as he drifted away.

Pushing the trends button on the monitor, she could see his blood pressure and oxygen levels were low. The wall clock said 1:00 a.m. as Nettie hung her shoulder bag in the small closet. Pulling the covers over Mr. Pepper's chest and arms, she dimmed the overhead lights and pulled a chair close to the nonbusy side of the bed. His journey back from the brink would take a while.

By 4:00 a.m., Mr. Pepper's vital signs had improved enough the rotating tourniquets could be removed. As Nettie and his nurse turned off the machine and removed the last Velcro cuff from his leg, Mr. Pepper woke, blinking several times as his eyes adjusted to the light.

"Nettie, is that you?" he asked hoarsely.

She took his hand. "Yes, sir. I'm here."

This time, he squeezed it. "Thank God." He raised his other hand and fumbled with his oxygen mask.

"Let me." She adjusted the mask on his chin so he could talk but still get oxygen.

"Thank you for coming," he whispered. "I was afraid I'd die—before—before I could tell you."

"Tell me what, sir?"

"In my Bible, there's a letter. If I die—would you see that it and the ring get delivered?"

"Of course." She squeezed his hand. "But don't plan on going anywhere soon. Your numbers are stabilizing. You'll probably be able to deliver both yourself."

He attempted to smile, but the corners of his mouth wouldn't stay up. "Please—promise me."

"I promise."

"Thank you." Relief smoothed the wrinkles on his face as he drifted off again.

THE SUN HAD JUST CLEARED the rolling skyline of the Blue Ridge as Nettie left the hospital early Saturday morning. It had been a long night, but Mr. Pepper's condition had stabilized. She might be able to catch a nap after lunch, but this morning there were things to do. She and Win were going to pool their money and buy a bottle of champagne. They wanted to help the Andersons celebrate.

A renewed energy filled the NAF office as they arrived.

"It may be grocery store champagne," Nettie quipped as she poured the sparkling liquid into their mugs, "but it still bubbles." She raised her cup. "To hope."

"Hear! Hear!" Mrs. Anderson said, taking a big sip.

"To hope," echoed Laura, Paul, and Win.

Win passed paper plates filled with buttered English muffins and fruit. "So, what happened? How did they find out Mr. Anderson wasn't MIA?"

"Remember Colonel Bell, the officer who was here a few weeks back?" Mrs. Anderson asked. "He was able to find out. He had his people gather all the information they could find on my husband and sent inquiries to different departments of the military, both here and in Southeast Asia. They found out that a POW who'd escaped several months ago reported being imprisoned with an air force pilot, a Major Anderson from Virginia, who'd been shot down near the DMZ."

Nettie took a sip of champagne to quell the flutter in her stomach. The DMZ—the very place where Andy and his squad were operating right now.

"The escapee was able to give the army an approximate location of the POW camp," Mrs. Anderson continued. "But by the time special forces arrived, the NVA and remaining prisoners had disappeared without a trace." Mrs. Anderson stopped to steady her voice. "On the bright side, Colonel Bell is now organizing a systematic network among all branches of the military that will update and coordinate information about POWs, MIAs, and KIAs as it becomes available."

Laura got up and hugged her mother. "All because a group of housewives refused to sit down and shut up."

Chapter 14

ANDY

Long hot showers, high and tight haircuts, fresh fatigues, and new boots gave Andy's squad the appearance of being prepped and ready, but their faces still showed the stress and fatigue of a three-month jungle patrol. He'd asked them to come to the operations building early so he could talk with them before General West and Colonel Clark arrived. He knew they'd need to vent.

"Okay, listen up," he said. "We have a special op that begins tonight."

Moans filled the room and quickly gained volume.

Andy let them blow off steam for a minute, then raised his hand and kept it up until silence settled across the room. "I share your frustration and your fatigue, but orders are orders."

"Why us, Lieutenant?" Chase asked. "We just got here."

"Because the op takes place at Ru Linh."

"Do they need more intel?" Strawberry asked.

"No. This op isn't recon, but it does require stealth."

The room went still. The odds of them making it back just dropped.

"In a minute," Andy continued, "General West and Colonel Clark will—"

"General West?" Hollis interrupted. "*The* General West? As in the guy in charge of this whole damn war?"

"The same."

"Geez! What kind of op is this?"

"One that has the potential to influence the course of the war," boomed a voice from the back of the room.

Andy's men jumped to attention as General West strode down the center aisle with Colonel Clark and Bien. Following them were Major Smith and the CSM.

"At ease, gentlemen," General West said. Once introduced, Bien took a seat, while General West and Colonel Clark provided an overview of the pending mission. As the general finished, he turned away from the maps and toward the room. "I'm aware that this squad is long overdue for a stand-down."

Major Smith stared straight ahead.

"So the fact I'm sending you right back out speaks to the importance of the mission and your role in it. When this is over, you'll get your break. A long one. Until then, we'll have your back. Good luck and Godspeed." As the general left the room, he motioned for his CSM to stay. "Make sure they get all the supplies they need."

"Yes, sir," the CSM replied, his expression indicating surprise at being reduced to a supply clerk.

Colonel Clark turned toward Andy and his squad. "We're confident the Quiet One helicopters can get you close enough to the village that you'll have time to hike to the cave before sunup. Flight logistics will be managed through my office; however, finalizing the operational details of who does what and when, I'm leaving to Lieutenant Stockton."

"Colonel," Major Smith said. "Perhaps I should—"

"No," Colonel Clark replied unceremoniously. "Lieutenant Stockton and his men are quite capable of planning what they need to do from this point on. After all, it's going to be their boots on the ground."

Andy heard his men stir at the acknowledgement.

"You can go, Major," the colonel continued. "Command sergeant major, you're free to go as well. Just meet these men at the supply tent in two hours. They'll know what gear they need by then."

"Yes, sir." The CSM cut his eyes at Andy as he followed an angry Major Smith down the aisle. Andy smiled and winked, causing the CSM to stumble into a chair.

Colonel Clark handed Andy the chalk and took a seat. "Lieutenant, it's all yours."

Motioning Bien and his squad up to the maps, Andy led the development of a step-by-step plan, integrating their observations and suggestions as he went. Two hours later the plan had been triple-checked for accuracy and contingency plans ironed out. They were ready.

"Good job, folks," Colonel Clark said. "I'll be on the other end of your radio. Now, get your supplies and some rest. We'll reconvene at the airfield at 2100 hours."

THREE SLEEK, JET-BLACK QUIET One helicopters sat on the moonlit tarmac with their lights off. The soft sounds generated by their spinning, odd-looking rotors emanating from the opposite direction, as if the machines were ventriloquists. Even stripped hollow, each chopper could carry six at most. Strawberry, Rawlin, Doc, Sirocco, and Quy would go in the first chopper and secure the primary LZ. Andy, Bien, and the rest of the squad would follow in the second chopper. A third chopper would remain on standby.

"Remember this sound distortion," Andy cautioned everyone. "It's going to matter if the LZ's hot when we leave."

Bien fluidly hoisted herself up and into the chopper without assistance. Dressed in close-fitting black pants and top, she wore a small, black waist pack, and had traded her sandals for flat ankle boots. The same ivory hairpin held her braided bun in place. As she moved into the chopper, Andy noted the sheath of a small knife stuck in the side of her boot. *Strong, flexible, and armed high and low. If she can move fast and quiet, our mission just got easier.*

Sitting near the door, Andy checked his men. Camouflage paint smudged their faces and hands. Their utility belts held extra ammo and a collapsible canteen. Their large rucks had been traded for small packs, and their freshly cleaned M16s stood cradled by their sides.

Moretti returned Andy's look. "I hope they're right, Lieutenant."

"About what?"

"About us getting R & R when we get back. Most of us are short-timers. If we're able to pull this off, maybe they won't send us back out."

"Maybe." He wasn't about to stomp on hope, especially his own.

Andy watched the shadowy dips and swells blanketing the sleeping jungle as his chopper circled a few klicks from the primary LZ, waiting for those in the first chopper to give the go-ahead to land. He wanted this mission over with.

"Chopper 2, LZ secure. Over." Strawberry's subdued voice was clear in Andy's headphones.

Andy gave the pilot a thumbs-up, nodded to Bien, and hand-signaled "on deck" and "wedge formation" to his men. The aircraft banked sharply, dropped, and skirted the treetops at blurring speed. They were on the ground in two minutes and off the chopper, running for the jungle in seconds. Strawberry and Quy joined Andy's group as Rawlin, Doc, and Sirocco dug in to monitor the LZ. Moving Bien to the cradle, Andy gave Strawberry the go signal.

Familiar beads of sweat formed on Andy's face as the dark jungle sauna closed in once again. Flying bugs and the constant threat of tripwires, booby traps, ambushes, snipers, and nature's predators kept them on high alert as they moved quickly but cautiously toward the river. The squad had perfected stealth movement during their months in the jungle, so the treetop canopy stayed relatively quiet as they passed. Andy checked on Bien frequently, but he needn't have bothered. She stayed right with him, moving quietly and more sure-footed than he.

A half klick from the river, Chase and Hollis split off to establish surveillance at the lake. They were to position themselves along the edge of the jungle behind the blue wisteria tree to support the abduction and ensure the escape path.

As planned, Bien took the lead at the bend in the river where the grove of majestic tualangs began. Moving gracefully around their wide trunks and sprawling roots, she stopped behind a root as tall as Andy's knee. Dropping down, she pointed and whispered, "The cave."

Using binoculars, Andy studied the riverbank. A narrow path coming out of the jungle ended on a small stretch of beach scattered with river chaff. Farther upriver, at the jungle's edge, sat a vertical outcropping of stones. "I don't see the entrance to the cave," he whispered.

"That's why it's a secret," Bien teased. "You'll see me slip into an opening that is not there."

Andy glanced at her sideways. He wasn't in the mood for riddles.

"Trust me, Lieutenant. It's there."

He had to trust her. He didn't like it but had no choice. Using hand signals, Andy had Strawberry, Cowboy, Moretti, and Quy spread out among the roots of the tualangs to provide as many lines of sight on the path and cave as possible. When they were in position, he looked at the canopy. Darkness hid the honeycombs and the giant bees who tended them.

"They're up there," Bien whispered. "Hear them? They're cooling the hives with their wings."

Using binoculars, he spotted dozens of large disc-shaped honeycombs nestled among the branches. The bee's hum a steady tone among the variable noises of the jungle and river.

"Let's hope they stay up there."

"They will. Unless you need them."

"What do you mean?"

"Should it become necessary, fire shots into the canopy, then run for the river. The bees will do the rest."

Andy and Bien settled in behind the tualang's root to watch and wait. As the hours passed, a sweet scented breeze swayed the canopy, giving Andy glimpses of a brilliant night sky. He thought of Nettie and their times on Allen's Hill— stargazing, talking about life, love, laughing, crying, arguing, and making up. He ached for her.

"You must love her very much," Bien whispered.

Startled, Andy quickly scanned the area. *Focus, Stockton, focus.*

Bien's face showed nothing but understanding.

"I, too, long for home, one that no longer exists. My parents, my husband, my life before the communists. The only remnant of a happy life is my brother. One day, he and I will cross the river of lotus and gather with our loved ones on the bank where willows never die and the darkest night always ends in light."

Andy couldn't fathom what it would be like to lose what Bien had lost—even the imaginary pain seemed too real. Yet, she still spoke of hope. A fish jumped in the river, startling them both. Andy quickly surveyed the jungle and riverbank again, then signaled "all clear" to his outposts. *Focus, Stockton, focus.*

Sunrise brought a reprieve from the incessant, palm-size mosquitos and other biting bugs that had plagued them during the night. It also marked the start of traffic on the river. Staying out of sight, Andy and his men monitored villagers poling sampans filled with second-harvest rice, as well as adults and children fishing with poles and handheld lines. As the morning wore on, an occasional villager came to the beach to bathe or wash clothes. By afternoon, the intensity of the heat brought an occasional swimmer, and by sunset, the traffic on the slow-moving river stopped. Overhead, an occasional low-flying jet could be heard.

No one had approached the rock ledge since they arrived. If the NVA were going to set a trap, they needed to get on it. If they were already in the cave and the squad's position got ambushed, Andy and his men would have no choice but to disrupt the bees hovering above and run for the river. If Bien didn't make it out of the cave, Chase and Hollis would head downriver as decoys while Andy and the others moved upriver. They'd doubled back to rescue her and capture or kill Trai.

At sunset, Bien straightened her clothes, readjusted her ivory hairpin, and made sure the hilt of her knife rested on the top of her boot.

"You're still confident this is not a setup," whispered Andy.

"Yes. However, one should be prepared for surprises, especially in the jungle."

"Let's go over everything one more time."

Bien patiently reviewed the operation again, step by step, including what to do if at any point she sensed a trap. "This is going to work, Lieutenant."

"I hope you're right, but as you said, one should be prepared for surprises."

Bien nodded. "I'll make sure Trai knows exactly what to do when he leaves the cave."

Signals from his men indicated movement on the path. Using binoculars, Andy spotted a slim, clean-shaven man with short salt-and-pepper hair and a relaxed gait coming down the path. His arms swung free, and his unbuttoned safari-like jacket revealed no visible weapons. Andy handed the binoculars to Bien.

Studying the man for a long moment, a slight smile curved her lips. "I believe that is my brother."

Once near the river, Trai turned off the path and crossed through the tall grasses to the rock ledge. Using only moonlight, he found small irregularities in the stone to climb toward the middle of the wall. Once there, he turned sideways and disappeared into a crack in the granite.

Andy did a quick status check with his men. So far, no one had followed Trai. "Okay, let's do this." Andy touched Bien's arm as she rose to leave, "If anything feels off, and I mean anything, signal me."

"I will."

Andy continued to hold her arm. "Bien, if this is a trap, we're not leaving you behind. Understood?"

Bien put her hand over his and nodded. Crouching low, she disappeared into the shadows, avoiding a direct approach to the cave to protect the squad's location. Once she reached the river, Andy found her with the binoculars.

Following Trai's steps, Bien nimbly scaled the face of the ledge and disappeared into the stone just as he had. Andy noted the time and quickly scanned the area again for movement or anything out of place. When all remained quiet, he signaled his men to get ready, they had fifteen minutes until the most dangerous part of the mission began.

Time ticked in slow motion as Andy watched the cave's entrance. At the fourteen-minute mark, he watched Bien leave the cave and move along the riverbank. Stopping frequently to ensure no one followed her, she turned into the jungle and made her way back to Andy. Her smile and tear tracks told the story.

"My brother has returned to me. He is ready to do what is needed to be free again."

"Bien, you're positive his loyalties are no longer with the NVA?"

"His loyalties were never with them. He did what he had to do to survive."

Andy nodded and motioned for Strawberry and Cowboy to escort Bien back to the LZ. "Whatever happens, get Bien on that chopper," he whispered.

Strawberry and Cowboy positioned Bien between them and took off as Andy joined Moretti and Quy near the path. Hiding in thick brush, Andy spotted Trai climbing down from the cave, his walk through the tall grass and onto the path to the village unrushed. Staying well back, Andy fell in behind him. Moretti counted to ten, then followed. Quy did the same. Nighttime jungle sounds and movements of nocturnal insects and wildlife were reaching a crescendo as Andy inched down the path.

Trai exited the jungle and sauntered across the moonlit clearing toward the lake. Stopping at the edge, he watched as the women from the village secured their lanterns and launched their boats.

Staying in the shadows, Andy, Moretti, and Quy turned off the path and joined Chase and Hollis across from the blue wisteria tree.

"Nothing unusual so far, Lieutenant," whispered Chase.

"Good. Remember, whatever happens, Trai gets on that chopper."

Everyone gave him a thumbs up.

Andy and Quy darted from the jungle into the hedge's shadow, then slipped under the thick, drooping branches of the wisteria tree.

Moments later, Trai turned from the lake and approached the bench. Stopping short, he turned toward the lake and put his hands in his pockets.

Andy tensed. Had Trai just signaled someone? He

followed Trai's gaze to a single boat near the water's edge. The woman inside glanced sideways at Trai, then swirled away. It had to be Cam. Trai turned, walked the few steps to the bench, and sat.

Staying low to the ground, Andy and Quy covered the distance to the bench quickly. Andy held the dull side of his knife against Trai's neck as Quy loosely gagged and cuffed him. Trai made a show of struggling but offered no real resistance. As they pulled him over the back of the bench, Cam yelled loud enough to garner the attention of the boaters but not loud enough to be heard in the village, successfully securing the witnesses needed to protect Trai's cover.

Half-carrying Trai, Andy and his men hurried south through the jungle. After fifteen minutes, they stopped to let Trai catch his breath.

"Quy, tell him the gag and cuffs have to stay on in case we're spotted."

Quy quickly translated.

Trai nodded as he gulped air. He had the same eyes as Bien. They looked grateful.

Andy replaced the gag, checked his compass, and pointed south. They grabbed Trai under the arms and took off again.

Nearing the primary LZ, Andy slowed and put everyone on a knee. Motioning Moretti forward, he grabbed the radio and whispered, "Bravo One, this is Alpha One. Over."

"Roger, Alpha One," Sirocco responded in a low tone. "Package one is with us. Be aware, possible hostiles at the opposite end of the LZ. We just spotted movement in the southwest corner. Over."

"Roger, Bravo One. How many. Over."

"Three, maybe four. Over."

"Roger, Bravo One. Package two proceeding to you. As soon as he's there, call the choppers."

"Roger Alpha One. Over."

Andy secured the radio and set his jaw. "Dammit." He didn't want to do what had to be done.

"I'll go," Chase said.

"Me too," added Moretti.

"Only two are going and I'm one. The rest of you need to get Trai on that chopper."

"I'm going with you, Lieutenant," Moretti said adamantly.

They had to move. "Okay. Chase, take over. You all join Strawberry. There may be more hostiles along the way, so be careful. Moretti and I will take care of whoever is at the other end. When you're in the air, let HQ know what we're doing. We'll rendezvous with the reserve chopper at the secondary LZ."

Trai bumped Andy's shoulder, his words muffled by the gag.

Andy pulled the gag down.

"Lieutenant," Quy interpreted, "VC monitor any place a helicopter can land. They will hide and come in behind you."

Andy nodded his thanks. Quickly repositioning the gag, he nodded to his men. "Go."

"Come on," Andy said to Moretti. "We'll backtrack and come in behind whoever's out there before they have a chance to get behind us."

Quickly retracing their steps, they turned until they were in a direct line with the edge of the clearing. One slow step at a time, they worked their way in. Andy heard the soft, wind-whipped sounds of the Quiet One helicopters echoing from the left, then the right, then from overhead, then from the left again. Hopefully, the distorted sounds would confuse the VC long enough for him and Moretti to spot them.

Andy watched the choppers touch down at the far end of the LZ. The rest of the squad, in two groups, headed for them on a dead run. Rapid-fire shots rang out from the brush line thirty yards in front of Andy, forcing those running for the choppers to hit the ground. Andy and Moretti blanketed the bushes with repeated rounds until the enemy guns fell silent. In a matter of seconds, the choppers were loaded, off the ground, and had sufficient altitude to make bullets irrelevant. The clearing stood eerily quiet. Andy and Moretti eased up and approached the brush line cautiously. Three bloody, lifeless VC lay twisted among the bushes, the entrance to their partially hidden tunnel a few feet away.

Andy scanned the edges of the clearing. "I didn't see Bien in the cradle for the second chopper, did you?"

Moretti shook his head and reached for the radio to confirm they had her.

"Not now," said Andy. "The VC and NVA will be all over this place in minutes. We've got to get out of here."

"Secondary LZ is likely to be hot as well."

"I agree. We'll come in from the north and see if we can smoke them out. Hopefully, the backup chopper is staying close by."

"And if it's not?"

"Then we have a hell of a hike back to Eagle. Let's go."

A twig snapped behind them.

"Look out!" Rapid-fire rang out as Moretti shouldered Andy to the side and swung his rifle around.

Searing pain tore through Andy's shoulder and chest as he fell in slow motion, bullet spray landing so close it kicked dirt in his eyes. Moretti slumped across his legs.

Andy heard brush rustling as the shooter closed in. Struggling to raise his M16 with one hand, he couldn't stop his slow slide into darkness, the glinting blade of a knife the last thing he saw.

Chapter 15

NETTIE

Nettie bolted upright in bed with a guttural cry, eyes wide and panicked. Her hair and nightgown were soaked in freezing sweat, terror squeezed her chest. Andy was calling her—over and over—as clearly as if he were in the room, but she couldn't find him. She searched everywhere, but all she could find were bodies of other soldiers covered in blood.

A full moon pushed eerie shadows through the window as she kicked frantically at the suffocating covers. Shaking uncontrollably, she pulled herself to the side of the bed and tried to take a deep breath, but the terror wouldn't yield. Standing on quivering legs and using the wall for support, she stumbled to the bathroom. Turning the shower on, she stepped into the warm water, leaving Andy's shirt wrapped around her. As the steam began to rise, she sank to her knees. Attempts to take deep breaths turned to sobs.

It's a bad dream. It's just a bad dream. Please Lord, let it just be a bad dream.

Nettie stayed in the shower until the hot water ran cold, then shuffled back to her room soaking wet. Collapsing on the bed, she jarred the lamp on the bedside stand and sent it crashing to the floor. Shattered glass slid everywhere.

Seconds later her bedroom door flew open.

"Nettie, are you okay?" Win asked, reaching for the light switch on the wall. Shock filled her eyes when she saw Nettie lying in a heap of disheveled linens, soaking wet, pale, and shivering. "Good Lord, what happened?" Dodging broken glass, Win quickly crossed the room to feel Nettie's forehead. "You're freezing." Helping her out of the wet shirt, Win wrapped a warm robe around Nettie's shoulders and rubbed her arms and back. "Are you sick?"

Nettie pushed wet hair out of her eyes. "It's Andy," she stammered. "He kept calling me, but I couldn't find him. There were bodies everywhere. He needed me and I couldn't find him."

"Oh, honey." Win hugged her tight.

"It was so real, Win. Something has happened to him. I know it."

Win rubbed Nettie's arms harder. "Don't go there, Nettie. It's a bad dream following a bad day."

Nettie pulled back enough to look into the eyes of the Monacan Indians' youngest medicine woman. "You of all people understand visions. What if this was one? A premonition that Andy is—"

"Then you'll deal with it as it comes, just like you've always done, my friend. And just like Andy would want you to."

Win held her friend until the shivering stopped. "Stay where you are. I'm going to get this glass up, then make you some chamomile tea. It will warm you up and help you get back to sleep."

As Win swept glass, Nettie slipped her arms into her robe and tied it tight.

The clock on the stove glowed 1:30 a.m. as the teapot whistled. Win poured steaming water over the triple tea bags in Nettie's cup. "You may need some extra help tonight," she explained.

Holding the warm cup in both hands, Nettie sipped the smooth liquid. A heart-sick calm slowly replaced the terror of the dream. Her thoughts drifted from Andy to the Andersons. "Paul, Laura, their mother—they live with this nightmare all day, every day, and have for four years. How in heaven's name do they keep going?"

"The only way anyone can," Win said. "One step at a time."

NETTIE STIRRED HER UMPTEENTH cup of coffee of the day as she waited for TK, Paul, and Dougie to join her for dinner at their usual table. Nothing along the serving line had looked appealing, so she'd plunked the only turkey sandwich left in the display on her tray. Fatigue caused by her nightmare-fueled fear for Andy's safety and her angry encounter with Mrs. Woods had turned her life into a twilight zone. She couldn't let go of the feeling that Andy wasn't okay, nor could she move past the fact that she'd resorted to black-mail to stop the vindictive supervisor from going after Paul. Wrong on the edge of right is still wrong. Her ongoing talks with God had resulted in more questions than answers, but the message she'd consistently opened her eyes to had stayed the same—the only behavior you can control is your own.

TK sat her tray on the table and slid her thin frame into the chair. Eyeing the dry, turned-up corners of Nettie's untouched sandwich, she asked. "Not hungry?"

"Nothing looked good." She hadn't said anything to TK about the nightmare. Talking about it made it too real.

TK touched Nettie's arm. "I don't know Andy well, but what I do know is that he wouldn't want you making yourself sick. Too much coffee, too little food and sleep, and that's exactly where you're headed." She moved a small dish of sliced apples from her tray to Nettie's. "You need to eat. Who knows what's around the corner."

"You're right. Thanks." *Shake it off, Nettie. You're not helping anyone this way, least of all yourself.* She picked up the sandwich as Paul and Dougie exited the serving line and headed their way.

"Good evening, ladies," Paul said with a broad smile.

"Evening," replied TK. "What are you so happy about?"

"Just a good day, that's all."

"Uh-huh," TK replied, knowingly. "What's up?"

Paul just shrugged.

Nettie wondered if his smile had something to do with Win. The two of them had been spending a lot of time together lately. Win would often leave notes that she and Paul were at the library studying or had gone for a walk on the riverfront. Nettie was happy for her best friend and thrilled that Paul finally had something to smile about. If he could smile, so could she.

THE NEXT DAY, NETTIE HURRIED through the eerie tunnel to the Godfrey Center. According to Mrs. Henry, Mr. Pepper had been moved back to his regular room that morning. Nettie knew it would cheer him up to see the progress Mr. Kalua had made on the garden while he was in CCU, so she came to the hospital early to give him a tour. Approaching Mr. Pepper's room, she stopped. Voices flowed through the crack in the door. Words like assets, trust management, and power of attorney made it clear the visitors were not routine. Going back to the nurses' station, she met Mrs. Henry returning with a medication tray in hand.

"Hi, Nettie. I figured you'd be along today. Are Mr. Pepper's visitors still here?"

"Yes, ma'am. They sounded official."

"Most lawyers and accountants sound that way."

"I figured that's who they were. It's hard to keep a business going from a hospital room halfway around the world."

Mrs. Henry motioned for Nettie to follow her to the medicine room, away from the other nurses, and closed the door. Putting the used pill cup in the trash, she unscrewed the empty syringe from the metal Tubex and put it in the sharps container. Washing her hands, she turned to Nettie as she dried them, her kind eyes and wrinkled face sad. "Mr. Pepper called his lawyers and accountants here for a different reason, Nettie. His cardiologist told him there was little more they could do for him; his heart has sustained too much damage. It's not a matter of years or months now, it's a matter of weeks, maybe days."

It took a moment for the words to register. Nettie knew Mr. Pepper was going to die. She'd known it all along, but hearing the finality of days hit her hard, almost as if she'd lost him already. She leaned against the door.

"Mr. Pepper didn't want to die in CCU," continued Mrs. Henry, putting her hand on Nettie's shoulder. "He wanted to come back here, to be close to the garden. His lawyers and accountants flew in from Hawaii to make sure the last of his affairs were in order."

"Does Mr. Kalua know?" Nettie asked quietly.

"I believe so. The two of them talked for a long time before the lawyers and accountants arrived."

WHEN HER SHIFT ENDED AT 11:00 P.M., Nettie went back to the Godfrey Center. Weary but knowing sleep would not come, she hoped Mr. Pepper would still be awake. Seeing the light on under his door, she took a deep breath, put a smile on her face, and peeked in. "Are you up for a late-night visitor?"

Sitting in bed, his Bible open in his lap, Mr. Pepper smiled and nodded. "I was hoping you'd come." He motioned to the wheelchair in the corner. "Let's go to the garden. Keona gave me a tour this morning. It's almost finished. I want to show it to you."

Nettie nodded. Hospital protocols and schedules were of little concern now. Moving the wheelchair into position, she helped him into his robe and slippers and supported him as he stood on weak and wobbly legs, pivoted, and sat. Unlocking the wheels, she turned the wheelchair toward the door.

"Wait," Mr. Pepper said. Leaning toward the bedside stand, he reached for his Bible and the framed picture of the couple by the pond. He cradled them in his lap as if they were precious cargo.

Mrs. Henry nodded and waved them on as they passed the nurses' station. Reaching the double glass doors, Nettie flipped on the two new wall switches. The first one turned on the soft, accent lighting in the garden and along the path. The second turned the waterfall and the underwater pond lights on.

Pulling Mr. Pepper's wheelchair backward through the door, Nettie pivoted it toward the garden and stopped, the night view too stunning not to savor. It hadn't taken long for the birds to find their way to the young garden; robins led the scattered nighttime chorus.

"Beauty soothes the edges of a troubled soul, doesn't it?" Mr. Pepper said, looking around the garden. "The prophet Isaiah foretold of the suffering servant who would guide us to a place of beautiful gardens and never-ending springs."

"The prophet of redemption and restoration," Nettie said, as the beauty and scents of the garden lessened her weariness a little.

"Indeed. This time last year, you told me I was a lucky man. That I'd been given a second chance to live and a second chance to die. Most important, you said I'd been given the gift of time to figure it all out." He reached back and patted her hand. "You were right, my friend."

Nettie pushed the chair at a snail's pace along the smooth, sandstone path, the lights and shadows blending the colors and contours of the garden in mesmerizing ways. Mr. Pepper's head moved back and forth slowly as if committing every image to memory. Up ahead, the soft sounds of the waterfall beckoned.

Reaching the bench Mr. Kalua had tucked among the greenery, Mr. Pepper raised his hand. "Help me over, please."

Shuffling into the same position as he was in the picture, he stopped to catch his breath while Nettie moved the wheelchair out of sight.

"You've heard the latest on my condition?" he asked as she sat on the stone rim of the pond.

"Yes, sir."

He gazed at the rippling light on the water. "Isn't it odd how you can know something is going to happen for so long and still be surprised when the time comes?"

"Yes, sir," Nettie replied softly.

Sighing, Mr. Pepper's business voice took over. "I've taken care of all the legal and financial loose ends of my life. And Keona and I have talked at length. I have no descendants, so my interests in our nurseries will go to him. They started with him, and they should stay with him. My home and gardens on the bluffs will be turned into a botanical education and research center and placed in a public trust which I have endowed and that he will oversee." He motioned to the garden surrounding them. "He will also oversee the care and upkeep of the garden and nursery here, albeit from a distance. He's already handpicked the staff who will manage things here. A separate trust has been established for this purpose, one the hospital benefits from but cannot interfere with. Otherwise, as soon as I'm gone, some eager beaver hospital administrator will bulldoze the healing garden and nursery to put up more parking garages. People need nature more than they need concrete."

Nettie nodded.

"The remainder of my fortune will also go to Mr. Kalua to be used at his discretion to support our other projects. My friend is a man of honor, so I'm leaving my estate in good hands."

Nettie nodded, glad her friend had such a friend.

"There's only one more thing that needs to be taken care of, and it's personal. I'm hoping you can help me with it."

"I'll do what I can," Nettie replied.

He handed her the picture. "That's me on the bench. A much younger me, of course, but just as handsome, don't you think?" he quipped.

Nettie smiled at the hint of his former spark.

Mr. Pepper's face grew somber. "The woman next to me is Vivi Allen, my fiancée. At least she was at the time. Danny, her older brother, and I had been best friends since childhood. Vivi adored Danny and used to follow us around like a puppy. As she got older, Vivi evolved into the most beautiful girl I'd ever known. I fell in love with her, and she fell in love with me. The day she said she'd marry me was the happiest day of my life."

Mr. Pepper's expression changed as his memories went in a different direction.

"At the time, Hitler was ravaging Europe, and most Americans, including Danny and me, felt it was just a matter of time before the United States entered the war. So, when we graduated from college, we joined the navy. Danny and I had earned degrees in telecommunication, so they sent us to a training center in Baltimore to learn how to use the navy's first radar system. Afterward, they stationed us at Pearl Harbor as part of the radar support group.

"I'd never traveled much, so from the moment I stepped off the plane on Oahu I was awe-struck. The island was the most beautiful place I'd ever seen. For months, Danny and I used our free time to explore the beaches, mountain trails, and waterfalls. We visited Diamond Head and watched the giant waves at Pipeline Beach. You name it, we explored it."

Mr. Pepper stopped to catch his breath.

"Of all the places we visited, Hanauma Bay was the most beautiful. Standing on the bluffs overlooking that magnificent turquoise water and coral reef, I knew I wanted to live there. Of course, we wanted Vivi to see it, so Danny and I pooled our money and paid for her flight to the island. Her first day on Oahu, we took her to the bluffs. Along the way, we stopped at a roadside nursery. I wanted to buy her a lei of red ilima flowers."

"Why ilimas?"

"In the Hawaiian culture, a lei of red ilimas represents love," he explained. "It's customary for a Hawaiian man to give one to his betrothed. I could hardly wait to give one to Vivi."

Nettie glanced at the picture, the engaged couple were not touching and the lei the woman wore was not ilimas.

"The nursery we stopped at was unlike any I'd ever seen. It had walls of trees, flowering vines, shrubs, and a roof of blue sky. It was like walking into nature's womb, a tapestry of glorious colors, heady scents, and serene sounds. The name of the nursery was Malama Nina, which means Nature's Nursery, and the owner was a man named Keona Kalua." Mr. Pepper smiled at the memory. "We had an instant connection, Keona and I. It seemed as if we'd known each other for years. As he gave us a tour of the nursery, I asked why he'd built it without walls and a roof. He said Hawaii *was* the perfect nursery—nature's nursery. It had the perfect temperature, the perfect amount of sun, and the perfect amount of rain. Everything needed to grow beautiful gardens.

"While Keona and I were talking, Vivi found a small pond full of lotus blossoms. She was so taken by them, she wanted me to buy her a lei of pink lotus instead of ilimas." He shrugged his lips. "It wasn't the lei of love, but it's what she wanted. Danny took this picture that day."

"Did she like Hanauma Bay and the bluffs?"

Mr. Pepper shook his head. "She wasn't nearly as impressed with them as I was, especially when I said I wanted to buy the land and build a house for the two of us. All she said was, 'That's crazy, Billy. Why would you want to live in the middle of the ocean?'"

Nettie hadn't realized Mr. Pepper's nickname was Billy until that moment, but it seemed to fit his lighter side.

"I should have known something was off, but when you're in love, you see what you want to see. The following Saturday, Danny and I put Vivi on a plane home. When I kissed her goodbye, she put a letter in my pocket and told me not to read it until I got back to the base. I foolishly thought it was a love letter. Turns out, it was a Dear John letter. Her engagement ring was in the envelope."

"That must have been heartbreaking."

"I was so upset I could hardly think straight. Danny couldn't believe his sister would do such a thing. We gave Vivi enough time to get home, then I called her. She refused to talk with me, so Danny got on the phone. They had a terrible fight. He was furious about the way she'd broken the engagement. He told her I deserved better, and that if she didn't love me, she should have had the courage to tell me to my face. The last thing he said to her was, 'God forgive you.'"

Mr. Pepper's eyes glistened.

Nettie stood to lay the picture on the bench and to give Mr. Pepper time to catch his breath.

"Danny stayed with me all night. By morning, he'd helped me begin to imagine a future without Vivi."

"Just like Naupaka," Nettie said.

"Yes, just like Naupaka. And like you said that day at the nursery, if you don't like your reality, build a new one. I did just that. I decided my future belonged on the bluffs above Hanauma Bay. Danny volunteered to cover my shift at the radar building so I could go back to the nursery to see if Keona knew who owned the land.

"As it turned out, the bluffs had been in Keona's family for generations. He said real estate developers had been trying to buy the land for years to build a vacation resort. He'd been able to resist their offers until the war and tension in the Pacific stopped tourists from coming to the island. Keona's financial situation had become so grim that he had to let his employees go and was having trouble paying his taxes. I had money my parents left me, so I asked Keona if he would sell the land to me if I promised never to build a resort on it. That way, he'd have money to pay his taxes and keep his nursery going. He liked the idea but wanted time to think about it."

Mr. Pepper's face went to a dark place.

"I was on my way back to Pearl Harbor when the Japanese attacked."

He looked up, seeing something Nettie couldn't.

"The sky was full of planes. Hundreds of them, wave after wave. By the time I reached the base, bombs were exploding everywhere. The whole waterfront was on fire. In the bay, ships were split in pieces and spewing orange and blue flames and black smoke as far as I could see. *The Arizona* exploded in a massive fireball in front of me. It sank so fast men were jumping into burning water to try to escape. Sailors and civilians were screaming, running everywhere, one direction then another, but there was no safe place to go. The bombs just kept coming. Stacks of fuel barrels and ammo dumps were exploding all over the base. Ash and fiery debris fell like rain, burning my skin and eyes. The air was so thick with smoke and the smell of burning oil I could hardly breathe."

Mr. Pepper had gone so deep into the memory, his eyes glassed over.

"Anti-aircraft guns were blasting nonstop, the noise was deafening. But they were too little too late. I was a hundred yards away from the building where Danny and I worked when the bomb hit."

Mr. Pepper rubbed the ring over and over.

"During the attack, the Japanese used armor-piercing bombs with delayed fuses. Ones that didn't detonate on impact. They wanted the explosives to penetrate their targets before detonating, to cause the most damage. The men and women in the building who survived the initial hit knew the terror of what was about to happen. When the building exploded, the blast knocked me to the ground and sent shrapnel flying everywhere. When I could finally lift my head, our building was nothing more than a crater full of splintered, burning wood."

Mr. Pepper swallowed and tried to sit straighter.

"I managed to get to the corner of the building where Danny's and my office had been—where Danny would have been working. Bodies—pieces of bodies—were embedded among the debris. I could see Danny under the rubble, his chest was impaled with jagged pieces of wood. His eyes opened when I yelled his name, but by the time I could clear enough debris to get to him, he was gone."

Mr. Pepper wiped his eyes with his sleeve, his voice tormented. "I blamed myself then, as I do now. Not a day goes by that I don't replay that morning from hell in my head. Only in my version, I'm the one who dies." He looked at Nettie, his eyes drowning in sorrow. "I know it's not logical— this self-blame. No one suspected the Japanese were coming, even those of us working with the new radar system. It was supposed to be just another day in paradise. And in the blink of an eye, it all changed. Danny and thousands of others died horrible deaths that day while I got to live."

Nettie stayed still, listening the best solace she could offer.

"I stayed with Danny for hours, unwilling to leave him in the chaos after the bombing. When I finally found someone to take care of his body, I took his signet ring and put it in my pocket. His parents had given him the ring the day he graduated from college, and I wanted to make sure it got back to them. I searched all over the base for a phone that worked. I didn't want them to hear about Danny in a military telegram. They were devastated. When I told them Danny had been covering for me when the bomb hit, Vivi became hysterical. She blamed me for his death, even called me a murderer. She screamed over and over that it should have been me, then slammed the phone down. We've not spoken since." Mr. Pepper looked at his hand. "After that call, I put Danny's ring on my finger and never took it off. It's a constant reminder that my life needs to give meaning to his."

Mr. Pepper glanced away, as if trying to silence the voices in his head. Taking a stilted breath, he continued. "After the war, Hawaii became my home. My parents were gone, Danny was gone, and Vivi had erased me from her life. Keona sold me the land above Hanauma Bay, and during the process we became good friends. Whenever the navy let me have a day off, I'd help him around the nursery. He was a patient teacher, and I was an eager student. He once told me that flowers were God's respite for the suffering, and that even when their beauty faded, their dust promised a future. Keona's friendship saved my sanity and his gardens helped me put the pieces of my life back together."

"Thank goodness you found him," Nettie said softly.

"When the war ended, we formed a partnership. Keona managed the nursery and I managed the business side of things. The economy took off again and in a matter of years, we were not only solvent, but had expanded the original nursery and built a second one on the other side of the island.

Within a decade we had nurseries on all of the major islands and had become one of the largest exporters of tropical plants and flowers in the world. I finally built my house on the bluffs, and Keona and I surrounded it with gardens."

Mr. Pepper studied the ring again. "Now you know my story. And you know why I was so anxious to get the ring back the night I met you."

Nettie gave him an understanding nod.

"The time has come to return the ring to Danny's family, and I need your help to make that happen."

"Are his parents still living?" Nettie asked.

"No, but Vivi is." The lines in Mr. Pepper's face deepened.

"Do you still love her?"

"There you go being nosy again," he replied with a smile. "I love what might have been—the Vivi of before. What I do now I do for Danny. It's time for his ring to go home."

"Do you want me to take it to her?"

"No. I want you to find her and bring her to this garden, so I can return it myself."

"Does she live near here?"

"Yes, very close, which is why I chose to come to this hospital." He handed Nettie the picture. "Show her this. Tell her I have something important to give her."

"Do you want me to tell her about the ring?"

"No. I want to do that. Tell her I'll be waiting right here a week from today at 9:00 p.m."

"Why then?" Nettie asked, puzzled by the delay.

"Because I want the garden to be finished. Keona says the lotus blossoms will be in full bloom by then, and the new, hybrid Naupaka tree, the one we named Hope, will have arrived. Keona is going to plant it here, next to the trellis."

"Are you sure you want to meet her at night?"

He nodded. "There are too many people around during the day. I want to talk with Vivi privately. Besides, the garden is stunning at night." He fingered a nearby leaf. "I tried to meet with her the day I arrived from Hawaii. I called her from the airport, but she hung up on me. I rented a car and drove to her house, but she slammed the door the moment she recognized me. I was going to wait to see if she'd open it again, but the chest pain became too intense, and the nitroglycerin wasn't helping. That's the night I came to the hospital. I've tried reaching out to her many times since I arrived, but she never responds. Every time the door to my hospital room opened, I had a split second of hope that it might be her. It never was." He sighed. "I want to try one last time, for Danny—and for me. Maybe she'll come if someone else asks. Maybe the idea of coming to the garden, this healing place, will make a difference."

That's why he built the garden—it's for her. Nettie had no idea what it would take to get this woman here, but she had to try. "I'll do my best."

"If she doesn't come, or if I die before then, I'd like you to make sure she gets the ring and my Bible with the letter inside."

"Of course."

"Thank you," Mr. Pepper said. "She should be easy to locate, she works here."

A gentle breeze stirred the garden, enveloping them in the faint scent of budding lotus.

Nettie straightened as she recognized the smell, her mind racing to a nauseating conclusion.

"She's a nurse," he continued. "Her nickname is Vivi, but her full name now is Genevieve Woods."

ALREADY WORRIED ABOUT ANDY, Mr. Pepper's request made Nettie's restless night worse. Not only did she have to deal with the fact Genevieve Woods was his Vivi, she had no idea how to get the woman who hated them both to the garden at the designated time.

Nettie and Win mulled things over as they walked to NAF office the next morning but came up with no viable options.

"Good morning, girls," Mrs. Anderson said.

"Morning, Mrs. A," they replied.

Paul gave Win a quick kiss as he shuffled boxes.

"Things are hopping," Laura said. "We're sending out double what we sent last week."

Grateful for the diversion, Nettie busied herself repacking big boxes as smaller, personalized packages. By noon, they'd already made two trips to the post office and would need to make a third trip before the work was done.

"If this keeps up, we're going to need a bigger cart," Win said.

Paul nodded. "All the media coverage and PAC activity across the country is paying off big time. The NAF Board just made their first round of presidential and senate campaign contributions."

"Thanks to Colonel Bell, even the Pentagon is coming around," Laura added. "Since he's gotten involved, Mom gets weekly MIA, POW, and KIA status updates. He's turned out to be a good guy."

As they were loading the last of the packages and donation requests in the cart, the bells over the front door tinkled.

"Good morning. May I help you?" Mrs. Anderson asked.

"Yes. I came to see Nettie. I understand she volunteers here on Saturday mornings."

Recognizing the woman's voice, Nettie's mind and body went into slow motion as she moved toward the breezeway. Win followed close behind.

Andy's mother stood in the middle of the front office, her face bearing heartbreaking news.

Mrs. Stockton wrapped her arms around Nettie. "Our Andy is missing in action."

Chapter 16

ANDY

Fuzzy, dust-filled light filtering through the slatted ceiling made Andy squint. Pain at a level he'd never known burned through his right chest. His right shoulder felt as if it were going to explode and he could barely feel his right hand. His neck and back ached from being propped against what felt like burlap sacks. Grateful not to be dead, he tried to clear his head. Who had captured him? The NVA, the VC? The phrase "KIAs don't talk, POWs do" floated through his foggy thoughts. He had to protect the mission. He had to keep Trai's defection a secret. Could he withstand the additional pain that would come with torture? Did he have the courage to do what he might have to do to keep from talking? He thought of Nettie.

"Don't even think about it," she'd say. "You promised to come back to me. I'm counting on it." Andy tried to sit up. *I'm not going to die, not now, not like this.*

Cool, gentle hands pushed him back down. "Lie still, Lieutenant. And keep your voice low," Bien whispered.

Relief coursed through Andy as Bien knelt close. Next to her sat a small, three-legged footstool with rolls of torn cloth bandages and a wooden tray piled high with different types of leaves.

"Moretti?" he asked hoarsely, denying what he already knew.

"I could not save your friend, Lieutenant."

Andy closed his eyes, but a rogue tear escaped.

"I'm sorry."

"Where is he? Did the VC take him?" Andy asked, unable to suppress visions of the VC dragging Moretti's body through the village, making an example of him to intimidate anyone who dared to speak or act against them.

"I don't know. We left his body at the clearing in hopes the VC would think he was the only one left behind and not come looking for you."

Andy said a quick prayer that his men had been able to come back for Moretti. He knew they'd try. Opening his eyes again, he realized what Bien had said. "Who's we?"

"Me and the couple who live here, Mai and Chi Phan."

"How did you—"

"First things first. I need you to drink." Bien helped him lift his head enough to get the cup to his lips.

The dryness in his mouth and throat eased as he drained the cup of cool, sweet-scented water. "More," he gasped. "Please."

"Slowly, Lieutenant. We want it to stay down." Bien refilled the cup from a wooden pitcher on the reed-covered floor.

Sipping his second cup, Andy leaned back and waited for the spike in pain to subside.

"I need to change your dressings, Lieutenant."

"Wait. My shirt, my things?"

"Looking for this?" Bien smiled and handed him the picture from his pocket. "Nettie is very pretty. She has kind eyes."

"How did you know her name?"

Bien smiled. "You've been calling for her for the past three days. Did you know her name is a gift? It can only be said with a smile."

"I never thought about it like that, but you're right. She chooses to be happy even when there is little reason to be."

"That says a lot about her and you."

Bien removed the blood-soaked bandages and leaves from his throbbing shoulder and chest and dropped them in a nearby bucket. "You've lost a lot of blood from the four bullet wounds in your chest and shoulder. We were able to remove two of the bullets, but the others are too deep and too close to your lung." Gathering fresh leaves from the bamboo tray, she tore them into small pieces, then sprinkled them in and over Andy's wounds. "This is a mix of cordoncillo leaves, which will help ease your pain, tawari tree bark shavings which help prevent infection, and lotus seeds which will restore your sức sống."

"Restore my what?" Andy asked.

"Sức sống. It means your spirit, your energy, your life's song."

"So, it doesn't help me sing any better?" Andy said, managing a little humor. "I can't sing a lick."

Bien chuckled. "In a way it does. We all are born with a song. Our spirit, our life's force is what enables us to sing it."

"Does it work?" Andy asked, hoping his song was strong enough to get him home.

"I believe most legends are based in some element of truth." She redressed his wounds and propped his arm on a bag of rice, keeping it above the level of his heart.

"Bien, why did you follow Moretti and me? You didn't have to. Trai was free. Staying behind doesn't serve your cause or the greater good."

"You and Moretti risked your lives to save my brother, me, and the rest of your men. There is no greater good than that." Bien rerolled the extra bandages. "I lost the love of my life to this soulless enemy. I want you to make it home to yours."

Andy noted the determination in her voice. "Thank you, Bien."

She helped him take another drink.

"I'm surprised my squad didn't stop you."

Bien refilled the cup. "Your friend with sun-colored hair tried. When I explained I had ways and means of helping you survive that the military did not, he let me go. I reached you at the same time as the last VC. He was so eager to kill you he never heard me come up behind him. I cut his throat."

Andy remembered the flash of a knife. "The area had to be crawling with VC and NVA by then. How did you get us out of there?"

"I stuffed a brown belt into your shirt to help stop the bleeding, then smeared blood on Moretti's knife and placed it near his hand. I pulled you to the tunnel where the VC had been hiding and pushed you in. I covered our tracks as best I could, then backed into the tunnel and pulled brush over the entrance. We hid there until the NVA search parties had come and gone."

Andy's eyes widened at her courage. "Quick thinking."

Bien gave him a wry smile. "The NVA does little by stealth, and they don't hide underground. I could hear them coming and knew they would not think of looking for a tunnel. We were lucky you were unconscious and didn't make a sound or we'd both be dead. They left the VC where they lay and continued searching for their missing commander."

"How did we get here?" Andy asked.

"When I was sure the search parties were gone and your bleeding had stopped, I left you in the tunnel and came to Mai and Chi for help. Mai is one of our observers, and their farm is near the clearing. We wrapped you in a blanket and put you on the back of their water buffalo. To the undiscerning eye, the animal's hoof prints weren't distinguishable from the cow prints all around the clearing, so the only tracks we had to erase were ours. We knew the VC and NVA would search the area again at daylight and possibly for days to come, so Mai and Chi hid us here, under their storage hut."

Andy looked around at the earthen walls. "They've hidden others here?"

"Yes." Bien gave him a spoonful of a rich broth. "The VC murdered Mai and Chi's twelve-year-old son because he refused to go with them. Since then, many children and adults have found refuge here until they could be moved safely to the south."

"Did you say we've been here three days?"

"Yes. There's been too much enemy activity to move you."

Andy's heart sank. The longer he stayed here the greater the danger for Bien, Mai, and Chi. Plus, the army would have already reported him as missing in action, which meant Nettie and his mom were going through hell. He tried to sit. "We have to get out of here." Shooting pain blurred his vision and caused a swell of nausea.

Bien helped him lay back. "You're too weak to walk, but we've worked out another plan."

"What? How?"

"If we can get more fluids in you and if we can get you up the ladder, we're going to take you back to Camp Eagle by wagon. With luck, we'll leave before sunrise tomorrow."

BIEN AND MAI PULLED ANDY's good arm from above and Chi pushed him from behind as Andy forced his legs to bend and move from one rung of the ladder to the next. Dizzy and weak, he leaned on the shorter people to walk the few steps to an old, big-wheeled wagon. Attached to the front was a feeble-looking water buffalo with loose bowels. Andy breathed through his mouth to avoid the worst of the stench as Bien, Mai, and Chi helped him into the wagon. He remembered what Bien had said about observers using old and sickly buffalos as a deterrent to the VC stealing their wagons. *I hope it works.*

Bien gave him a long drink of water, then positioned him on the hard planks toward the front. Using a bag of tea as a pillow, they disguised his form by surrounding him with bags of rice and tea. Bien slid a smooth-handled knife into Andy's good hand. "This was my husband's. You may need it." She then covered him from neck to toe with lightly filled bags of tea, leaving enough space around his face for him to see and breathe. Even so, dust from the bags clogged his mouth and nose. The wagon's hard floor intensified the throbbing in his shoulder and chest, but with luck, nosy villagers and the enemy would see nothing more than two farm women on their way to market.

Underneath the cloth bandages, Bien had covered Andy's wounds with a fresh layer of medicinal leaves. He knew the beneficial effects would not last all the way to Camp Eagle, should they be lucky enough to get there.

Chi opened the doors of the storage hut as Mai climbed on the wagon's seat and grabbed the reins. Dressed in one of Mai's skirts and blouses, Bien tied a peasant's scarf over her head and wrapped it around her lower face and neck. She couldn't take a chance on being recognized by her scars. Lurching forward into the somewhat cool predawn, the cart creaked and moaned with each clop of the water buffalo's hooves. Painful minutes stretched into mind-numbing hours as the wagon jostled along dusty, rutted roads, stopping only long enough to water the buffalo or for the women to sell tea to an insistent passerby. Bien had planned for such stops by placing salable bags of rice and tea in the very back of the wagon, away from Andy. When they reached deserted sections of road, Bien climbed in the back to give Andy water and broth.

While the predawn hours had been tolerable, the searing heat of the afternoon cooked Andy from the outside in. His lips were cracked and bleeding, and he had no saliva to ease his parched throat. Memories were his only escape. He and Nettie swam in the cool, blue waters of Sweet Briar Lake, waded in the rocky shallows of the James River, body surfed at Sandbridge Beach, and hiked the shady paths along the Blue Ridge. They walked the tree-lined streets of Amherst, had a cookout in his mother's backyard, and watched lightning bugs flit among the trees while eating homemade strawberry ice cream.

By evening, memories of Moretti filled Andy's thoughts, his feistiness, smiling face, corny jokes, sharp eye, quick wit, creative cooking, and hard-to-explain loyalty.

Nighttime brought some relief from the heat, but not from the traveling. Bien and Mai stopped in the shadows of the jungle long enough to feed, water, and rest the buffalo and give Andy water and a cup of thick mush. They then pushed on through the night. How the old animal kept going hour after hour defined beast of labor. Andy slept fitfully and by the next morning, there wasn't one part of his body that didn't ache.

On the second day, as the sun approached high noon, the swaying wagon came to an abrupt halt. Angry shouts were coming closer, fast. Mai responded over and over, her voice calm, but the shouting increased. Bien stayed silent.

Andy forced his stiff hands to find the smooth handle of the knife Bien had given him and pointed the blade up, unsure if he had the strength to use it.

The front of the wagon jerked downward as the angry voice climbed on board. An audible blow sent Mai off the wagon with a loud moan and hard thud. Andy froze as the sounds of burlap bags being sliced open moved closer to him. Within seconds, he locked eyes with an upside-down VC. Backlit by intense sunlight, the man raised his curved machete. Andy tightened his grip on the still hidden knife. His only chance would be to plunge the blade into the man's chest as he leaned over to strike.

Smirking, the man never saw Bien's ivory hairpin coming.

Bright red blood spurted from his neck as he collapsed in slow motion across Andy, his feet still draping the seat.

Bien quickly pulled the man off Andy, then jumped to the ground to check on Mai. Andy could hear them talking in hushed tones. A few minutes later they both climbed into the back of the wagon.

"Bien," Andy called, his hand still gripping the knife. "VC rarely work alone. Make sure there aren't others."

"We already did. There are no more. We think he was scouting American activity going in and out of Camp Eagle." Bien cleaned her hairpin on the VC's shirt, twisted her hair back into a bun, and secured it with the pin. Grabbing the dead man's arms and legs, she and Mai pushed him over the side. Jumping to the ground, they dragged the body off the road and into the jungle. When the women returned, Andy heard leaves rustle as they disguised their tracks and covered the blood.

Climbing back onto the wagon, Mai covered the bloody gash on the side of her head with what looked like the VC's cloth belt while Bien flipped bags over to hide his blood. She then washed Andy's face.

"That's the second time you saved my life, Bien. Thank you."

"Our life songs crossed, Andy," she replied. "And because they did, I have my brother back. And you have Nettie. We can be thankful together."

Andy squeezed her hand. "Please tell Mai I'm grateful to her, too."

"I will, but she already knows."

"What was that guy ranting about?"

"He demanded to know why we were selling tea and rice on the road leading to the American base. He said American soldiers don't drink tea and they don't eat rice."

Andy's eye widened at the simplicity and accuracy of pattern analysis that almost got them killed.

Bien nodded. "We'll not make that mistake again. Thank goodness he was alone."

"If we're lucky enough to make it back to Camp Eagle, I need to be sitting up front so the sentries can see me. Otherwise, they may think you and Mai are carrying weapons."

"We'll move you up when we get closer. When it's safer."

By late afternoon, Bien pulled the bags away from Andy's face.

"We are near the camp. It's time to get you up front." He gave a slight nod, dreading the spike in pain moving would bring.

Bien gave him a long drink of water, then she and Mai pulled the rest of the bags out of the way. Linking their arms behind Andy's back and being careful of his injured shoulder, they lifted him to a sitting position. His damaged muscles screamed, but he refused to give them voice.

"Can you stand?" Bien asked.

"Yes," Andy replied, taking deep breaths through his mouth. The little bit of sweat he had left ran down his temples in thick, rust-colored drops.

"Once you're on your feet and steady, back up two steps and sit on the seat," Bien said. "We'll swing your legs around."

"Okay. Let's go."

Andy's head swirled as the women helped him to his feet and onto the wagon seat. Bien swung his legs toward the front, then positioned herself at his back to help him stay upright. With a one-handed, white-knuckle grip on the plank seat, Andy focused on scanning the sides of the road for signs of the enemy. Mai climbed next to him, patted his hand, then slapped the reins on the buffalo's back. Growing circles of bright red spread across Andy's bandages, the exertion opening his wounds. A half-mile later, wooden barriers blocked the road as sentry dogs barked and pulled frantically against their MP handlers. A half dozen men with M16s aimed and ready approached the wagon.

Andy raised his good arm as they came closer. "Stand down fellows. I'm Lieutenant Andy Stockton, 101st 2nd 502nd. I'm wounded. These women saved my life."

Chapter 17

NETTIE

Nettie's life blurred the moment Andy went MIA. Every phone call, every knock on the door caused surges in her battle between hope and despair. Andy's mother had taken her anguish home, Nettie's family had come and gone, the Andersons were staying in touch with Colonel Bell, TK had given her as much time off as she needed, and Win stayed close. Cloaked in heartbreak, the only thing Nettie could do to help Andy was pray. On her knees, pacing, moving from chair to sofa to chair, and flat on her back staring at the ceiling, she reached out to God.

In the wee hours of another sleepless night, Nettie leaned against her bedroom window gazing into a smokey-moon sky. "Lord, please wrap Andy in your loving arms. If he's hurt, ease his pain. If he needs a friend, please send one. If he's lost, help him find his way home. If he's already with you, hold us both close. And Lord, please bring Mr. Anderson home to his family. They've dealt with this pain for so long. Please give them respite." Lastly, Nettie prayed for her broken heart and trampled spirit. Sending her worries upward helped loosen the feelings of injustice and anger, but the sense of loss would not yield, perhaps it never would.

"One step at a time, one day at a time," Andy had said, and Win had said, and Laura had said. "Please Lord, help me find my footing again so I can take that step."

Her weary mind moved to Mr. Pepper. He'd lived a lifetime without the love of his life, mired in unwarranted guilt and regret. Now, his time was short and he wanted Nettie's help to leave this earth in peace. She pulled Andy's shirt snugly around her. If the situation were reversed, Andy wouldn't be walking around in a daze. He'd be keeping his promise. It was time for her to do the same. *Hang on just a little while longer, Mr. Pepper.*

Being careful not to wake Win, Nettie found the phone book and thumbed through the names beginning with W. The phone company had finally become progressive enough to list wives' names along with their husbands', so finding Genevieve Woods's address wasn't a problem. Putting the address in her bag, she pulled the old wing chair close to the window, curled up under an afghan her mother had knitted, and waited for sunrise.

"ARE YOU SURE ABOUT THIS?" Win asked.

"Do I want to be face-to-face with that woman again? No. But it's the only way I can keep my promise. I can't help Andy, but I can try to help Mr. Pepper." The clock on the stove said 9:00 a.m. With luck, Mr. Woods would be at work and Mrs. Woods would still be home since she worked evenings.

"Are you sure you don't want me to go with you?" Win asked as they walked to the door.

"I'm sure. If this goes wrong, I don't want you caught up in it." She gave Win a quick hug.

Finding the right street, Nettie tracked house numbers until she located Mrs. Woods's. Pulling to the curb, she studied the austere brick house with its manicured lawn and sculpted shrubs. The garage doors were closed, so there was no way to know how many cars it held. Hoping for the best, Nettie grabbed Mr. Pepper's framed picture and headed for the front door. She straightened her shoulders as the door chimes echoed through the house.

The sheer curtains covering a panel of sidelights moved. Seconds later, an angry Mrs. Woods jerked the door open. Dressed in a light green robe and matching slippers, her hair pushed back with a cloth headband, she appeared less menacing than when in uniform. The lines around her eyes and mouth were more prominent without her usual makeup. "How dare you come to my home!"

"I need to talk with you, ma'am." Nettie handed her the picture.

Mrs. Woods stared at the image. A myriad of emotions flashed across her eyes, settling somewhere between furious and tortured.

"He wants to see you. He has something to give you."

Mrs. Woods pushed the picture back into Nettie's hands. "That man knows I have no desire to see him. Don't ever come to my house again."

Nettie put her hand up to stop the door from slamming shut. "Mrs. Woods, you know as well as I do, Mr. Pepper has very little time left. Please."

"Get off my property or I'm calling the authorities." Hands shaking, Mrs. Woods tried again to close the door.

Nettie didn't budge. "Mrs. Woods, the love of my life is missing in action in Vietnam. I may never see him again. You're the love of this man's life, and he's waited a lifetime to see you. Please."

"The love of my life isn't lying around some fancied-up hospital room waiting to die, he lives right here."

The cruelty of the woman's words burned. "Really? So, that's why you sneak around the hospital in the dark with another man?"

"How dare you!"

"Billy is dying. You have a shared history. The picture shows you were at least friends once. Won't you please give him a few minutes of your time?"

"He killed my brother."

"No, he didn't. You know he didn't. You've known it for over thirty years."

Mrs. Woods glared at her. "Get off my property, now!"

"In heaven's name, please. Whatever the reason for your anger, won't you forgive him and come."

Mrs. Woods pushed the door closed, her eyes glistening. Nettie laid her forehead against the painted wood. "Please. Please come to the garden tonight at nine. He'll be there. He has something important to give you."

BACK AT HOME, NETTIE FORCED herself to stay busy—cleaning, washing clothes, ironing, cooking, studying—anything to keep the stomach-churning angst for Andy and the coldness of the encounter with Mrs. Woods at bay. She knew she'd crossed a line, but it was one she didn't regret crossing. She had to try.

At sunset, Nettie said goodbye to Win and drove to the Godfrey Center. Her heart sank when she realized Mrs. Henry wasn't on duty. Mrs. Franks, the relief charge nurse, sat at the counter in the nurses' station. This woman didn't come close to having Mrs. Henry's empathy, understanding, or energy. Mr. Pepper had become so weak, Nettie knew she'd need help getting him to the garden.

"Hi, Mrs. Franks," Nettie said from the doorway. "I'm here to take Mr. Pepper to the garden. It's a beautiful night. Do you have time to help me get him up?"

Mrs. Franks barely glanced at Nettie before turning her attention back to the stack of charts in front of her. "No. I do not. Besides, it's too late and he's too ill to get out of bed."

"Yes, ma'am. But he asked to go."

"Patients don't dictate their care," she replied dryly, closing one chart and reaching for another.

"Ma'am, Mr. Pepper knows how ill he is. He wants to go. Please, it's important. I'll be with him, and we won't stay long."

Mrs. Franks swiveled her chair toward Nettie.

"Young lady, what part of no did you not understand? Now good night."

Nettie left the station under the charge nurse's irritated stare. Determined to get Mr. Pepper to his garden, she scrambled to think of a way. Passing the open door to the linen closet gave her an idea. Hurrying through the tunnel to the main hospital, she headed to the laundry room where Dougie dutifully went back and forth filling tall, metal carts with stiff, white sheets, pillowcases, and bedspreads, all neatly folded and smelling of industrial-strength detergent.

"Hey, Dougie."

"Miss Nettie, what are you doing down here?"

Scanning the room to make sure they were alone, Nettie whispered. "I need your help."

PUSHING AN EMPTY WHEELCHAIR, Nettie followed Dougie and his tall silver cart through the tunnel toward the Godfrey Center. As he approached the nurses' station, she hid behind the cart and remained there as he turned the cart toward the north hall. Dougie waved and smiled at Mrs. Franks, then pushed the cart to the door of the linen closet and angled it to obstruct her view. Scurrying down the hall with the wheelchair, Nettie and Dougie entered Mr. Pepper's room without knocking. He lay on his back, eyes closed, his skin damp and deathly white. An open bottle of nitroglycerin tablets lay on the bedside stand. Gently placing her hand on his shoulder, Nettie called his name.

Mr. Pepper's eyes fluttered open. "Nettie, thank God," he whispered. "My time is close. Is she coming?"

Nettie hesitated, but he had to know. "No, sir, I don't think so. Whatever her reasons for not wanting to see you before are still there. I told her you'd be in the garden at nine. Maybe she'll reconsider."

"She saw the picture?"

"Yes, sir." Nettie returned the picture to his bedside stand.

"What did she say?"

"Nothing. But she had tears in her eyes."

Mr. Pepper's expression turned to one of resignation. "Nettie, I don't want to die in this room, and I don't want to die in that wheelchair. Please take me to the garden."

It unnerved her that he spoke of imminent death, but she'd seen it before. Dying people had a way of hanging on when they had something important to do and then letting go when it was over. She quickly explained that Mrs. Franks was on duty and did not want him out of bed. "But we're going anyway. Dougie is going to help us."

"Hey, Mr. Pepper." Dougie stepped forward to squeeze his friend's hand.

"Thank you."

Nettie positioned the wheelchair next to the bed. "Do you want to take the nitroglycerin tablets?"

He shook his head. "No more."

Moving Mr. Pepper to a sitting position and swinging his legs over the side of the bed made him short of breath. His physical decline since the second bout of congestive failure had been dramatic. Nettie slid his arms into his silk robe, tied the belt, then knelt to work his swollen feet into his slippers.

"Do you think you can stand?" she asked.

"With help."

Motioning for Dougie to follow her lead, Nettie stood at Mr. Pepper's side, put her foot in front of his so he wouldn't slide, then put one hand under his shoulder and the other on the back of his belt. "We stand on three, pivot toward Dougie, then sit," she said. "Ready?"

Both men nodded.

"Okay. One, two, three."

Nettie expected Mr. Pepper to be weak, but not dead weight. She and Dougie struggled but managed to get him up, turned, and eased into the wheelchair. Grateful he wasn't in a heap on the floor, Nettie put his feet on the metal rests, unlocked the wheels, and turned the wheelchair toward the door.

"Wait," Mr. Pepper said weakly, pointing to his bedside stand.

Nettie put his Bible and the framed picture in his lap. The clock said 8:58 p.m. This was it—Mrs. Woods's last chance. Nothing short of a miracle would change the woman's mind. But miracles happened, and Mr. Pepper deserved a shot at one.

"Okay," she warned. "Nobody talks until we're in the garden. Mr. Pepper and I will stay behind the cart until we reach the linen closet on the south hall. Dougie, angle the cart like you did on this side. Maybe Mrs. Franks will have her nose stuck in charts and won't notice how long the cart is there."

"Got it," Dougie said.

Nettie took a deep breath, then motioned for Dougie to open the door. "Let's go."

Mrs. Franks was on the phone as the cart and hidden wheelchair eased passed the station, the entrance to the tunnel, and down the south hall. Reaching the linen closet, Dougie angled the cart to block her view, then led the way as Nettie scurried Mr. Pepper's wheelchair toward the exit. Flipping on the accent lights in the garden, they eased the wheelchair out the door, and along the sandstone path. Reaching the lotus pond, they lifted Mr. Pepper to the bench, the move taking whatever energy he had left. Somewhere in the distance, a robin and whip-poor-will called.

"Thank you, Dougie," Nettie said. "We couldn't have done it without you. Now, take the cart and get back to the laundry room before Mrs. Franks figures out what's going on."

"Won't you need help getting him back inside?"

"I don't know how long we'll be, plus I don't want to take any more chances with you getting in trouble. Mrs. Franks refused to help me get him here, but she can't refuse to help me get him back."

Dougie looked doubtful. "But you'll get in trouble."

"Right now, that's the least of my worries. Now hurry."

With tears in his eyes, Dougie gave Mr. Pepper a hug. "I'll miss you—and our talks."

"Be happy, Dougie," Mr. Pepper whispered.

Nettie moved the wheelchair behind the bench as Dougie disappeared inside.

"I've put you through a lot these last months, Nettie," Mr. Pepper whispered. "I'm sorry."

"Don't be. I wanted to be here. I still do."

"I'm so grateful our paths crossed." He gave her a weak smile. "This time, I'm ready."

He turned half-mast eyes to the path, still looking for someone who wasn't coming.

There was nothing to say as his last flicker of hope went out.

He grimaced with pain. "Nettie, the ring."

"Yes, sir. I'll take it to her."

"The letter."

"Yes, sir. The one in your Bible. I'll see that she gets it."

"Thank you," he whispered. "For everything."

"I should be thanking you, Mr. Pepper. You're a wonderful teacher."

Mr. Pepper's shoulders drew in as the pain in his chest hit harder and lasted longer. His eyes turned glassy and his expression became disoriented as the weakening beats of his heart failed to deliver enough oxygen to his mind.

Nettie fought back tears as her friend's life slipped farther and farther away. She'd been with people in the ER as they died, watched as their eyes and minds went places she could not see. But this time, it was her friend who was leaving. Helplessness crushed her already broken heart.

Mr. Pepper's unfocused gaze came to rest on the glittering pond. "Gardens—magical," he mumbled. "Happiness—waits there." His eyes closed, his chest barely moving.

Nettie leaned over and whispered in his ear. "You're right, Billy. Happiness waits in the garden."

Mr. Pepper struggled to open his eyes, the light behind them almost out. His unseeing gaze landed on her. "Vivi? Vivi is that you?"

"Yes, Billy, I'm here." Nettie squeezed his hand.

"So glad—been—so long." Tears spilled from his setting-sun eyes. "Danny—forgive me."

"I'm the one who needs to be forgiven, Billy. War caused Danny's death, not you. I was wrong to blame you for so long."

"The baby. I forgive you."

Nettie's eyes widened. *Baby? Vivi was pregnant when she broke their engagement?*

"I love you, Vivi," his words barely audible.

"I love you too, Billy."

Mr. Pepper's eyes closed, the lines in his face smoothed, and his last breath eased from his lips.

As his soul went home, Nettie squeezed his hand, holding on against a tsunami of sadness. A soft breeze stirred the leaves surrounding them, the lush aroma of the garden enveloping Nettie like a hug.

Voices and footsteps in the distance broke through her swirling grief. Bright beams of light moved back and forth across the garden as two security guards hurried down the path.

The consequences of her choices were about to begin. Pulling herself together, Nettie quickly slipped the signet ring off Mr. Pepper's finger and into her pocket and slid his Bible onto her lap. Brushing tears from her cheeks, she shielded her eyes against the security guards' bright flashlights.

"Ma'am," one of the guards said, "Mrs. Franks reported that this patient was taken from the hospital without permission."

"His name is Mr. Pepper, and I had his permission. He asked me to bring him here."

The security guard nudged Mr. Pepper's shoulder. "Sir, it's awfully late for you to be—" The guard leaned down, looked at Mr. Pepper, then at Nettie. "Is he asleep?"

Nettie shook her head.

The guard jumped back. "You mean he's dead? You're sitting out here with a dead man?"

"No, I was sitting here with a man who was dying. He just completed his journey."

Chapter 18

ANDY

The MPs guarding the road to Camp Eagle quickly overcame their shock at seeing a bloodied and weak officer sitting atop an old wagon with two Vietnamese women. One MP radioed for help, while two others helped Mai guide the wagon behind the protective barrier. Within minutes a military ambulance arrived with two corpsmen who helped Andy to the ground. Sitting him on the vehicle's rear bumper, they started to cut the crude dressings off his shoulder and chest but stopped at the sight of the leaves and bark.

"Leave them for now," Andy said.

The corpsmen reinforced the seeping bandages with compression pads and tape as Mai turned the wagon to leave.

Standing on wobbly legs, Andy motioned for the MPs to stop her. "Bien, tell Mai to come with us. She's hurt and needs food and rest. So does the buffalo. Tell her the soldiers will take care of the animal and the wagon until she's ready to go home."

Mai nodded her gratitude as Bien translated.

Andy called to the closest MP. "Get a support detail out here to feed and water that buffalo, then move him and the wagon inside the camp. Be sure to tell them to clean all of the blood out of the back of the wagon and wash the bloody bags for her."

"But sir—"

"I didn't stutter, Corporal. Make the call." At that moment, the buffalo's loose bowel delivered an audible splat in the middle of the dirt road. Despite his pain, Andy grinned. "And see if one of the docs at the hospital can treat this animal's diarrhea. Biology is biology."

The MP looked at the old animal as if hesitant to touch it.

"Corporal, if anything bad happens to this animal or wagon, I'm holding you personally responsible. Understood?"

"Yes, sir. But how do I—"

"It's not brain surgery, Corporal, figure it out."

Once Andy, Bien, and Mai were in the ambulance and heading toward Camp Eagle, a corpsman pulled out a syringe and started cleaning Andy's good arm with an alcohol wipe.

"What's in that syringe?" Andy asked.

"Pain med."

"Not now." Andy pulled his arm away. "I need to be alert a little while longer."

"But sir—"

"No buts. Tell the driver to take me to headquarters."

"Sir, you're headed to the operating room as soon as we can get you to the hospital. These wounds look rough."

"You heard me, soldier. Headquarters." Bien needed to be reunited with her brother, if he hadn't already been shipped elsewhere, and Andy needed a favor that required a rank higher than his. Maybe Major Loring would help.

"But sir—"

Andy gave him a withering look.

"Yes, sir."

The corpsman relayed the message to the driver who relayed it to someone else inside Camp Eagle.

"Sir," the driver called over his shoulder. "The triage doc says we are to bring you straight to the hospital."

"Tell him okay, then take me to headquarters."

"Sir?"

"You heard me."

"Yes, sir."

The radio squawked loud and often as the ambulance drove past the hospital. By the time it pulled in front of headquarters, Major Loring wasn't the only one on the steps waiting for them. Colonel Clark and General West had joined him.

General West climbed into the back of the ambulance and shook Bien's hand, holding hers in both of his. She introduced him to Mai.

"You and Bien were incredibly brave," General West said. "Thank you." He looked at Bien. "After Mai's cut is taken care of, my driver will take you both to Trai. I'll join you later." Moving farther into the ambulance, he sat across from Andy.

"Sir, did we recover Luca Moretti's body?" Andy asked before the general could speak.

"Yes. Your squad did. They've been looking for you and Bien since. We just informed them you're here. The Quiet Ones are on their way to pick them up now."

"In broad daylight?"

"The NVA are gone, Lieutenant. They packed up and left the next day. Your squad watched the village from both sides as they loaded the trucks but saw nothing to indicate that you and Bien had been captured or killed. In fact, they found things at the landing zone that convinced them you all were alive. They found a VC tunnel with drag marks and blood but no body. The entrance to the tunnel was camouflaged with brush after the fact. The throat of one the VC had been cut low, as if by someone short, but they couldn't find Bien's boot prints anywhere. The knife next to Moretti wasn't the one used to kill the VC, and it had been staged next to his right hand when he was left-handed. Your squad also found deep buffalo tracks intermixed with cow tracks along the edge of the clearing. It looked as if the buffalo might have been carrying something heavy. That's quite a recon squad you have, Lieutenant."

"Yes, sir, they're very good. Sir, may I have Moretti's address in Brooklyn?"

"I'll see that you get it. Your men also retrieved this for you." The general handed Andy the copy of the New Testament he'd given Moretti.

Andy ran his thumb over the crinkled cover. "Thank you, sir."

"Now, it's past time to get you to the hospital. They're waiting."

"Sir," Andy said, "would you approve the securing of a healthy water buffalo for Mai and her husband? They risked everything to get Bien and me here, and their animal is on its last leg."

"Done."

"And, sir, one more thing. I need to call home, to let them know I'm not missing. The Comm Center won't let me—"

"Yes, they will, but you'll make the call from the hospital, understood? We'll talk more after the docs get you patched up."

"Yes, sir. Thank you."

General West stood. "No, Lieutenant, thank you."

Once Andy reached the hospital, things happened quickly. Corpsmen removed the temporary dressings and cut off what was left of his pants. They irrigated leaves and bits of bark from his wounds, then covered his chest and shoulder with green surgical towels. Using a field shower wand and liquid soap that smelled like olive oil, they scrubbed and rinsed the rest of him until every speck of dirt was gone. After taking X-rays of his chest and shoulder, one of the corpsmen tried to start an intravenous line, but the needle kept bending against Andy's tense arm.

"Lieutenant, if you don't relax, I'll never get this line in. I need to give you something for pain before I scrub these wounds."

"No pain med until after I make a call."

"But they're holding an OR table for you, sir."

"Do what you have to do, private, but no pain med until after I make that call, understood?"

"But, sir, it's going to hurt like hell."

"Like what I've been living with the last four days hasn't hurt like hell?"

"Yes, sir." The corpsman irrigated Andy's wounds for another five minutes, then opened a bottle of orange antiseptic and a sterile pack containing a bristled brush. "Sorry about this, sir." He gave Andy a roll of gauze to bite on and scrubbed the gaping wounds. Andy clenched his teeth and his good hand, digging his nails deep into his palm until the corpsmen finished. Flushing the wounds for another five minutes, the corpsman had just covered Andy's chest and shoulder with sterile towels when a man in green OR scrubs and a lab coat appeared with X-rays in hand.

"Lieutenant, I'm Captain Hill, one of the trauma surgeons. You're a lucky man. Those bullets tore the hell out of a lot of muscle but only partially collapsed your lung. With a little luck, we'll be able to remove the remaining two bullets, re-expand your lung, remove the debris that found its way into your wounds, and put your shoulder back together. Whatever those women packed into your wounds stanched the bleeding and kept infection away. They saved your life."

"Yes, sir."

"Now, we need to get you to the operating room."

"Captain, I need to make a phone call first."

"That's what I understand. Someone from the Comm Center will be here shortly. Make it quick, Lieutenant, you should have been on an OR table days ago."

Chapter 19

NETTIE

The immediate aftermath of Mr. Pepper's death in the garden and Nettie's role in the process lasted for hours.

"I need you to leave," Mrs. Franks insisted as Nettie helped the orderlies move Mr. Pepper's body back to his room.

"Ma'am, Mr. Pepper left explicit instructions about what needed to be done at the time of his death. Mrs. Henry put them in his chart weeks ago, so I know you've seen them."

"Yes, but what you did here tonight—"

"Mrs. Franks, I intend to follow those instructions to the letter, including the part about notifying his lawyer. Once I'm done, I'll come talk with you."

"Humph." Mrs. Franks turned and stormed out of the room.

After helping the orderlies perform post-mortem care, Nettie used the phone in Mr. Pepper's room, to call his lawyer, Jake Cooper.

"Thank you for letting us know, Nettie. We'll be on a flight to Virginia tonight. Would you remind all necessary personnel that Mr. Pepper's body is to stay at the hospital until we get there? And please let the hospital administrator know we'll need to meet with him tomorrow."

"Of course. What about Mr. Pepper's room? His things?"

"We'll have people pack up his personal belongings tomorrow. For now, please ask security to keep an eye on his room."

"Okay."

"Nettie, were you with him when he died?"

"I was."

"Did he die in the garden?"

"Yes."

"And you have his ring and Bible?"

"I do."

"Good." Jake paused. "Nettie, Mr. Pepper said it's not your nature to be sad, so try not to be now. He wanted you to be happy for him. He said for you to spend some time in the garden, and that you would know why."

Nettie could hear Mr. Pepper's voice in her head. "I will. Thank you."

"Mr. Cooper, was Mr. Pepper happy in Hawaii?"

"I think he was as happy as he could be. He was more concerned about the happiness of those around him, especially those who'd lost loved ones in the war. He did everything in his power to help them. He used to call it the 'Danny Rule.'"

Of course. "Thank you, Mr. Cooper. Have a safe trip."

Numb with loss, Nettie sat by the bed until the orderlies returned with a stretcher to take Mr. Pepper's body to the morgue. She placed her hand on his one last time. "Take good care of heaven's gardens, my friend." With his ring in her pocket and his Bible and letter in her shoulder bag, Nettie went to face Mrs. Franks.

"You intentionally disobeyed me and sneaked that dying man outside."

"Yes."

"Why?"

"Because Mr. Pepper didn't want to die in a hospital room."

"So, you took it upon yourself to ignore me and hospital policy."

"Yes."

"From what I understand from the evening supervisor, Mrs. Woods, this is not the first time you've shown contempt for this hospital's policies and its nursing leadership."

"There is no hospital policy that says you can't honor the reasonable wish of a dying man when the charge nurse and supervisor are too disinterested to care."

Mrs. Franks looked as if she'd been slapped. Nettie refused to look away.

"Well, we will see about that," the woman snapped. "I'm reporting you to the Vice President for Nursing."

THE MOON WAS SETTING WHEN Nettie made it back to the garden, the always present robin the only one left to sing. Emotionally and physically drained, she sat on the bench and stared at the stars. She longed for Andy and she missed Mr. Pepper. He had wanted to leave this life with a sense of peace, and she'd had to sneak around and pretend to be someone else to make it happen. "Lord, please forgive Mr. Pepper of his sins, known and unknown. Nourish his soul and welcome him into the beauty of your eternal gardens." Nettie searched for words. Praying for enemies wasn't always easy. "Lord, I don't understand why Mrs. Woods would do and say such mean-spirited things. And I don't understand why Mrs. Franks turned a blind eye to the last wish of a dying man. Who does that? Enter their hearts and souls, Lord. Forgive them, and forgive me for not loving them right now, because I know You do. Not their actions, but them. Please help me find my way there, too. Amen."

Nettie fumbled getting the key in her apartment door as the phone continued to ring, hope battling the fear surging in her chest. *Don't hang up!*

Sleepy-eyed, Win ran from her bedroom as Nettie threw everything to the floor and grabbed the receiver. "Hello?"

"Nettie? Honey, it's me, Andy. Over."

"Oh God." Relief took Nettie to her knees, and for a moment she forgot how to breathe.

Win sank to the floor next to her.

"Andy—I thought I'd lost you," Nettie stammered. "They told your mom you were missing—over."

"I was for a while," Andy replied, "but I'm back at Camp Eagle now. I wanted to make sure you and Mom knew I was okay. I'm so sorry you all had to go through all of this. Over."

"Are you all right? Are you hurt? Over."

"Just a little banged up. Over."

"Banged up? How? Over."

"My shoulder's hurt, that's all. I'm at the hospital now. Honey, Linda's here; she wants to talk with you. Over."

"Hey Nettie," her friend said. "I know you must be relieved beyond words. Over."

"Linda, I'm so glad you're there! Is he okay? Over."

"He has a shoulder and upper chest injury that we need to take him to the OR to repair now. And he'll need physical therapy after, but with luck, he should be up and going in a few days. Try not to worry. We're going to take good care of him. He'll be able to write to you soon, and so will I. Take care. Over."

"Thanks, Linda. Over."

Andy's voice came back on the line. "Honey, I have to go. Please call Mom for me. Over."

"Of course. I'll call her right away. Over."

"I love you, Nettie. Over."

"I love you, too, so much. I can't wait for you to be home. Bye. Over."

Win gave her a long, happy hug, then went to the kitchen to put the kettle on. This time the chamomile tea would be for celebrating. Nettie slumped against the sofa, holding onto the receiver long after the connection ended. In a matter of minutes, she'd gone from despair to ecstasy. She closed her eyes and thanked God for the sun, the moon, the stars, and Andy. Hitting the button to get a dial tone, she called Andy's mom.

Chapter 20

ANDY

Andy walked his right hand up the support pole of the makeshift physical therapy department of the MASH. Ignoring the pain, he forced his fingers an inch higher than last time. Walking them back down took as much control but hurt less. He'd started physical therapy for his shoulder as soon as he woke up from surgery, determined to make a full recovery.

"That's enough for today," Linda said, appearing in the doorway.

"Nope. Ten more."

"No can do. Overdoing it can be as bad as doing nothing at all. Besides, there's a driver outside waiting to take you to headquarters."

Andy grabbed his hat and followed Linda to the front entrance of the hospital.

Linda gave him a quick hug. "Fingers crossed this means good news. If it is, swing by before you leave. I have some things for you to take to Nettie."

At headquarters, General West, Colonel Clark, and Major Loring were waiting in the anteroom when Andy arrived.

Andy raised his right arm to salute, making it as far as his shoulder before the pain stopped him.

"Go on, Lieutenant, finish it," General West said.

Andy forced his hand to his cheek, then his forehead, holding it for barely a second before having to ease it down with his other hand.

"Good job. Glad to see the docs were right."

"Sir?"

"They said in due time, you'd be good as new."

As they entered Colonel Clark's office, Bien, Trai, and Cam rose from the sofa. Andy's chest tightened at the sight of the man whose life cost Moretti his. *What kind of man is he? Is he worth the price Moretti paid? Am I?*

Trai looked different now, a gray tunic instead of a uniform, longer hair, and a mustache and beard forming on his face, the beginning of a new identity.

"Andy," Bien said coming forward to hug him. "I'm so glad to see you."

Andy kissed both of her cheeks. "Thank you again for all you did, Bien. I will be forever grateful. Did Mai make it home all right?"

"Yes. She and her old water buffalo, plus two young ones. General West and Colonel Clark were very generous. They even arranged for a couple of undercover ARVN regulars to see that Mai and the animals got home safely. She and Chi came back two days ago to bring Cam."

Andy gave Cam a respectful nod, then turned to his former enemy, keeping his hands at his side.

Bien translated as Trai spoke. "Lieutenant, you lost a friend and risked your life to return me to my family, to the life I once had. No amount of gratitude will ever repay that debt, but I will honor the sacrifice the rest of my life."

Andy nodded but stayed quiet, not trusting his voice.

"Let's sit, shall we?" Colonel Clark moved more chairs close to the coffee table.

When everyone had been seated, Andy turned to Bien. General West and Colonel Clark would not be happy with what he was about to ask, but he needed answers. "Would you ask your brother what he did to earn his rank in the North Vietnamese Army?"

Bien looked back with understanding eyes, then translated.

"My value to the NVA from the beginning lay in the fact that I could read and write, something our father insisted Bien and I learn to do. Most NVA soldiers, then and now, cannot. I was also good at mathematics, which made me valuable to their mapping and intelligence divisions. I was trained to shoot and carried a rifle I never fired."

"Did you ever conscript children?" Andy asked.

"No. With my first intelligence command, I began recruiting boys from within the NVA ranks who I knew had been conscripted. They were taught how to read, write, and do mathematics. Not only so they could do the intelligence work, but so they could find their families and build a better life for themselves after the war."

"Is that why you chose to occupy Ru Linh as a forward intelligence base? Because your family was from there?"

"In part. My main motivation was to see if any of my family survived the raid. However, as my unit traveled the southern edge of the DMZ, I noticed women along the roads and at intersections who always seemed to have plenty of rice, tea, and vegetables to sell regardless of the season. I suspected they were monitoring the roads coming in and out of the DMZ, but I didn't tell anyone. I knew what the NVA and VC would do to the women if they knew."

Andy looked at Bien, alarmed that her network's cover might have been blown.

"Don't worry," she said. "We've already sent word to our observers to adjust the amounts of their supplies and to sell only what is in season. Trai also suggested the villagers start harvesting and selling tualang honey since it is harvested between growing seasons. He believes it will draw even the most reclusive enemy into the light."

Andy turned back to Trai. "So, how did you end up at Ru Linh?"

"I recognized Cam as one of the women selling tea. I was thrilled she was alive. It gave me hope that some of my family might have survived as well. I convinced my superiors that Ru Linh was strategically located to support reconnaissance to the south without being obvious. They did not know Ru Linh was my home." He took Cam's hand. "Coming home, being with Cam, and learning my sister was alive, I knew my decision to defect from an army I never joined was the right one. I knew the only way for me to leave without causing deadly consequences for those in my unit and the villagers in Ru Linh was for the NVA to think I'd been abducted. That's when Cam went to Saigon to find Bien. At the time, I did not know Bien's married name, and I did not know she was part of the observer network." He smiled at the two women. "They protect their network at all costs, as they should. When Cam came back with the abduction plan, she did not know my sister would be the one meeting me in the cave. We were told it would be an American soldier. When I saw Bien—when I saw her scars—"

Bien stopped translating until her voice steadied.

Trai handed Andy the carved dove Bien had shown him the day they met. "My grandfather made this for me. I kept it with me every day I was away from my family. It made me feel as if they were still with me. If possible, I would like you to give it to the family of the man who died helping me." Trai touched Bien's arm to stop her from translating, then with a heavy accent said, "Luca Moretti."

Andy's throat tightened. "Of course."

"In honor of Luca," Bien continued interpreting, "I will be joining my sister, Cam, and other freedom fighters in Saigon to help stop the enslavement of Vietnam's children."

"It's dangerous for you to stay."

"I've been given a second chance to live the life I was meant to live, Lieutenant. There is much work to be done, and it must be done here with my family."

The ache around Andy's heart eased just a little. Moretti would have liked this man.

Bien smiled as she looked from her brother to Andy. "Vietnam has been brutally occupied by foreign armies for over a thousand years. The Japanese, Chinese, French, and now the communists, occupiers who want only to exploit our resources and our people. American involvement in this war is the only military operation in Vietnam's history with the expressed goal of helping us become a free nation. We've never known the freedom you and other Americans have. But someday we will."

"Even if we leave before the job's done?" Andy asked, refusing to look at his commanding officers.

"The legacy of war is seldom known at the time fighting starts and stops," Bien said with a wry smile. "It is unveiled in the decades that follow. Thanks to the United States and her allies, the seeds of freedom have been sown here and there is no going back. It will take time to eradicate the communists, but we will. Until then, thousands of us will continue the work. Maybe one day you'll be able to return to help us celebrate our own Fourth of July."

Andy nodded. "I'll look forward to that."

Major Loring and two MPs entered the office. "General, the helicopter is ready."

Trai stood and bowed to Andy. "*Ban toi.*"

"It means my friend," Bien interpreted.

Andy rose and shook Trai's hand. "Ban toi."

Colonel Clark motioned to the MPs. "Unfortunately, our kidnapping ruse needs to continue a little while longer in case there are spies in camp. Trai will be flown to ARVN intelligence headquarters for additional debriefing, then he'll join Cam and Bien in Saigon."

The two MPs loosely handcuffed and blindfolded Trai, then escorted him from the office.

Major Loring turned to Bien and Cam. "If you ladies will come with me, your helicopter will be leaving shortly as well."

Andy shook hands with Cam. "Goodbye. I wish you and Trai the best."

Bien hugged Andy and whispered, "Be well, be happy, and live a long and love-filled life, my friend."

Andy held her an extra moment. "You, too, Bien. God be with you."

When the door closed, General West motioned for Andy to sit as he and Colonel Clark returned to their seats.

"Lieutenant, your squad's mission, while costly, was an incredible success," Colonel Clark said. "Trai has spent the better part of two weeks sharing valuable intel with us. Not just about the offensive the NVA and VC are preparing to mount, but also about their leadership, their capabilities, resources, long-term strategies, and how they handle conscripted children."

"I'm glad about that, sir. But we're not going to finish the job here, are we?" The loss of Moretti and others in the platoon and the wounding of Gus haunted Andy. Had their sacrifice and that of thousands of other soldiers been worth it?

General West's expression changed to one of contemplation. "In the traditional military sense, no. But we will win the peace. Initially, we hoped Vietnam would turn out like Korea, with a free, democratic southern half. Had it just been the North Vietnamese we were fighting, that goal would have been met years ago. They wouldn't even have an army if it weren't for conscripted children from the north and south. Things changed when Russia and China started bickering and vying for dominance in Southeast Asia, each trying to outdo the other by sending money, weapons, and a never-ending supply of men to help the NVA. As a result, we either have to end the war or risk it escalating into another world war, one where all three sides have nuclear weapons. The public's media-fueled discontent may be influencing the timeline, but it has little to do with the reasons for ending the war."

The general leaned forward. "The good news is that Bien was right when she said freedom and democracy will win the day eventually. Despite the doom and gloom surrounding the potential spread of communism, global economists, politicians, and ideologues say communism isn't sustainable, and that it's already showing fundamental flaws that will lead to its demise. They predict the Eastern Bloc, led by Germany, will fall within the next twenty years, followed by Russia, and eventually China. Bien, Trai, and Cam may not see a free Vietnam in their lifetime, but future freedom fighters will. As Bien said, the seeds of democracy have been sown here and there is no turning back."

"We've never lost a war."

"No, we haven't. In fact, this war marks a paradigm shift for our country and in war itself. The days of declared wars where battalions fight battalions are over. Undeclared wars in jungles and deserts where cultures, religions, histories, and self-serving politics combine to create insidious enemies who move fluidly across borders and anonymously through the airways will constitute the wars of the future. Our military needs to redefine itself within that context."

Major Loring entered the office and handed a small black box to Colonel Clark and another one to the General.

Colonel Clark opened his box first. "Lieutenant, according to your doctors, your injuries are such that rehabilitation is going to take longer than the remainder of your tour.

Consequently, you are leaving tomorrow for the army hospital in Japan. They'll help you rehab that shoulder, then send you home. And you'll be going home as a captain. Congratulations." The colonel snapped the captain's bars on Andy's collar.

"Thank you, sir."

General West stood and opened the second box. Inside lay two medals, a Silver Star and a Purple Heart. "They say these medals prove you were smart enough to think of a plan, stupid enough to try it, talented enough to make it work, and lucky enough to survive it or save someone else in the process. You were smart enough to alter our plan on the fly and brave enough to implement it, knowing you would likely be outnumbered. You and Moretti sacrificed yourselves to make sure Trai, Bien, and the rest of your squad made it out alive. That's the definition of courage. The mission succeeded because of you. And because it succeeded, the NVA's intelligence capabilities have been set back months if not years and Bien, Trai, and Cam are alive to continue their work. Well done, son."

"Thank you, sir."

"These medals were given to me when I was about your age. On behalf of the army, I'd like for you to have them."

"Sir, Luca Moretti deserves—"

"Yes, he certainly does. I've already sent a personal letter and medals to his mother. These are for you." The general pinned the medals on Andy's chest.

"Thank you, sir."

"Captain," said Colonel Clark, "your company commander's position is open. Any chance you'd re-up and take it?"

The day after his surgery, Andy's men told him Major Smith had been reassigned to a non-combat desk job in Saigon. Soon after, Andy had sent the banana slug bullet back to Gus along with a note saying he'd be in touch once he made it back to the States.

"I'm honored you'd ask, sir, but no."

"I understand," the Colonel replied.

"What about a job at the Pentagon?" General West asked.

"Sir?"

"The Pentagon has initiated a program to seek out and track information across all military branches related to personnel identified as POW, MIA, or KIA. They're starting with Vietnam but the program will eventually include those lost in all modern wars. Organizers are looking for someone with frontline experience to help. Interested?"

Andy thought of Moretti and all those who wouldn't make it back to their families. The decision was easy. His engineering career could wait a couple of years. "Yes, sir. I'd appreciate the opportunity."

"Good. I'll have my staff make the arrangements."

Andy turned to the colonel. "Sir, who will take over my squad?"

"Any recommendations?"

"Yes, sir, Ronnie Mays, call name Strawberry. He's re-upping and he's ready. Keep them together, and you'll have the best recon squad in Vietnam."

"Done."

"And, sir, about Quy Tran, our interpreter. Will he be able to keep his position with the squad?"

"Bien has invited Quy to join her in Saigon. He'll be working as an ARVN liaison with her and Trai," Colonel Clark replied.

Andy smiled and nodded. *Quy has a family now.*

"Good luck to you, Andy," General West said.

"Safe travels home, Captain," Colonel Clark added.

Using his injured arm, Andy shook hands with both men. "Thank you, and good luck to both of you, as well."

Leaving headquarters, Andy went in search of his men. They were nearing the end of their stand-down and were scattered all over camp. He wanted time with each of them.

Chapter 21

NETTIE

Nettie had an odd sense of calm as she entered the hospital's administrative conference room. Andy was safe and would be home soon. Little else mattered. Mrs. Adams, the hospital's frumpy but respected Vice President for Nursing, sat at the head of the long table. Dean Fraser sat to her left.

"Welcome, Nettie. Thank you for coming," Mrs. Adams said. "Have a seat."

Dean Fraser patted the chair next to her.

"I asked to meet with you because Mrs. Franks, one of the Godfrey Center's charge nurses, and Mrs. Woods, one of the evening supervisors, have accused you of misconduct surrounding the death of a patient, Mr. William Pepper."

"Yes, ma'am."

"I understand you sneaked Mr. Pepper out of his room and took him to the garden outside the Godfrey Center after being told by Mrs. Franks that it was too late and he was too ill to leave his room."

"Yes, ma'am."

"But you felt you knew better and did it anyway?"

"I knew Mr. Pepper had asked to go. He didn't want to die in a hospital room or a wheelchair."

"So, you were able to get this weak and dying man to the garden by yourself?"

"No. I had help."

"Who?"

"Ma'am, the decision to take Mr. Pepper to the garden was mine, no one else's."

"I see." Mrs. Adams looked at the dean, then moved on. "I take it you and Mr. Pepper were close."

"He was my friend."

"I understand you were helping him and his partner, Mr. Kalua, with the garden and nursery."

"Yes, ma'am."

"Did you receive money in return for your help?"

"No, ma'am."

"Gifts?"

"Mr. Pepper gave me a peach gardenia in a nice planter a few months ago."

"Any other gifts?"

"No, ma'am."

"Did you ever ask Mr. Pepper or Mr. Kalua for anything?"

"No, ma'am."

"When Mrs. Franks turned down your request for help, did you think of contacting the evening supervisor, Mrs. Woods, for assistance? I believe she was on duty that night."

"No, ma'am."

"Why?"

Nettie hesitated. "I didn't think I could convince her in time."

"I see. Did you know Mrs. Woods reported you to security before Mrs. Franks even knew Mr. Pepper wasn't in his room?"

Nettie didn't like where the questioning was leading. "No, ma'am."

"Do you know how Mrs. Woods knew you and Mr. Pepper would be in the garden?"

"Ma'am, does it really matter? It doesn't change the fact that I'm the one who disobeyed Mrs. Franks."

"We don't believe the situation is that simple."

Dean Fraser turned to Nettie. "After you came to see me a few months ago, I had a long private conversation with Mr. Pepper. I told him about the letter Mrs. Woods wrote criticizing you and asking that you be transferred. Without going into detail, he validated what you told me. He also indicated he knew Genevieve Woods and that her attempts to discredit you may be because of him. If true, that may be why she is making accusations now."

Mrs. Adams leaned forward. "And, when I came in this morning, there was a delegation of people waiting for me. Mrs. Henry from the Godfrey Center, TK, your preceptor from the emergency room, Paul Anderson, one of the surgical residents, and a laundry department worker named Dougie. All of them were worried that Mrs. Woods might be targeting you unfairly."

"Nettie, it's time you told us what's going on," Dean Fraser said.

Nettie hesitated. Part of her wanted to see Mrs. Woods held accountable for the injustices she'd inflicted on innocent people while trying to cover up her affair and for the cruelty she exhibited toward Mr. Pepper. But Nettie wasn't her judge and jury, and if this meeting became about Mrs. Woods, there'd be little hope of keeping her promise to Mr. Pepper. "Ma'am, we're here because of my choices, no one else's."

The dean and Mrs. Adams exchanged futile glances.

"In retrospect, do you feel your choices that night were appropriate?" Mrs. Adams asked.

"No disrespect, ma'am, but that night wasn't about me. It was about Mr. Pepper. He was of sound mind. He knew he was running out of time, and he knew how and where he wanted to die. He asked me to get him to the garden, and I promised I would."

"Nettie, I hope you are around to take care of me when my time comes," Mrs. Adams said. She hit the intercom button on her phone. "Please ask Mr. Cooper to come in."

A tall, distinguished man with an expensive-looking briefcase walked into the room.

"Dean Fraser, Nettie, this is Jake Cooper, Mr. Pepper's attorney."

Jake reached across the table to shake hands with Dean Fraser and Nettie before sitting. "Nettie, it's nice to finally meet you in person. Mr. Pepper was a fan."

"Nice to meet you, too, sir." She recognized the kind voice she'd talked with the night Mr. Pepper died.

"Jake," Mrs. Adams said, "please share with Dean Fraser and Nettie what you shared with me earlier this morning."

Jake pulled an official-looking document from his briefcase. "This is Mr. Pepper's advanced directives for activities following his death. It covers the details of a substantial trust that has been established to benefit this hospital and support the long-term maintenance of the healing garden and nursery, as well as the experienced personnel to manage both. It also includes caveats under which financial support of the hospital will end should anyone employed by or affiliated with the hospital attempt to act in a manner inconsistent with the intent of the trust. Mr. Pepper made sure this document explicitly protected anyone working at his direction, even at the time of his death."

"Nettie," Mrs. Adams said, "this document supports what you told us about Mr. Pepper's wishes. From an administrative standpoint, as an intern, you should never have been put in a position of having to help him by yourself, which is something I will be looking into. Therefore, the accusations against you have been dismissed."

Nettie breathed a sigh of relief and gave Mr. Pepper a mental hug.

Jake pulled an envelope from his briefcase and handed it to the dean. "Perhaps you'd like to tell Nettie about this."

Dean Fraser smiled, pulled a document from the envelope, and handed it to Nettie. "During my meeting with Mr. Pepper, he made arrangements to start an annual scholarship for nursing students at our school. He wanted you to be the first recipient. Consequently, your past student loans have been paid, and you have a full scholarship to cover the remainder of your education. He insisted you not be told about this until after his death. He didn't want you hesitant to accept."

It took a moment for the dean's words to register. When they did, Nettie fought to keep the tears at bay.

Jake leaned over and handed Nettie his card. "Mr. Pepper also said you were getting married soon. He wanted to offer you and your fiancé his home on Oahu for the wedding and or honeymoon. It will take months for the property to be transitioned into a public trust. Until then, the house and gardens will be empty. He wanted you to enjoy both. In particular, he wanted you to see the view of Hanauma Bay from the bluffs, visit the original nursery that Mr. Kalua built, and see the tea ceremony at the lotus pond."

Nettie fumbled getting a tissue out of her pocket.

"Mr. Pepper and Mr. Kalua would also like to donate the flowers for your wedding, whether here or there. Mr. Pepper specifically said you and your fiancé were to be given all the leis of red ilimas you wanted. He said you'd know why. My phone number is on the card, give me a call, and we'll work out the details."

"I don't know what to say," Nettie said, tears overflowing at her friend's generosity.

Jake grinned. "Now, that's a surprise. Mr. Pepper said you were seldom at a loss for words and didn't hesitate to put him in his place whenever he needed it. If I'm not mistaken, I think you even called him a smelly, pessimistic jackass when he was being less than cordial."

Laughing through her tears, Nettie glanced at the surprised faces of her dean and Mrs. Adams. "I guess you had to be there."

As the meeting broke up, Mrs. Adams walked Nettie to the door. "Young lady, you have a healthy respect for a patient's right to self-determination. Don't ever lose it."

NETTIE HURRIED THROUGH THE cafeteria line, paid the clerk for her coffee, then slid onto a chair between Win and TK.

"There you are," TK said. "I hope you have good news for us."

Nettie quickly filled the group in on Mrs. Adams's decision. "Thank you all for helping me."

"I'm so glad things went well," Win said, giving her a hug.

"Did they say anything about me?" Dougie asked.

Nettie shook her head. "Thankfully, they were more interested in what Mrs. Franks and Mrs. Woods did and didn't do than in what we did."

Dougie looked relieved. "Good. I was afraid they'd move me back to the day shift."

"But you helped me anyway."

"Mr. Pepper was my friend."

Dougie didn't know it yet, but Mr. Pepper had left him the scenic pictures hanging in his hospital suite, the ones Mr. Pepper had told him grand stories about. Jake Cooper said the pictures would be delivered to Dougie next week along with a note from Mr. Pepper.

"Well, Dougie, I don't think you need to worry about Mrs. Woods anymore," TK said, patting his hand.

Paul turned to Nettie. "Mrs. Adams was really interested in what was going on between you and Mrs. Woods. We could only tell her what we'd witnessed. I hope you filled her in on the rest."

"We mostly talked about Mr. Pepper," Nettie replied, diverting the conversation. "But I suspect Mrs. Woods and Mrs. Franks will be interviewed, too."

As the others chatted, Nettie's thoughts drifted back to what Mr. Pepper had said the night he died. *What made Vivi do what she did? What made her go from someone in love and having a baby to a cruel, angry woman?* There had to be more to the story.

"Well, I think things are changing for the better," Paul said with a grin.

"For sure," Win replied, putting her hand on Paul's arm.

Nettie sat straight and grabbed Win's left hand. "Oh my gosh!" A small, princess-cut diamond circled Win's ring finger. Nettie looked at Win, then Paul, then Win again. "I'm so happy for you two!" she said, giving them both hugs.

Paul slid over and put his arm around Win's shoulders. "Looks like we all have something to celebrate."

SATURDAY MORNING, NETTIE WALKED with a lighter step and a smile on her face as she and Win picked up bagels and headed to the NAF office. Andy would be home in a few days, and school was almost out for the summer.

Mrs. Anderson waved as she and Win walked in, then continued an in-progress phone conversation. In the back, Paul and Laura were stuffing the wall bins with updated packets, Paul filling A-M and Laura filling N-Z. Boxes overflowed the room.

"It won't be long before the NAF is going to need a bigger office," Nettie said, working her way through the maze to pour coffee for everyone.

Paul stopped working long enough to give Win a kiss good morning.

Laura winked at Nettie. "I don't know how much of these love birds I can take." She ducked as Paul threw a T-shirt at her. "They're not getting married for a year, so I guess I'm stuck having to watch them be all kissy-kissy."

"Don't worry," Win laughed, "when you start nursing school in the fall, you'll be too busy to care."

"I'm really nervous, but as soon as I started shadowing you two, I knew that's what I wanted to do."

"Well, you'll have lots of help along the way," Nettie added. "Win and I are good tutors."

Mrs. Anderson came through the breezeway. "Good morning, girls."

"Morning, Mrs. A."

"That was a great interview you had in the newspaper yesterday," Win said. "It's so cool the President of the United States is going to keynote the NAF conference in the fall. I'd say the PAC worked. Everyone is paying attention now."

"I especially like how you ended the article," Nettie added. "'The NAF is the only organization working to put itself out of business.'"

"We can only hope," Mrs. Anderson replied as the bells over the front door jingled. Going back to the breezeway, she stopped suddenly, her hand going to her chest, her eyes focused on the door.

Paul and Laura rushed to her side. Win and Nettie followed. They could see Colonel Bell, walking toward them, hat in hand. The devastated look on his face broadcasted the news none of them wanted to hear.

"Ann, Paul, Laura, I'm so sorry—"

Mrs. Anderson held up her hand, not wanting to hear the words. She pulled her children close and held them tight. The three whispered to each other in an emotional language only they understood, a language bred from years of not knowing if your loved one was dead or alive, if he was being repeatedly starved and tortured at the hands of his captors, if he believed he'd been forgotten. One in their grief, there was nothing Nettie, Win, or the colonel could do or say to ease their loss of hope.

Colonel Bell laid his cap on the counter and went to hang the closed sign in the door, but Mrs. Anderson stopped him. "We stay open," she said, her voice even. "As long as other families have hope, we stay open." She took a deep breath and steadied herself. "Steve would want it that way." Kissing her children, she went back to her counter.

With Win at his side, Paul returned to the worktable, mindlessly folding T-shirts, his eyes glistening.

Laura eased into a chair at the table, her hands trembling as she picked up a pen to address envelopes.

Nettie gently took the pen. "I'll write. You seal."

Colonel Bell hung his coat on a hook, rolled up his sleeves, and started opening boxes.

As usual, Nettie's pace slowed the moment she entered the lush greenhouse. Diffused light from the glass ceiling and nature's misty, intangible energy enveloped her as she moved along the sandstone path. Leaves waved in the low breeze produced by the ceiling fans. Scattered bees and butterflies flitted from flower to flower, while pulses of tantalizing smells pulled Nettie from one section of the path to the next. Tension she didn't realize she had slipped away with each step, just as it did every time she came. Mr. Pepper was right about the healing power of gardens.

Per his request, Nettie, Mr. Kalua, Mrs. Henry, Dougie, and Jake Cooper had taken Mr. Pepper's ashes to a little Presbyterian church in the beautiful Northern Shenandoah Valley and scattered them over his parents' graves. Now, there was only one more promise she had to fulfill. She had to get Mr. Pepper's ring and letter to Mrs. Woods and do it in such a way the woman wouldn't accuse Mr. Pepper of being a ring thief and throw his letter in the trash. It had taken a while, but Nettie had finally figured out a way to get the woman in the same room with her, but she'd need help to make it happen.

Slipping through the overlapping walls at the back of the nursery, she found Mr. Kalua checking moisture levels in a cluster of small coco pots full of beautiful plumeria. In the next row, the assistant who would take over when Mr. Kalua returned to Hawaii did the same. Each person visiting the greenhouse or garden during the grand opening on Saturday would receive one of the plumeria pots and directions on how to care for it. Tied around each pot was a ribbon containing the Hawaiian Ho'oponopono Prayer for healing of the mind, body, and spirit. "I'm sorry. Forgive me. Thank you. I love you."

Standing, Mr. Kalua brushed the dust from his knees, then walked toward Nettie. "Good evening, young lady."

"Hi, Mr. Kalua. Do you have a few minutes?"

"Of course. Let's talk by the pond."

Once again, his Hawaiian accent reminded her of rainforests, waterfalls, and an unhurried life.

As they settled on the bench, Nettie looked at the new hybrid Naupaka tree nestled among the white and pink dogwoods, its bright white blossoms edged in spring-like green.

"Billy's tree of hope," Mr. Kalua said, following her gaze.

"It's beautiful. I'm so glad he got to see it before he died. Did he ever figure out a new ending for the Naupaka legend?"

Mr. Kalua chuckled. "He didn't need to. Billy knew better than most that the legend was never about lost love. It's about choices, consequences, and courage. Billy had the courage to build a new life in Hawaii and he had the courage to come home again. Not only to deal with the consequences swirling around choices he, Vivi, and Danny made decades ago, but to face his own death. Along the way, he found faith, forgiveness—"

"And hope," Nettie said.

"Indeed."

"Mr. Kalua, I need help keeping a promise I made to Mr. Pepper."

"Danny's ring? His letter to Vivi?"

"How did you know?"

"Billy and I had few secrets, especially where Danny and Vivi were concerned. Those two were with him the day we met, and Billy and I became partners in their aftermath."

"If you know Vivi, wouldn't it be better if you gave her the ring and letter?"

"The ring, maybe, but Billy wanted you to give her the letter."

"That may not be the best idea." Nettie hesitated. Mr. Kalua didn't need to be pulled into any more of Vivi's secrets. "Mrs. Woods and I haven't gotten along for months. I couldn't even convince her to say goodbye to Mr. Pepper when he was dying."

"I see."

"I still can't understand why she would be so cruel to a dying man."

"People rarely forgive you for what they do to you."

Nettie sat straighter. "You mean—"

"The choices Vivi made in 1942 that started all of this caused an incredible amount of pain for everyone, especially for Billy. His lasted a lifetime. Unless I miss my guess, hers has too. Otherwise, she would never have refused to see him."

"Seems like he wanted to end the pain for both of them and she couldn't be bothered."

The wise old Hawaiian nodded. "Pain is a chameleon, my friend. It hides behind many faces. Being constantly reminded of the pain you caused someone else can be a tormenting burden, especially if it plays out for a lifetime."

Nettie couldn't bring herself to feel empathy for the woman, at least not yet. She took Danny's ring and Mr. Pepper's letter out of her pocket. "I understand Mr. Pepper's reason for wanting to return the ring. But, if Vivi wanted nothing to do with him, regardless of her reasons, why was he so intent on getting this letter to her?"

"Billy came home to find peace at the end of his life. Maybe the letter is about helping her do the same."

"So how do we give a ring and letter to someone who doesn't want them?"

"The only thing we can do is use the ring to open the door, and hope she'll come through it to receive the gift Billy left her."

THE NEXT EVENING AT CLOSING TIME, Nettie joined Mr. Kalua in the wall-less office in the back of the nursery. She had checked with the ER, and Mrs. Woods had the evening off, which meant there was a good chance she'd be home. Nettie sat on the edge of her seat as Mr. Kalua dialed the supervisor's home number, then hit the button for the speakerphone.

"Hello," Mrs. Woods's edgy voice answered.

"Vivi? Hi, this is Keona Kalua."

Nettie started counting silently. She reached ten before Vivi spoke.

"Hello, Keona. It's been a long time." Her voice sounded different, softer.

"Yes, it has, Vivi, too long. How are you?"

"Fine. And you?"

"I'm well, thank you. Do you have a minute to talk?"

Nettie counted through another long silence.

"Yes, of course."

"I'm sure you're aware our friend Billy Pepper died recently."

"I'm aware," her voice barely there.

"Before he passed, Billy asked that something be returned to you, a ring that belonged to your brother, Danny."

"A ring? What kind of ring?"

"It's a signet ring." Mr. Kalua didn't give her a chance to interrupt. "I have it with me at the greenhouse. Would you like to come over?"

"Maybe," Vivi replied, hesitantly.

"We're getting ready for the grand opening so I'll be here until six. I'd love to show you around."

Nettie had counted to twenty before she heard Vivi's quiet reply.

"I'll be there in a few minutes."

"Wonderful. I look forward to seeing you."

Nettie sighed as Mr. Kalua hung up. "Now let's hope she doesn't see me and leave."

"She's coming to a healing garden, remember? Once Vivi and I are seated on the bench at the pond, stand behind the trees so you can see and hear. You'll know when to join us."

A half-hour later, Nettie heard a car pull up. She saw Mrs. Woods come through the main entrance. Dressed in capris and coordinating blouse with her hair in a ponytail, she looked like the girl in the picture, more like Vivi than Mrs. Woods.

Vivi studied the atrium up, down, and around. Her tense expression transformed to one of amazement. Closing her eyes, she took a slow, deep breath.

Mr. Kalua stayed back until she opened her eyes. "Hello, Vivi."

"Keona, this is beautiful."

"Thank you." Mr. Kona put a lei of pink lotus blossoms around her neck and kissed both cheeks.

"You remembered," she smiled. "It's just as beautiful as the first one."

"I hoped it would be."

Vivi lifted the flowers to her face. "Back then, I'd never smelled anything like it. After the war, someone sent me a sample of Paradise perfume. It smelled just like this. I've worn it every day since." She held out her wrist for him to smell.

"Very nice," Mr. Kalua said. "When we became partners, Billy suggested we grow flowers for the international perfume houses. Lotus were the first flowers we produced commercially. Billy knew you loved the scent. He wanted you to have one of the first bottles made with flowers our company had grown."

Vivi's eyes widened. "You mean Billy sent me the perfume? After the war? It came from him?"

Mr. Kalua nodded. "He had it sent from the distribution center in New York."

Vivi gently rubbed her wrist. Nettie couldn't tell if she was rubbing the scent in or off.

Mr. Kalua took Vivi's elbow and guided her along the sandstone path, pointing out interesting plants and features as they went.

Once they'd settled on the teak bench near the lotus pond, Vivi took a deep breath. "May I see Danny's ring?"

"Of course."

Nettie had cleaned and polished the ring and Mr. Kalua had placed it in a small, intricately carved wooden box.

"Is this Koa wood?" Vivi asked.

"It is. Koa is native to the islands and is sacred in our culture."

"I remember Billy telling me about it."

"The name means warrior," Mr. Kalua added. "I thought it would be a fitting home for the ring of a soldier."

Vivi slid the top of the box open and removed the ring, running her fingers over the swirly initials at the top. "I remember my parents giving this to Danny the day he graduated from college." She put the ring on her finger. "You said Billy had it? Why? Why didn't he send it to my parents with the rest of Danny's belongings?" Blame still resonated in her tone.

"As you know, Billy loved Danny like a brother. When he died, Billy was devastated. The morning of the attack on Pearl Harbor, Danny volunteered to cover Billy's shift so he could come see me about buying the land above Hanauma Bay. Billy was almost back to their office when the attack began. He saw the bomb hit the building. Despite the danger, he found Danny in the rubble. Your brother died before Billy could get him out. Billy stayed by Danny's side through the remainder of the attack and for hours during the chaos and confusion that followed. Eventually the navy sent trucks to gather up the dead, but Billy refused to let them throw Danny on a pile of bodies. He carried his friend over a mile to the hospital, where a makeshift morgue had been set up. Once there, he refused to leave until Danny's body had been cared for."

Vivi pressed fingers to her lips as the lines in her forehead deepened.

"Billy put the ring on his finger the day Danny died, and it didn't come off until the day he died. Billy knew better than anyone that he was supposed to be in the building that morning. That his life had been spared at the cost of Danny's, the heartbreaking, unintended consequence of an innocent choice. To Billy, the ring served as a constant reminder that his life needed to give meaning to Danny's. Every day, it motivated him to keep working. To do things Danny would have been proud of. After the war, Billy made it possible for us to employ hundreds when well-paying jobs with benefits were scarce. He never had children of his own, but he quietly funded the education of children who lost parents in the attack."

Pulling a tissue from her pocket, Vivi blotted her eyes.

"Because of Billy, my family was able to not only protect our ancestral land, but also form a public trust to protect Hawaiian heritage sites all over the islands. He worked hard to be worthy of the gift he'd been given, and he wanted Danny to be with him on the journey. That's why he kept the ring." Mr. Kalua paused to give Vivi a moment. "He also made it clear that the ring and all it represented should be returned to you when he died."

"I blamed him for so long." Vivi's shoulders slumped. "For everything. I knew he wasn't responsible for Danny's death, but I blamed him anyway and I told him so." She leaned forward, elbows on her knees. "Blaming him made it easier to live with what I'd done—I never had to tell the man I loved that I'd been unfaithful."

"He knew, Vivi," Mr. Kalua said softly.

Vivi sat straight. "What?"

"Billy knew you were pregnant when you broke the engagement and that the baby wasn't his."

"He knew? All this time? How? Danny?"

Mr. Kalua nodded.

"I didn't want Billy to know—not until I figured out what to do. I thought I could tell him once I was on the island, but I couldn't. He was so excited about our future, about getting married and living in Hawaii. I just couldn't tell him, not face-to-face. I was so ashamed." Vivi twisted the tissue. "I knew he wouldn't want to marry me once he found out what I'd done, so I gave him a Dear John letter right before I got on the plane to come home."

Vivi's hands trembled as she stemmed more tears.

"Billy called me right after I got back to Virginia. He begged me to tell him why—what happened—what he'd done. But I refused to talk with him. Danny got on the phone. He was so angry. We had an awful fight. He kept asking why I would break the engagement like that? 'Billy deserves better,' he said. 'If you didn't love him, you should have had the courage to look him in the eye and tell him. Instead, you let him believe everything was fine, then stuck a Dear John letter in his pocket on your way out of town. How could you do such a horrible thing?'" Vivi shook her head as if to stop the voices. "Danny wouldn't stop yelling at me. I was so mentally and physically exhausted from the pregnancy, the stress of keeping it a secret, and from flying all day that I just blurted it out. I told him that I was pregnant and the baby wasn't Billy's. I begged Danny not to tell, not Billy, not anyone. The only thing he said was, 'God forgive you,' and hung up. Those were the last words my brother ever said to me. He died the next morning."

Nettie felt a wave of empathy for the girl Mrs. Woods once was, making the foolish, life-altering, irreversible mistakes of the young.

"After the bombing, Billy called my parents and me to tell us what happened. I was in so much pain, I refused to see his. I screamed awful things at him. I blamed him for Danny's death, the broken engagement, for everything. I told him I never wanted to see him or talk with him again. In the weeks that followed, I talked myself into believing everything I'd said. It was easier to deal with the pain and guilt if I wasn't the cause." Vivi pushed a strand of hair out of her eyes and sat straight. "I lost the baby soon after I got home. My parents never knew. My friends didn't know, and the father had already disappeared. For the longest time, I couldn't look at myself in the mirror. I floated from man to man and finally married a nice guy I didn't love just to have something—someone—to hang on to."

Vivi stood and walked to the Naupaka tree, touching one of the white and green blossoms. "When Billy showed up here last spring, all the suffocating guilt I'd kept at bay for decades came rushing back. The only way I could breathe was to churn up old anger and blame him all over again. I can't tell you how many times I stood outside his door but couldn't make myself go in. I didn't give him a chance to tell me anything. And I didn't deserve the chance to tell him I was sorry—and that I loved him."

Nettie recognized the unintended cue. With Mr. Pepper's letter in hand, she walked toward the lotus pond.

Vivi heard the noise and turned. "What are you doing here?"

The lack of acidity in her voice took Nettie by surprise. "You want to know what Billy had to say? Well, here it is. He asked me to give this to you."

Mr. Kalua disappeared quietly among the trees.

Vivi didn't reach for the letter, so Nettie laid it and Mr. Pepper's Bible on the bench, then sat on the stone wall surrounding the lotus pond.

"I can't seem to get you out of my life," Vivi said, with more resignation than condemnation.

"It's been no picnic for me, either."

"Why would Billy want you to give me these things?"

"I don't know, but he asked, and I promised."

Vivi looked Nettie in the eye. "I had to meet with Mrs. Adams and your dean this morning."

Nettie braced.

"I went in fully expecting to have my life blown to hell. To lose my job, my marriage, and any shred of self-respect I had left." She sat on the edge of the bench. "Why didn't you tell them? You were protected. You could have told them everything. Why didn't you?"

"My meeting with them was about the consequences of my choices not yours," Nettie replied. "Besides, it's impossible to work on forgiveness and retribution at the same time."

Vivi scoffed. "You are such a Pollyanna." She pressed the shredded tissue against her eyes. "There's no forgiveness for what I did to Billy, my husband, you, and heaven knows how many others."

A breeze eased through the open glass panels in the wall, stirring the leaves and soft scents.

"And to yourself," Nettie added, realizing for the first time why Mr. Pepper wanted her to deliver the letter. "No one is beyond forgiveness. Not me, not you, not Mr. Pepper, not anyone. He struggled for a lifetime to find forgiveness for a debt he never owed. He was still looking for it a year ago when he came home to die. What he found instead was the gift of time. Time to figure out what he'd been looking for all along, a way to forgive himself—and to forgive you."

Nettie rose to leave. "Mr. Pepper never told me what was in the letter or why it was so important for you to read it, but if my guess is right, he's showing you the way to do the same thing."

Leaving Vivi to read Billy's letter in private, surrounded by what he loved, Nettie walked outside with a sense of freedom she hadn't felt in a year. She'd kept her promise to her friend, a promise more important than she'd ever imagined. *What was it Mr. Pepper had told her?*

"Winter doesn't last forever, and spring doesn't skip its turn." With eyes wide open and arms raised, she looked to heaven and thanked God.

Chapter 22

NETTIE AND ANDY

Loud, shirtless boys playing softball in the littered street scattered as the cab pulled up in front of the old brick building in Brooklyn. Open windows, some propped up with fans, others with curtains half in and half out, speckled its six-story face. The smell of an outdoor market whose produce needed refreshing greeted Andy as he paid the driver and stepped into the steamy heat and humidity. Stepping over beer cans and smoldering cigarette butts, then maneuvering around curious adolescent girls with bare midriffs and too much makeup, he made his way up the disintegrating concrete steps.

Inside, the only improvement was the smell. The delicious scents of Italian dishes greeted him as he went up flight after flight of stairs. No wonder Moretti was so strong and could cook a good meal with next to nothing. Stopping in front of apartment 6E, Andy removed his cap, took a deep breath, and knocked.

A petite, wiry female with kind brown eyes and tightly permed, graying hair opened the door, her worn dress covered by a clean but stained flowered apron. Her eyes glistened when she saw Andy's uniform.

"Mrs. Moretti?"

She nodded. "You must be Andy."

"Yes, ma'am. Andy Stockton."

"Please come in." She wiped her eyes with the hem of her apron as she closed the door. A window air conditioner hummed in the corner and the smells from the kitchen made Andy's mouth water. Mrs. Moretti ushered him into a living room filled with colorful plants and flowers. Some were clustered in the windows and others were placed on little tables scattered around the room, even the sofa had a slipcover of roses. Nestled among the plants and flowers were pictures of Moretti growing up. On top of the bookcase were his high school diploma, his military picture, a tri-folded American flag in a glass case, and a large cross. His Silver Star and Purple Heart sat next to the flag. Scattered along the shelves below were colorful, intricately coiled and quilled paper figures—stars, trees, hearts, birds, a dragon, and a lotus flower. Moretti must have sent them from Camp Eagle.

Andy sensed Luca's presence in the room—his smile, his laughter, his friendship. He even felt Moretti teasing him about visiting his mother.

"It's so kind of you to come see me," Mrs. Moretti said. "Would you like some tea?"

"Yes, ma'am, that would be great."

Given the summer heat, Andy assumed she meant iced tea, but the small tea service she sat on the table held two delicate, cobalt blue cups, saucers, and a teapot, all intricately decorated with lotus flowers.

"Luca sent me this set along with several tins of lotus tea. He wrote about how beautiful it was to watch the women swirl around the water at night putting tea in the flowers."

"It is a magical thing to see." Andy took a sip from his cup. "And it's good tea."

Mrs. Moretti studied her cup for a moment. "Luca thought the world of you, Andy. Every letter he wrote included something about you—the first time he met you at Fort Benning, when you chose him to be part of your squad, when you went to bat for him when he got into trouble, even when you and the others saved him from drowning. His last letter said if he had to be in that awful war, he was glad it was with you."

Andy clenched his jaw to control his emotions. "He was my friend."

Mrs. Moretti smiled and nodded. "I'm glad to hear you say that. Luca had a hard time making friends. With his father gone and his being so small, he was picked on a good bit. But he always fought back. He used to tell me he didn't start the fights, but he finished them his way."

"He did the same thing in the army," Andy chuckled.

"When he enlisted, I worried that he'd simply traded one kind of fighting for another. But he loved the army. He felt like he was part of something special; it gave him a sense of belonging."

"Mrs. Moretti, he was part of something special, and he was one of the best soldiers I ever served with."

"He would be so proud to hear you say that."

Andy pulled his copy of the New Testament from his pocket and looked at what Moretti had written inside of the back cover once more. "Luca and I shared this while we were in Vietnam. I'd like you to have it. He wrote a note in the back."

Mrs. Moretti set her cup on the table, then read Luca's message aloud. "Thanks, Andy. I'm not alone anymore." She closed her eyes for a moment, rubbing her thumbs over the crinkled cover.

When she finally looked up, a hint of peace shown in her eyes. "Now, Andy, please tell me how my Luca died."

He pulled the carved dove from his pocket.

ANDY SLID HIS AVIATORS INTO his pocket and closed his eyes as the plane lifted off for the short flight from New York to Virginia. Up to now the flights to get home had been on military planes, and he'd been spared the ugliness of the antiwar protesters he'd heard so much about. However, this flight was a domestic one, and the airport he flew out of allowed protestors to yell and spit at any uniform that went by. Andy ignored them like he did the crack along the rim of his aviators, only to be seen if he chose to look. After what he and his men had been through, the protestors' obscene banter and desire for drama was little more than background noise, the price paid for living in a free society.

There was no way the protestors could understand the motivation and sacrifices of the majority of returning soldiers who'd served on the front lines. Andy had led a reconnaissance team of men he now called brothers, in a country whose people and sacrifice he'd come to respect, during a war whose value would be determined in the decades to come. No war is victimless and neither side is blameless, but he, Moretti, and the others had been part of the only military action in Vietnam's history whose sole purpose was to help a freedom-starved people escape continued oppression from yet another ruthless invader. In the process, they'd helped delay a communist offensive, helped Bien and her underground network of freedom fighters continue their work, rescued her brother from forced conscription in the NVA, and saved two innocent little boys from the same fate. *Never underestimate the power of what you leave behind.*

He'd soon be with the woman who was a part of him. The one who kept him sane and focused during the oppressive days and terrifying nights. The woman who was the right to his left, the up to his down, his port in a storm, his breeze on a hot day, his gift from God. And, blessing of blessings, he was hers. They had a future to plan, one free of the weight of the past year.

Pressure pushed Andy against the seat as the plane banked and turned to line up with the runway at Dulles. He looked at his watch the moment the plane's wheels touched the tarmac. 12:00 noon. Home.

NETTIE ROLLED THE CAR WINDOW down as she cruised along scenic Route 50 in rural Virginia, barely controlling her excitement. Just a few minutes more and Andy's plane would be on the ground. He'd be home. She knew he'd been through hell on earth while in Vietnam and that he would need time to adjust. His mother and Mrs. Anderson had shared the wisdom only experienced military wives would know about how to help him.

"Give him time to get his feet back on solid ground and his mind back in a safe place," they'd said. "Let him talk if and when he's ready. Some of what he went through he may never want you to know about, and that's okay. He's coming home to the love of his life, and that's the best tonic there is."

The same advice worked for her. Andy would want to know about her year. So, while they vacationed for two weeks at home in Amherst, she'd tell him about school, her internship, and her wonderful friends, TK, the Andersons, Mr. Pepper, and Mr. Kalua, and about the generous wedding and honeymoon gifts the two men had given them. The saga with Mrs. Woods would not be mentioned. Nettie refused to give the ugliness of the past year one more second of her life.

When she and Andy returned to Northern Virginia, she'd take him to the healing garden, the nursery, and the NAF office before he started his job at the Pentagon and she resumed her internship. So much had happened since he'd been gone. Some good, some not, but all of it helping to sculpt the type of person she wanted to be and the kind of life she wanted to live.

"Just a few minutes more," she repeated as she turned onto the road to Dulles, Virginia's newest international airport. In the back seat sat a picnic basket full of Andy's favorite foods, a small cooler containing a bottle of champagne and lemonade, and the engagement quilt she and Andy had said goodbye on. After a long, dangerous year, they'd soon be together again. She'd see his warm smile, touch his handsome face, and hold him for real. They'd take a leisurely drive south along Route 29 to Amherst, where they'd spend the afternoon picnicking at River's Rest just as Andy said they would a year ago. This evening, they'd celebrate a summer Christmas with Andy's mom, then tomorrow and for the next couple of weeks, they'd stargaze on Allen's Hill, walk the streets and paths of their childhood, put the finishing touches on their wedding, and re-blend their lives one step at a time, one day at a time.

"If we have to do this, let's do it our way," Andy'd said the day he went to war. And that's exactly what they'd done.

Pulling into the airport parking lot, the grand contemporary glass and concrete building with its landmark, white, up-sloped roof, and multi-layered space-age control tower seemed to sing to the future. What was it Mr. Pepper had said? *Those who wish to sing will always find a song.* Well, she and Andy had one and they would sing it together. Jumping from the car, Nettie ran for the terminal.

AUTHOR'S NOTE

The Easter Offensive mounted by the North Vietnamese in the summer of 1972, was the largest and last enemy offensive of the Vietnam War. US and South Vietnamese military leaders anticipated the offensive, but underestimated the size, intensity, and scope of the simultaneous three-front attack.

While US and South Vietnamese troops were able to repel the invasion, the North Vietnamese gained a foothold within the borders of South Vietnam, which improved their bargaining position at the Paris peace talks.

No war is blameless or victimless, but time often gives us a clearer view of what was actually won and lost.

In his article "The Vietnam War in Hindsight" (published April 27, 2000), Richard N. Haass of the Brookings Institution indicated that the United States may have "lost the war but won the peace." He further asserted that despite the withdrawal of troops, the war's outcomes could not have turned out better if we had won. Vietnam is now mostly democratic. Important alliances with countries such as Japan, South Korea and Australia are robust, and the United States remains the dominant power in the Asia-Pacific region. Even the postwar predictions related to the spread of communism did not materialize. When the Vietnam war ended, communist states began to fall like dominos, "as one country after another pushed communism aside in pursuit of freedom."

Life Dust

BOOK CLUB QUESTIONS

1. What moment in Nettie's story prompted the strongest emotional reaction, and why?
2. What factors contribute to Nettie's ongoing reluctance to reveal Mrs. Woods's affair?
3. Why do you think Nettie bonds with Mr. Pepper when others are unable to deal with him?
4. What aspects of Mr. Pepper's illness and death are comforting, and why? Which are uncomfortable, and why?
5. In what way does Nettie's development reflect the 1960s/1970s women's movement?
6. What factors play into Andy's initial trepidation about going to war?
7. What aspects of Andy and Luca Moretti's personalities contribute to their friendship?
8. How do the hardships that his squad endures in the jungle change Andy over time?
9. What about Bien's story reflects the humanity and inhumanity of war?
10. Do you think Andy comes home a changed man? If so, how?
11. What is unique about the bond between Nettie and Andy?

12. What about Nettie and Andy's shared history sustains them during their darkest moments?

13. How have Nettie and Andy changed by the end of the story?

14. How is symbolism used throughout the story?

15. Where do you see Nettie and Andy in ten years?

16. Was this your first time to read a book with dual narrators and alternating viewpoints? How was that for you?

17. Which scene(s) are you most likely to remember, and why?

18. Was there something about the writing style in this story that you particularly liked or didn't like?

19. Do you think differently about the following after reading this story?
    - The Vietnam War
    - Bullying
    - Death and dying
    - Guilt and forgiveness

20. If you read *The Wiregrass* and *Moon Water*, was *Life Dust* a satisfying conclusion to the trilogy?

ACKNOWLEDGMENTS

Vietnam Veterans Who
Served with Distinction

This includes my husband, Jeffrey Michael Webber, who served in combat in the jungles of Vietnam, endured the unimaginable, was seriously wounded, yet came home the most optimistic human being I've ever known.

The National League of
POW/MIA Families (The NLF)

According to their website, the NLF was formed in 1970 with the purpose of obtaining the release of all prisoners, the fullest possible accounting for the missing, and the repatriation of all recoverable remains of those who died serving our nation during the Vietnam War. As of April 28, 2022, the number of Americans still missing and unaccounted for from the Vietnam War is 1,584. Without the League, America's POW/MIAs would have been forgotten long ago.

The work of the NLF's founders and membership motivated the creation of the Department of Defense's POW/MIA Accounting Agency in January 2015. Advances in DNA technology, increased access to battlegrounds and crash sites, and ongoing international negotiations continue to bring more and more of our soldiers home.

In 1979, Congress declared the third Friday in September to be National POW/MIA Recognition Day. In 1982 the POW/MIA flag started being flown over the White House, and by 2018, Congress required the flag to be flown year-round at the Vietnam Veterans Memorial, the World War II Memorial, and other selected federal sites.

The Founders of the NLF

Sybil Stockton, Jane Denton, Louise Mulligan, Angela Rander, Helen Knapp, and Phyllis Galanti

In 2019, Heath Hardage Lee authored a book titled *The League of Wives: The Untold Story of the Women Who Took On the US Government to Bring Their Husbands Home.* This compelling documentation of what the founders of the NLF and their families went through to gain the release of their husbands from North Vietnam is a worthy read for anyone who loves history and respects the power of women and love. Lee's book provided valuable insight into the development of some of the fictitious characters in *Life Dust*.

Mr. Hal Borland

"No winter lasts forever;
no spring skips its turn."

This beautiful phrase was penned by Hal Borland (1900-1978) and published in a *New York Times* editorial titled "April's End" on April 29, 1956. Mr. Borland was an American author and former editor of the paper.

ABOUT THE AUTHOR

Pam Webber is the best-selling author of three historical novels—*The Wiregrass*, *Moon Water*, and *Life Dust*. *The Southern Literary Review*, Historical Novel Society, and Ingram's Book Buzz "highly recommend" her work because of the memorable characters, engaging stories, and immersive settings.

As a second-career novelist, Pam is a popular speaker for book clubs, writing circles, and civic organizations. She has had the honor of being a featured panelist at Virginia Festival of the Book, the Library of Virginia, and James River Writers.

Pam is also an internal medicine nurse practitioner and former nursing educator. She and her husband, Jeff, are avid travelers and especially love visiting World Heritage Sites and US national parks. They live in the beautiful Northern Shenandoah Valley of Virginia.

For updates on Pam's next novel, visit her at www.pam webber.com.

Author photo © Merrissa Hill, Portrait Lady Photography

SELECTED TITLES FROM SHE WRITES PRESS

She Writes Press is an independent publishing
company founded to serve women writers everywhere.
Visit us at www.shewritespress.com.

Moon Water by Pam Webber. $16.95, 978-1-63152-675-6. Nettie, a gritty sixteen-year-old, is already reeling from a series of sucker punches when an old medicine woman for the Monacan Indians gives her a cryptic message about a coming darkness: a blood moon whose veiled danger threatens Nettie and those she loves. To survive, Nettie and her best friend, Win, will have to scour the perilous mountains for Nature's ancient but perfect elements and build a mysterious dreamcatcher.

The Wiregrass by Pam Webber. $16.95, 978-1-63152-943-6. A story about a summer of discontent, change, and dangerous mysteries in a small Southern Wiregrass town.

Wild Boar in the Cane Field by Anniqua Rana. $16.95, 978-1-63152-668-8. One day, a baby girl, Tara, is found, abandoned and covered in flies. She is raised by two mothers in a community rife with rituals and superstition. Poignant and compelling, her story contains the tragedy that often characterizes the lives of those who live in South Asia—and demonstrates the heroism we are all capable of even in the face of traumatic realities.

Murder Under The Bridge: A Palestine Mystery by Kate Raphael. $16.95, 978-1-63152-960-3. Rania, a Palestinian police detective with a young son, meets cheeky Jewish American feminist Chloe at an Israeli checkpoint—and soon becomes embroiled in a murder case that implicates the highest echelons of the Israeli military.

Other Fires by Lenore H. Gay. $16.95, 978-1-63152-773-9. Joss and Phil's already rocky marriage is fragmented when, after being injured in a devastating fire, Phil begins to call Joss an imposter. Faced with a husband who no longer recognizes her, Joss struggles to find motivation to save their marriage, even as family secrets start to emerge that challenge everything she thought she knew.

Split-Level by Sande Boritz Berger. $16.95, 978-1-63152-555-1. For twenty-nine-year-old wife and mother Alex Pearl, the post-Nixon 1970s offer suburban pot parties, tie-dyed fashions, and the lure of the open marriage her husband wants for the two of them. Yearning for greater adventure and intimacy, yet fearful of losing it all, Alex must determine the truth of love and fidelity—at a pivotal point in an American marriage.